"Why play a game just to tie?" Alan asked.

"As we move up in age and level, the games aren't just about winning." Easton said. "They're more about learning something. Sometimes you learn more from losing or a tie."

"Losing should teach you how not to do something." Brandon said. "Doing it differently might get you a win. You should always try to win."

"Even when it's impossible?" Easton asked.

Brandon flashed a grin. "*Especially* when it's impossible."

The rest of the group laughed and nodded

Books By TERRY SCHOTT

The Game is Life Series
The Game
Digital Heretic
Interlude - Brandon
Virtual Prophet

Also available at Amazon.com
The Gold Apples
Harvest *
Flight *
Timeless *

*short stories at the moment... well worth the 0.99

Interlude-Brandon

Terry Schott

This is a work of fiction. Names, characters, businesses, places, events and incidents are either the products of the author's imagination or used in a fictitious manner.
Any resemblance to actual persons, living or dead, or actual events is purely coincidental.

Interlude - Brandon Copyright ©2012 by Terry Schott

Editing by Alan Seeger

April 2013

Well, I have certainly been writing some words down.

Stephen King says you should write for a primary reader; someone who gets the way you think and likes your writing enough to read it, and then helps you make it better with your honest feedback. A "First Reader" is what he calls that person.

Thanks to Karen Schott for being my first reader and my biggest fan ever since I began to post chapters of The Game. Your encouragement, feedback and honest opinions have been extremely valuable to me during this entire process. I could fill a chapter with all the help and encouragement you've given me on this journey of writing... but I will simply say thank you so very much, Karen. I'm truly grateful for your support.

Next I want to thank my blog readers. To name you all would be difficult, so I will name those of you who posted comments on my blog (hint, hint... post comments on my next book during the blog phase and I will mention you here for your dedication!). Thanks to Sarah-Marie, Xandra, Sean, AJ, Tony, Brittany, Euph, Derek and Cloud Evangelist! If I missed you, please e-mail me and I will revise this.

Also thanks to those who follow me on Facebook and have left so many encouraging comments! I love to hear from people that like the story so far, and the e-mails and Facebook comments make my day when I get them. Thank you so much, everyone! I appreciate it.

Thanks also to Alan Seeger for editing, and to Kerstin Campagna for all your computer assistance and magic!

I hope you enjoy this one... it was a blast to write.

Terry

1

"**It would be** better if the boy could stay with you, sir. We do our best, but he would certainly have a more normal life with you as his guardian. That's something he will not receive here at the South Western Children's Centre."

The man felt his cheeks flush with embarrassment as he looked at the small boy through the one-way glass. Just two years old, with dark brown hair and eyes, the child was sitting on the floor playing with some blocks. Occasionally he would look up and glance around the room as if searching for someone before returning to his task.

He's looking for me, the man thought, but quickly shook his head in denial. *No, it's his parents he's looking for.*

The child's parents were dead. A horrible accident had claimed them over a year ago. The man had done his best to take care of their son — his nephew — but after struggling for a year, he knew that he couldn't do it. He was too young to raise a child on his own. He had a business to build, and plans for a future that he could not — would not — sacrifice. He couldn't offer the boy anything.

He'll be better off here, the man repeated the lie once more in his head.

"Keeping him isn't an option," he said. "I've researched these facilities and found yours to be best there is."

"Even the best of our facilities are lacking in many areas, sir. Perhaps if..."

"Enough," the man said. "I have to go. Let's stop this useless chattering and finish the paperwork."

The Centre administrator nodded his head. "Of course, sir." He pushed three documents across the table to the man, along with a pen. "If you will just sign these release forms, our business will be concluded and you'll be free to leave. The first transfers control of the funds you are offering. 500,000 credits, to be paid to our facility."

"Which will be used to provide for the boy's needs," the man said. He'd made this perfectly clear, but wanted to make certain there was no misunderstanding.

"Absolutely, sir," the administrator smiled. If the uncle had been paying closer attention, he'd have recognized the lie, but he was distracted.

"The second form transfers complete guardianship of the boy over to us until he is eighteen years of age." He waited politely while both were signed. "The third document surrenders any rights you have to ever know where the boy is, or how he is doing. You will not be able to contact him again, sir."

The man paused with his pen over the paper. It seemed as if he might ask a question, but then he shook his head and scratched his signature above the line.

He stood up and looked at the boy through the glass a final time, hoping that he'd done the right thing, and then walked towards the door.

"Sir?" The administrator called after him. The man paused and turned back to face him.

"What is the boy's name?"

The man almost sobbed. He knew he shouldn't leave. He knew deep inside that this wouldn't turn out well, but instead he took a deep breath and opened the door.

"Brandon," he said. "His name is Brandon."

2

"**It's a great** honour to meet you, General."

"I can assure you that the honour is entirely mine, Mr. Thorn."

"Please, General — call me Samson."

"Only if you call me Donovan."

The two men shook hands and sat beside each other at the long main table of the crowded banquet hall, which was filled with people eating and conversing.

"So what do you think of the evening so far, Donovan?"

"I think it's everything one could expect it to be," he said. The conversation paused while a servant filled their glasses with red wine.

"A colossal waste of time and a pain in the ass?" Thorn asked.

The General laughed loudly, startling those around him and attracting looks from people throughout the room. Thorn smiled politely and took a sip of wine.

"Your assessment is perfect, Samson," the General said. "It boggles the mind... how can we be such an intelligent society, and yet remain so pompous?"

"People enjoy gathering to celebrate their heroes, General," Thorn said.

"They're here tonight to celebrate me, and I thought you were supposed to call me by my name — Mister Thorn."

"Right you are," Thorn smiled. "You deserve this party tonight, Donovan. You've led our nation from the brink of world war into an era of absolute peace. That's cause to celebrate, no matter who you ask."

"There's no such thing as absolute peace," Donovan said. "We currently have a bigger gun pointed at the rest of the world. When that changes, then this 'peace' will quickly disappear."

"I agree," Thorn replied. "I've been trying to meet you for months now to discuss exactly this topic, Donovan."

"That's not possible." The General shook his head. "If you'd requested a meeting, I would have accepted instantly."

"Repeated attempts to meet with you have all been denied," Thorn said.

"My assistant knows that I'm a fan of yours. If he's responsible for keeping us apart..."

"I'm surprised you've even heard of me," Thorn admitted.

"You're being modest," Donovan said. "You've taken the world of computing and information processing to miraculous levels."

"Yes, well, thank you."

"No, Samson, thank you." Donovan leaned in close and whispered. "Did you know that it was your technology which helped to win this war?"

"What?" Thorn was genuinely surprised. "I had no idea."

The General nodded as he reached into the inner pocket of his suit and pulled out a cell phone. He smiled pleasantly as he dialed and then put the phone to his ear. "Yeah, I've been waiting for you to contact me. I'm so busy that I never had time to seek you out, but I figured you would come looking to meet me. It's a horrible excuse, I know, but when you're in my position you can get away with it."

Thorn started to reply, but Donovan held up his hand for silence. "Hello, Brad. No, everything is fine at the dinner. Listen, Brad I'm sitting beside someone who you know I've wanted to meet for a long time. No, not him; I'm talking about Samson Thorn."

The General smiled as he listened to Brad on the other end of the line. Thorn smiled, too, as he imagined Brad stammering and apologizing, trying to extricate himself from the trouble he was in.

After a few moments, the General spoke up. "That's all well and good, Brad, but the fact is that you knew how badly I wanted to meet Mr. Thorn, and yet you have apparently gone out of your way to prevent it."

The General listened to Brad's frantic excuses on the other end of the line, but it was apparent from the look on his face that it was all in vain. "Mm-hmm. Stop talking now, Brad, and listen very carefully to what I'm about to say. Are you listening...? Excellent. You have one-half hour. Good luck to you, Brad." The General hung up the phone and tucked it back into his pocket.

"There, now where were we?" he asked.

"He has one-half hour for what?" Thorn asked.

The General lowered his voice. "Brad has just been fired. He has a half hour to get as far away from me as he possibly can. Then I will hunt for him. Don't worry, I won't hunt that hard. If he's stupid enough to cross any paths that I influence..."

"Sounds nasty," Thorn said.

"Brad's a clever guy," the General shrugged. "He'll likely be fine. What was it that you wanted to meet with me about?"

"I'm quite intrigued by your use of games in training and development," Thorn said.

"What a coincidence," The General said. "I wanted to meet with you concerning the exact same thing."

"You want to use computers and my knowledge to develop games for your use?" Thorn guessed.

"Great minds think alike, it seems," the General smiled.

"Perhaps we should enjoy this evening and meet soon?"

"How does tomorrow morning sound?"

"Tomorrow would be perfect," Thorn smiled. "Should I just show up at your office, or call for an appointment... with Brad?"

The General loosed another loud laugh and took a drink from his glass.

3

Brad sat in first class looking out the window and smiling with pleasure at the progress he'd made. It had been nearly seven hours since he'd spoken to the General, and he was still alive.

He'd known from day one that becoming the General's aide was a deferred death sentence. The General had pleasantly disclosed this fact at the beginning of his employment, seven months earlier. The General was a straight shooter who insisted on entering into important agreements with all pertinent information laid out. Like every other person who had optimistically accepted the position of General's aide, Brad was convinced that he would be different. He was extremely intelligent, and there had been no doubt in his mind that he would quickly become indispensable to the General.

Brad's dreams had come crashing to a halt just a few hours ago, when he picked up the phone and heard the General speak the dreaded five words, "You have one-half hour."

Not one to waste time, Brad had hung up the phone and immediately grabbed his emergency bag. It contained his passport — forged, of course — different types of currency, and several stolen but valid credit cards. He knew the General was a man of his word; there would be no one looking for him until half an hour had passed.

Brad had walked out the front door of his apartment, walked past his regular automobile, and strolled to another car parked two blocks away. He'd thrown his bag onto the passenger seat and driven away, leaving his old life behind.

Fifteen minutes later, he'd arrived at the local airport. He'd been busy during the drive, making one call after another on a never-before-used and unregistered cell phone. He pulled up to the main doors of the airport, got out of the car with his bag, and walked calmly into the terminal. He glanced casually behind him and noticed a man already getting into the car he'd left running. The General had a complex network of workers; Brad had learned very well from his boss, and had built a small but effective network of his own.

By the time his half hour grace period was up, Brad was in the air, flying towards another country. It would be the first of many flights and car rides over the next several hours which would eventually bring him to his final destination.

Brad went over his escape progress so far, ticking off the tasks that he'd completed during his journey. His first order of business had been to escape the General's sphere of influence. Second, Brad had contacted the most powerful friends he'd been able to cultivate over the years. He was careful not to talk to anyone he'd met or befriended since his time with the General, as their loyalties would probably lean towards his ex-boss. Brad's road to becoming the General's aide had been complex and intricate. A person didn't acquire a position like this without the assistance of many others. News reporters, politicians, military leaders — Brad had cultivated deep and mutually beneficial relationships with all sorts of people. These were the individuals he'd spoken with during his flight. With the reporters, he'd shared top secret facts and details about his time in the General's employ. The General would soon be informed of the damaging news stories which would go public if anything unfortunate were to happen to Brad. Next he spoke to his politician contacts. Brad informed them about key strategies that the General and his friends intended to implement over the next few years. Finally, he'd spoken to his military allies. Soon the General would be busy on multiple fronts; he would have no time to pursue Brad.

He leaned back and smiled with satisfaction. The General had made a mistake firing him, and now Brad was going to show him what kind of damage a truly brilliant opponent could do.

Brad's cell phone rang, startling him from his thoughts. He answered it quickly, not wishing to disturb the other passengers in first class.

"Hello, Brad." The General's voice sounded cheerful on the other end of the line.

"Hello, Donovan." Brad said.

"So we're on a first name basis now, are we?" the General asked.

"Why not?" Brad asked. "I no longer work for you."

The General chuckled. "That's true. I received instructions from one of your allies. They said to call you at this number, and that's what I'm doing. What is it that you would like to say to me?"

"You weren't supposed to call me for another twelve hours..." Brad was concerned; his instructions required precise timing in these matters.

"Yes, your source was quite clear on that point. I wish I could have waited that long, but we simply can't wait twelve hours. Time is running out, Brad."

"What time is that?" Brad asked.

"Your severance time," the General answered.

"My... severance time?"

"Yes, I give all of my aides a sort of... bonus package after they are let go." The General said. "One hour for every month you spent in my employ. You were with me for seven months, so you had seven hours to live, and that time has now run out. Any last words?"

"You can't kill me," Brad sputtered. "I've put complex safety measures in place. If I'm harmed, you'll be ruined. I'm about to land in your enemies' territory. They'll protect me from you. It's impossible for you to get to me now."

"Are you that naive, Brad?" the General asked. "They won't help you any more than I would help an aide of theirs who tried to defect. As far as the other measures you've put into place...I've counteracted all of them. If, by some stroke of luck, a couple were missed... that's of no concern to me. I'm glad you had a fun little game, Brad, but time's run out."

"How?" Brad asked.

"You have an RFID chip implanted in you." The General said. "I activate it; you die."

Brad believed the General, and instantly his spirit was crushed. "Everything I did was for nothing," Brad said. "I wasted my time."

The General heard the despair and hopelessness in the young man's voice and he smiled. He pressed the button that activated the chip, knowing that Brad's implanted device would receive the signal within seconds no matter where he was on the planet.

"I'm glad you finally learned something, Brad. Goodbye."

4

"**How can a** five-year-old boy get into so much trouble?" the Administrator asked. He looked at the youth worker sitting across from him, waiting for an answer.

Wesley squirmed in his chair uncomfortably. He knew that stating his opinion would only bring more unwanted attention. During his three years of employment with the Centre, he'd learned a number of startling and disturbing facts about this institution. If anyone discovered how much he'd been able to piece together, they would have him fired...or much worse.

The South Western Children's Centre was more than a simple orphanage. Wesley had uncovered evidence that it was a feeding tank for the military. The children were raised and nurtured in specific ways, molded and steered both physically and psychologically, to be used in various military experiments.

When he'd stumbled onto what was going on, Wesley wanted to quit. After a few days of soul-searching, he chose a different option; he decided to stay and gather information so that he could eventually take it to the public and help free these children from their fates. The key to his success remained being hidden from suspicion, and sitting in front of the Administrator being reprimanded was not a very effective way to fly under on the radar.

"He's very clever, sir," Wesley said. "A few of the others don't like it, and they bully him."

The Administrator pursed his lips. "If the others are bullying him, please explain to me how they are the ones in the infirmary, while he appears to be healthy and unharmed."

Wesley shrugged his shoulders. "Like I said, he is very clever."

"He's too young to be moved into other programs, yet he appears to be too advanced to remain with those in his age group." The Administrator tapped his fingers together in thought. "You have a special interest in this boy, Wesley; what do you suggest we do with him?"

Damn it! Wesley thought to himself. Showing a special interest in him is dangerous for both of us. I have to try something to convince them I don't care about the boy.

"He's too young to possess much physical strength," Wesley said.

"Tell that to the boys and girls with broken limbs and concussions," the Administrator chuckled.

"Yes, well, he didn't inflict the actual injuries himself," Wesley said. "He had his older friends do it."

"What?" The Administrator leaned forward and his eyes widened in concern. "How is that possible? We keep the little ones separate from the others. Until they are five years old, they aren't allowed to be with the older children. He turned five only two days ago. There's no way he could have befriended older children, and convinced them to him hurt the others so quickly."

Wesley hid his smile, pretending to stifle a yawn. "Yet that's exactly what he did, sir."

"Fine — I'll take your word for it." The Administrator waved his hand. "He's clever. Now answer my question... what do you suggest we do with him?"

Wesley hated himself for what he was about to say, but it was the only way the boy would have any chance of making it through this hell of a school and retain some small part of who he was. "Send him to the Games Facility, sir."

The Administrator stared at Wesley, opening and closing his mouth like a fish out of water. Finally he said, "That's a ruthless recommendation, Wesley. Children don't get invited to try out for the Games until they are at least ten years old."

"I've seen the Games, sir," Wesley said. "The boy is as capable as any of the ten-year-olds, perhaps smarter than all of them combined."

The Administrator considered the idea. He was frustrated with this particular child, but he also recognized great potential in him. The General would pay handsomely for this one when it came time to enlist, so long as they didn't ruin him.

"What the hell," the Administrator said. "I haven't gambled on a student like this in years, and if there was ever one worth taking a chance on, it's him."

He pressed a button on his phone. "Send him in, please."

The door opened and the boy walked in. He was of average height for boys his age, with sandy brown hair and dark brown eyes. His clothes were standard issue grey and brown. He walked in with his head down, but when the door closed behind him, he raised it slightly, looking towards the Administrator. Both adults could see that he was biting his lip in an attempt to look contrite, but his eyes twinkled with the promise of mischief.

"Brandon, I'm tired of seeing you in this office," the Administrator said.

Brandon lowered his head and nodded. "Yes, sir."

"Wesley and I have been trying to figure out what to do with you."

The boy said nothing. He'd visited this office often enough to know that they would do as they pleased; speaking up would only earn him a more severe punishment.

"Wesley has an idea, and I rather like it."

Brandon looked up with genuine interest in his eyes. He was fond of Wesley; the man had shown him small kindnesses over the years, defending him when he could, and giving him special treatment when possible. Brandon hoped Wesley had enough influence to place him where he wanted to be.

"We're allowing you to apply early to the Games Facility."

Brandon's expression changed from eager to afraid. The Administrator pretended not to notice, but secretly he was pleased by Brandon's reaction. "You will report to the entrance trials in three days. Good luck, Brandon, I know you'll do your best."

The Administrator looked down at his paperwork, dismissing the boy with a wave of his hand.

As he turned away to leave, a satisfied grin spread across Brandon's face.

5

"**How can I** help you, Donovan?"

The General grimaced in discomfort. "I'm afraid that during business hours I must insist that you refer to me by my official title."

Samson smiled and nodded. "Of course. Please forgive me."

The General shook his head dismissively. "Oh, there's nothing to forgive. If I had things my way, it wouldn't be so formal."

"I understand entirely," Thorn said. "Don't give it another thought. How is it that I can assist you, General?"

"You've been spending considerable time and resources developing virtual reality technology," the General said.

Samson smiled, "There are many companies spending considerable time and resources developing virtual reality technology."

"Yes, but word is that you've actually done it, Samson."

Thorn grimaced, perfectly mirroring the General's facial expression from a few moments ago. "I'm afraid, General, that during business hours I must also insist on being addressed in a more formal manner." There will be no confusion here, Donovan, Thorn thought. I am not inferior to you. At the very least, I'm your equal. If you want to play games with me, then I will play back.

The General's eyes became flat and he closed his mouth abruptly.   could see his jaw clenching and relaxing rhythmically.

The moment passed, and the General's smile returned. "That is entirely understandable... Mr. Thorn?" he asked.

Thorn nodded.

"Are the rumours correct then, Mr. Thorn? Have you perfected virtual reality technology?"

Thorn wasn't sure how much information he wanted to share. Success in being first to introduce virtual reality to the world would make the company to do so a major global player. Everyone would want access to this technology, and whoever controlled it would be in a position of unlimited potential for power and dominance. Thorn knew enough about the General to be concerned about partnering with him in this matter.

The General understood Thorn's hesitation. He lifted his hands in a soothing gesture. "I don't want control of the technology for myself, Mr. Thorn."

"I find that hard to believe," Thorn said.

"As you know, I am a powerful man."

Thorn laughed. "Yes, General, I'm aware of your power, and I really do want to work with you. I believe that both of us could benefit from a partnership, but it would need to be just that — a partnership."

The General considered Thorn's words carefully, and then nodded. "I understand, Mr. Thorn, and I agree one hundred percent."

"What would you do with VR technology, if it were yours to command?" Thorn asked.

The General went to the large conference table which occupied one corner of the room and pulled out a chair. Thorn nodded his thanks and sat down. The General sat down across from him and poured them each a glass of water, taking a sip before answering Thorn's question.

"I've always been a fan of games, Mr. Thorn," The General said. "Not long after I was promoted to General, I attended a university competition. Engineering students were competing to see who could build a structure capable of keeping an egg intact while being dropped from extreme heights. I was amazed at the results."

Thorn nodded. He was familiar with the type of contest the General was referring to.

"One of my divisions had a challenge that they assured me was impossible to achieve. I'm sure that a man such as yourself would agree that there's no such thing as impossible, but the group working on the challenge was at a significant roadblock. I devised a game with challenges that exactly duplicated the problem we needed to solve, and then sent invitations to all universities to compete."

"How quickly did they solve your problem?" Thorn asked.

"The invitation was sent out, and three months later the game was held. The fourth team to play solved our 'impossible' challenge."

"Remarkable," Thorn said.

"Indeed," The General agreed. "Even more remarkable is the fact that seven other teams also presented us with solutions during the same competition. A challenge that we had worked unsuccessfully on for over a year, employing the world's best and most intelligent scientists, solved in three months — by kids."

"Impressive results," Thorn said.

"I realized that this strategy could be applied to most, if not all, areas of the military. I formulated a proposal and approached the government for funding. They gave me the money I asked for immediately, and with the appropriated funds, I was able to start my own division. Our results have been overwhelmingly positive."

"Infinite Solutions Division," Thorn said.

"Changing The World Through Play," the General said, finishing the Division's motto.

"So you want to use my virtual reality technology to allow your gamers to play and learn more safely?" Thorn guessed.

"The uses are limitless," The General said. "If I could train a soldier, put him in absolutely real combat repeatedly. Every time he dies, we don't lose him; instead, he comes back to be debriefed and then reinserted. After ten virtual reality simulations I would have a combat hardened veteran, a battle seasoned professional who has died many times, and killed his enemies thousands."

"Which is only the tip of the iceberg," Thorn said.

"Exactly!"

"So I will still own the technology?"

"Absolutely, Mr. Thorn. I don't have the time or the energy to worry about the technology. All I want is to be your most important and number one customer. If we can solidify a deal, I promise to make you the richest man in the world, and also one of the most powerful."

Thorn pretended to think about the proposal for a few moments. The truth of the matter was that he had thought about this partnership for months. He knew what it could mean for him and his company.

"Okay, General," Thorn said. "Let's solidify a deal."

"Does this mean that you possess fully functioning virtual reality technology?" the General asked.

"Yes," Thorn smiled. "That's exactly what it means."

6

Brandon smiled as he sat on a bench in the hallway outside of Wesley's office. He swung his legs gently back and forth, pleased that he'd been able to encourage the adults to let him into the Games early. Brandon wasn't sure what to expect in the games section of the Children's Centre, but he wasn't nervous. No matter what happened, he was excited about the opportunity.

Life wasn't normal for orphans growing up in the Centre. It was more like a military academy than a children's home. Their needs were met, and they all received an excellent education. By the age of five, each child had been tested and assessed thoroughly. Then they were placed in a program that was judged to be most beneficial to their strengths. Intelligent children were steered towards training that would someday involve office work and intellectual tasks. Physically apt children would be groomed for manual labour and field work. Those who excelled at both, like Brandon, were tagged for the Games. The goal of the Centre was to produce the best product possible, and over the years they had become very proficient at their craft.

Brandon was able to read and comprehend anything his instructors put in front of him. He was best in his group for solving puzzles and in spoken communication drills. It seemed that Brandon was a natural at any task set before him. If he was intelligent when it came to books and formal education, the boy was brilliant when it came to the intangible 'street smart' aspect of life.

Brandon was popular with almost everyone. He was funny, kind, and generous to his fellow students, and always willing to stop whatever he was doing to assist his peers. Not only did Brandon have an uncanny ability to comprehend and perform all tasks, but he was also able to teach these new skills to his classmates better than most instructors could.

There were a few children who hated Brandon no matter how hard he tried to win their friendship. He'd done his best to stay out of their way, and when that had finally failed, he had taken steps to show them that it would be best to leave him alone.

The office door opened, and Wesley emerged. "Good morning, Brandon," he said. "Are you ready for orientation?"

Brandon hopped off the bench and stood at respectful attention. "Good morning, Instructor Wesley," he said. "Ready and waiting for orientation, sir."

Even after three years in his position, Wesley still found it a bit unsettling to see these young boys and girls acting like adults. Kids their age should be learning the basic rules of life, playing and worrying about nap time in a regular school, but that wasn't how life was for children inside the Centre. Here they were required to be much more. The Administrator believed that all children could be more. In his opinion it was simply poor and lazy parenting that prevented children from achieving their true potential. Wesley disagreed — silently, of course. Some of his fondest memories were from his childhood. The children who grew up at the Centre would never have memories of playing outside all day, climbing trees, or doing any of the other normal things that regular kids did.

"Let's get going," Wesley said. He led Brandon down the hallway to the elevator. When it arrived, they descended to the basement level. From there, the two walked down a long hall that emerged into an underground subway.

A small train with three cars was waiting. Inside the cars were perhaps two dozen boys, all of them 10 years old. Outside of the train stood five older boys who appeared to be around 15 or 16. As Wesley and Brandon got closer, one of the boys stepped forward and saluted Wesley. Wesley stopped and returned the salute.

"Hello, sir. My name is Cadet Walsch, and I've been instructed to escort Brandon to his orientation."

Wesley nodded. "Very well, Cadet Walsch. I require a moment with Brandon alone. I'll send him over to you in just a moment."

Walsch frowned as if he wanted to deny the request, but he nodded instead. "Very good, sir." He saluted again and moved to stand beside the train door.

Wesley looked at Brandon and smiled. "Give 'em hell, boy," he said.

Brandon smiled back. "Thank you, sir. I will try my best." He stuck out his hand, and Wesley paused for a moment before he grabbed it and shook. "I hope to see you again someday, sir," Brandon said.

"You'll see me very soon, Brandon," Wesley said. "They promoted me to Game Instructor. I'll be one of your first teachers in just a few days."

"Oh," Brandon said, his expression making it obvious to Wesley that he was pleased to hear this. "Then I look forward to learning more from you, sir."

Wesley smiled warmly. "I look forward to learning from you as well, Brandon."

"I don't think I have much to teach," Brandon said.

"I believe you will teach others more than they will ever teach you, Brandon." Wesley replied.

===

Brandon walked to the door of the train and stopped in front of Cadet Walsch. He saluted, holding the gesture until Walsch returned it.

"At ease, Gamer," Walsch said with an amused smirk on his face. "I'm going to take you to join the group of new candidates." Walsch paused for a moment. "But before we get on this train, I have one question."

"Sir?"

"I can only assume that you wanted to become a Gamer," Walsch said.

Brandon stood quietly. He'd been told there would be a question coming, but so far he'd only heard a statement.

Walsch chuckled and nodded his head. "Why would you be in such a rush to start playing games, Brandon?"

"I'm not in a rush to play games, sir," Brandon said. "I haven't lived a long life, but from what I've been able to learn so far, it seems to me that life is a game. Everything I do seems to be part of some sort of game. There are rules, and moves, and reactions, and strategies to refine and perfect. There are even scoring methods for measuring success and failure. Life is all a big game, sir." Brandon smiled. "I figured it would be best to get somewhere that acknowledges this fact and start building myself some points or credits. The Centre's Game Facility is the only place that I've managed to find so far that fits the bill."

Walsch looked at Brandon for a few moments, and then he smiled. "Well, Brandon, you might not have lived that long, but you've figured out some tricky concepts in your short time. I think you'll be one to watch closely in the Games. Come on, let's go."

Walsch led Brandon onto the train and pointed out a seat for him to take, away from the other boys. The older boys stopped talking when Brandon came aboard, watching him quietly as he sat down. Each boy silently told himself that they would easily beat the tiny five-year-old that dared join them in the Games.

Brandon smiled confidently at them, as if reading their minds and inviting them to give it their best shot.

7

Samson Thorn lowered himself into the plush leather chair in the General's office and swirled his brandy around in the glass. The General had just taken him on a day-long tour of the advanced training facilities. The exercises and drills as well as the final products that the General was turning out, using games as a foundation, were an intricate operation.

The General entered the room and removed his jacket. He handed it to his new aide and walked over to join Thorn in the sitting area. "So, Mr. Thorn, what did you think of the facilities?"

"They're quite impressive," Thorn said appreciatively. "I had no idea how much thought and planning went into some of the training; I would be surprised if there are any better soldiers in the world."

"There aren't," The General said. "It isn't just soldiers, Thorn. If you look at any significant leader in this country, you'll discover that they were also trained by us." The General held up his ring for Thorn to inspect. It was a gold signet ring, with the symbol for infinity embossed into its surface. "Now that you've seen this ring, you'll likely begin to notice that many powerful and influential people wear it."

"It does look familiar," Thorn said.

"Any person you see wearing this ring is a graduate of Infinite Solutions Division," the General smiled, "which means that they owe the majority of their success to me."

Thorn considered the implications of the General's statement. Without coming right out and saying it, the General was letting him know how powerful he was on the world stage.

"How much are you currently worth, Mr. Thorn?" the General asked.

Thorn shrugged. "I'm wealthy enough that if I had children, then their children would never have to work a day in their lives."

The General smiled. "So it isn't money that motivates you."

"Money motivates everyone," Thorn said. "It's not my only motivating force, though. I simply want to do my part to help this country remain the great power that it has always been. If I should happen to make a few billion credits as a result," he shrugged, "I would consider that fair compensation for the benefits that I can bring to the table."

"What benefits do you think you can offer us , Mr. Thorn?" the General asked.

"I thought you'd never ask." Thorn produced his laptop computer and turned it on, positioning the screen so that both men could view it. He typed some commands on the keyboard and brought up the graphic of a tropical island. He pressed a key and the image of a person appeared in the middle.

"I can put you into this scene, General. Our process for immersing a subject into a virtual reality matrix has been perfected. You lie on a table and close your eyes. When you open them again, you will find yourself in a different body, and discover yourself in this place. You'll hear every sound and see every detail as if you were truly there. If desired, I could even block the knowledge that you exist somewhere else and have been placed inside a false reality."

"Interesting," the General said.

"Yes," Thorn agreed. He pressed one key at repeated intervals, and each time he did, aspects of the scene disappeared. Eventually the screen was entirely white with only the graphic of the person remaining. "I can remove any or all of the items in this reality. They can be replaced easily with whatever scene the imagination can conceive."

Thorn typed a command and a dragon, large and fierce, stood in front of the person. A few more typed commands filled in a medieval landscape, complete with a damsel trapped in a tall stone tower. With a final keystroke the entire scene became animated; the dragon started to move towards the person, breathing fire and roaring in rage.

"When you are inside the simulation..." the General started to ask.

"It's as real as if we were sitting here at this table," Thorn assured him, "just a bit warmer when the dragon's fire burns the flesh from your bones."

"Incredible," the General said. "So the sky's the limit when it comes to what can be simulated?"

Thorn chuckled and typed on the laptop. The medieval scene disappeared, replaced by the same man floating in the void of outer space. "The sky isn't the limit, General. Only your imagination is."

"Can you replicate exact conditions? Our gravity, physical and scientific laws, bodies that react identically to our own?"

"Absolutely," Thorn assured him.

"Are there any limitations?" the General asked.

"Yes," Thorn said. "We can only put a few individuals into the same simulation at once, and the more complex the simulation, the fewer players that can occupy it."

"Is there a way to address that?"

"Absolutely," Thorn said. "Build and equip more powerful computers with larger capacity. I already have technicians working on the details. If we had enough money, then we could solve these issues very easily."

"How much money do you want to come and work with me, Mr. Thorn?"

Thorn handed him a sheet. "The amount I require is at the bottom of this page, General."

The General glanced briefly at the page, then looked back at the computer screen with the simulation running on it. He looked at Thorn seriously. "This is more money than a decade's worth of GNP for most countries." He paused for a moment, then nodded and smiled grimly. "Nonetheless, I can guarantee that amount for you."

Thorn suppressed a smile of triumph. He'd expected more resistance.

His happiness was abruptly halted by the General's next sentence.

"However, for that amount, I will require greater control of the project."

Thorn smiled calmly and said nothing while the General waited for an answer.

Thorn stood up and closed the laptop.

"I understand that you are a very powerful man, General, and I have the utmost respect for you. It's your prerogative to insist on such control. I'm sure that dealing with civilians is unpleasant, mostly because we aren't required to stand at attention and say, "Thank you, sir," when you kick us in the teeth like enlisted people are. But if you intend to change the rules of the game whenever you like, then I'm going to have to pass on this partnership."

The General said nothing as Thorn left the room. After a few moments he reached for the phone and dialed a number. "Thorn just left. It seems that he's willing to walk away rather than concede control to us."

"Is there no one else with this type of technology?" asked a woman's voice.

"No," the General said.

"Do we need Thorn alive, Donovan?" she asked.

"It appears that the answer to that question is yes, at least for now."

"Okay, then. Get him back on board," she said.

"He has other offers on the table," the General said. "I think after what just happened he'll decide to explore them first."

"We can at least eliminate the others who are making offers, right? Don't tell me we can't kill anyone right now; I don't need to hear that kind of negative talk from you."

The General smiled. "Yes, we can do that."

"Excellent." The General could hear the pleasure in her voice. "Then get to work, Donovan, and let me know when he's back in line. I'd like to see things moving forward in less than a month."

"Yes, Madame President," the General said, and hung up the phone.

8

Brandon's first day in the Games Facility was not what he had hoped for.

There were no games to be played; instead the children spent both the morning and afternoon touring the facility and listening to their guides. The wealth of information on the details of the Facility and its procedures were a bit overwhelming; Brandon was positive that he would forget most of it, and from the looks on the other kid's faces, he guessed he wouldn't be the only one. By day's end they had learned everything they would need to live in the Game Facility. Brandon knew where he would sleep, eat, learn, play, and compete. Their guides were very thorough in their orientation.

Cadet Walsch and the other senior gamers from the train were their tour guides for the day. The recruits learned that there would be minimal adult involvement during a normal day in the facility. Adults acted primarily as instructors and referees for the older gamers. The new kids, or Baggers as they were called, were to be kept together. Baggers were expected to learn from the older and more experienced Gamers about the basics. They could expect help getting started in the simple, entry level games.

After dinner they were shown to their barracks where each kid selected a bunk that would be theirs until they moved up in rank. There were a dozen newcomers in Brandon's group, eight boys and four girls. The beds were standard, military issue bunks with thin mattresses and rough woolen blankets. At the foot of each bed was a small locker. Brandon opened his and found a bar of soap, two towels, underwear, socks, and some plain pants and shirts.

Lights out occurred not long after that. Brandon lie down on his bunk, closed his eyes, and promptly went to sleep.

===

A strange sound caused him to open his eyes. Brandon sat up in his cot and looked around the room. It was dark; everyone else was asleep. A faint light shone from the bathrooms at the far end of the barracks where the sounds seemed to be coming from. Brandon stood up and walked carefully toward the source of the noise.

He walked through the doorway and stood in the center of the room. Suddenly, the doorway behind him became a solid wall, and the lights dimmed. The floor began to shimmer, taking on a dark silvery colour, like black sand on a beach. Brandon heard a skittering sound, and three small whirling patterns formed on the floor in front of him. They darkened in colour as they spun and began to emit a high pitched whine. The whining stopped abruptly, followed by a distinct popping sound as the circles on the floor exploded upwards. A black rat emerged from each hole. They looked uglier than normal vermin, with ragged, oily fur, long claws, and yellowed teeth. Brandon noticed that their eye sockets were empty, which made them look even uglier. The three rats remained very still, making eerie chittering sounds and slowly turning their heads from side to side in a searching motion.

Brandon sensed another presence to his right. He turned his head very slowly and discovered that the wall beside him had opened onto a lush, tropical rain forest. The green landscape was tinged with a faint but noticeable golden glow.

In the tree closest to him, Brandon noticed a giant sloth gazing at him as it hung lazily from a large branch.

"Don't move," the sloth said. Its voice was deep and rich, and the tone of its command made Brandon obey without hesitation. "Don't make a sound or move an inch. If they hear you, they will attack."

Brandon followed the sloth's advice and remained frozen in place. The rats didn't move, but continued to chitter excitedly, stopping simultaneously every few seconds to move their heads and listen.

How long will I have to stand here? Brandon thought to himself.

Sensing his thoughts, the sloth replied. "Not very long. They will soon move along to continue their hunt."

Would they eat me? Brandon asked silently.

"They most certainly would," the sloth said. "A small boy like you, with no protection or knowledge of the world you are living in...? Yes, they would eat you, and be pleased with their good fortune at finding such a tasty morsel."

After a few tense moments, the rats abruptly dug down into the floor, disappearing as quickly as they had materialized. As they vanished, Brandon felt the golden glow from the rain forest begin to fade as well. He looked toward the sloth, but the jungle scene was slowly fading as the bathroom wall began to reappear.

"Farewell, young one," the sloth said, raising one arm. "I will see you again soon."

What is this place? Brandon asked. *Where are you going?*

The sloth chuckled. "It is you who are going, Brandon. This is a dream, and you are leaving this place to go back to your other dream."

I feel like I'm waking up, Brandon thought.

"So young, and so naive," the sloth said. "You are simply moving from one dream into another; goodbye for now."

Brandon opened his eyes and found himself lying on his bunk. The other students were waking up around him. He felt like he'd only been asleep for a few moments, but the night had passed entirely.

It was time for his first day of gaming lessons.

9

The mess hall was a huge, underground cavern with tall walls and a rough natural stone ceiling. It looked like the great halls described in books that Brandon's last teacher used to love to read to the class. He imagined bats or owls suddenly swooping from the dark rafters and causing havoc.

Brandon was an instant celebrity among the rest of the facility, but it hadn't been a positive thing so far. He sat alone at a table in the back, ignored by the other students as they laughed and joked around him throughout the giant room.

An older student bumped Brandon's table as he walked past. "This the baby superstar?" he asked his friends as he passed. The other boys laughed and slapped the student on the back.

"More like a toddler," Brandon said.

The student stopped, turned around, and walked back to Brandon, towering over him. "What did you say, snot?" he asked.

Brandon stuffed his mouth full of food, then looked up at the boy with a big smile on his face. "I said," he crunched loudly, food dribbling down his chin as he spoke, "That I'm more like a toddler. I'm almost out of diapers; that's how I know I'm not a baby."

The other kids laughed at Brandon's joke, but the main boy silenced them with a dark scowl.

The boy leaned forward until he was only inches from Brandon's face. He was tall with brown hair and dark eyes. He looked around 13 or 14, his nose was normal width and length, and cruel, thin lips formed a straight line as he glared at Brandon. "I hope by some strange miracle that you advance enough to face me in the Games, little one. When I'm done with you, you'll be wearing diapers for the rest of your life."

Brandon said nothing. Instead, he continued to smile and chew loudly, not appearing concerned that an older and much larger boy was in his face uttering threats.

"Come on, Lohkam," one of the other boys said. "Leave the brat alone. He'll wipe out of trials and be gone before the week is out."

"Yeah, Lohkam," Brandon said. "Leave the superstar alone. Save it for the Games. I'll never catch up to a smart guy like you."

Lohkam glared silently, then straightened up and smiled at his friends. "I hope you do, puke," he said to Brandon as he walked away.

Brandon smiled and continued eating. He was just finishing up when a silence swept over the room. Five men walked into the dining hall, casually strolling through the room as if they owned the place. They were talking and laughing as they walked, calling out names and exchanging comments with students. It seemed like everyone in the room knew who these men were, and adored them.

Brandon leaned over and got the attention of a girl at the table beside him. "Who are those guys?"

"Those are the A's," she said. "The right hand of the A's."

Brandon looked at the men in awe; of course everyone knew who they were. Brandon had never dreamed of seeing them this close up.

Each year, a group of Centre children turned 18 and were released from the Centre as adults. Their years of training and conditioning often resulted in them entering the military where they excelled over their peers. The best graduates were offered prestigious positions working directly for General Donovan. Each year he selected graduates to fill 20 spots. Not all were filled from this Centre; there were many Centres around the country for the General to select from. The twenty spots were broken down into four groups of five, and named after the body. Five became the right hand, five the left hand, five the heart, and five the soul. Collectively they were known as the Avatar of the General. When it was announced to the public that the General had infiltrated a rebel group and destroyed them, or the General was delivering supplies to assist a starving nation, these elite groups were the ones they were speaking about. No one knew for certain how many Avatars of the General currently operated in the field, but they were given letters to distinguish them. Brandon could recall hearing about Avatar H one time on the news.

The A's were the best of the best, and the Right Hand of the General were the top five of that group of twenty.

That's who Brandon was looking at in the mess hall; the five most skilled soldiers in the entire world.

Brandon sat in his seat and silently watched them from the back of the room. It became apparent that the Hand of the General had a leader, and that's who Brandon found himself watching the most.

He was a tall muscular man who appeared to be in his late twenties. His skin was tanned with a few white scars visible on various parts of his body; his features were sharp and handsome. His short cropped hair was white and looked stylish despite its messy appearance as it stood up at various angles. Even from this distance the man's most remarkable characteristic were his eyes. They were a blue colour unlike any that Brandon had seen before, and they twinkled with clever mischief wherever they looked.

Brandon watched the General's Right Hand work the room until it was time to go to class. As he stood up to leave the room, he heard a friendly voice from behind him.

"Nervous on your first day?"

Brandon turned around to find himself face to face with the man he'd been watching. Brandon wanted to say something witty, but he couldn't seem to make any sound.

The man grinned, and continued to speak. He was obviously used to receiving this type of reaction. "I wanted to come over and meet you, young man. It's Brandon, right?"

Brandon recovered his voice and answered. "Yes, sir," he said.

The two shook hands. Brandon swore that he felt a tingling in his hand from the contact.

"Don't call me sir," the man said. "I'm not some old fart. Call me by my name; I'm Cooper."

"Oh, I know who you are, sir. I mean, Cooper." Brandon said.

Cooper smiled and slapped the boy on the shoulder. "We got here late today, and you likely have to get to your class."

Brandon nodded.

"I won't keep you long," Cooper said. "We stroll through here whenever we get the chance, which isn't as often as we would like. I had to talk to you. I noticed you and felt it, so I had to come over."

"You felt what?" Brandon asked.

"The spark," Cooper said. He leaned forward and put his hand on Brandon's shoulder. "When I feel the spark, I'm compelled to approach that student and offer a word of advice; something that the General himself said to me when I was just a young ward of the Centre."

Brandon looked around wondering who might have this spark that Cooper was speaking about. Then he realized that Cooper was talking about him. He looked at Cooper hopefully.

Cooper nodded, "Yes, I sense that spark in you, Brandon. Are you ready for your words of advice?"

Brandon nodded silently.

"Okay, then," Cooper said, "here they are. Relax. It's all just a game."

Brandon stood there waiting for the advice. Cooper watched him with an expression of amusement. After a few moments it appeared that Cooper had nothing more to say.

Brandon wanted to tell Cooper that he knew it was a game. The school itself was called the Game Facility, after all; there was nothing surprising in what he'd said. Cooper's look told him there was a message in his words, even if he didn't understand it.

Brandon simply smiled and nodded his head. "Thank you, Cooper, I appreciate the advice. It was great to meet you."

Cooper smiled at Brandon's politeness. Every kid asked him what he was talking about when he gave his advice. He wasn't sure any of them ever got it, although he was fairly certain that most never did. Brandon seemed different, though. Was it possible that this young one was better than all the others? Only time would tell. He patted the boy on the back and sent him on his way, turning to go rejoin his brothers.

He would be keeping an eye on young Brandon.

<u>10</u>

The General was reading reports when his phone rang.

"General, Mr. Thorn is here to see you. He says that you are expecting him?"

The General smiled and nodded. "Yes, Sarah, please send him right in."

A moment later the door opened and Thorn walked in. He didn't waste time with polite greetings or small talk. "It would seem that no one wants to work with me, General," he said. "Do you really think you can force me into a partnership with you?"

"I told you that I was a very powerful man, Mr. Thorn," the General replied. "I don't want to force you into a partnership, but I will certainly not allow you to work with anyone else and leave me out of the equation. That wouldn't be acceptable to me, or to your country. You either work with me, or you go it alone."

Thorn started to speak, but he caught himself in mid-sentence, took a slow breath, and smiled. He went to the bar and, without asking for permission, poured himself a drink. Thorn walked over to the desk and sat down, taking a sip. The General sat calmly and watched Thorn with a pleasant look on his face. Both knew who the winner was, but the General saw no point in gloating over his victory.

Thorn finished his drink and set the crystal glass down on the desk with a loud thunk. "It's been three weeks since our last meeting," he said. "I assume that you have the money I require and the computers built?"

The General looked slightly confused. "I've built the computers as specified in the instructions provided when we last met. I thought that the money you requested would be used to build the computers, so I went ahead and did the work for you. Since you have the computers, you don't need the money."

Thorn smiled coldly. "My price to work with you has doubled, General. Now I require the computers *and* the sum of money quoted."

"Very well," the General said.

"Just like that?" Thorn asked.

"Just like that," the General nodded. "Look, Mr. Thorn, I don't want bad blood between us. If paying the credits on top of building you the computers puts us on good terms then it's a small price to pay, as far as I'm concerned. I can have that sum credited to you within the hour. Would you like to confirm receipt before we get to work, or do you trust me enough that we can begin now?"

"I'm not sure I will ever trust you, General," Thorn said. "However, I'm willing to get started now."

"Excellent," the General said. He opened a desk drawer, pulled out a small box, and passed it to Thorn. Inside was a platinum pin fashioned into the shape of the infinity symbol; the General's mark. "If you wear this at all times, it will help our work progress more quickly. I bestow these pins on very few individuals, Mr. Thorn, and anyone who works with me will recognize it as a symbol of authority. Your orders will be followed without question while you wear it... as long as your orders don't counteract my own."

"Thank you, General," Thorn said. "This will certainly help save time."

"How soon will we be able to put my people into virtual reality?" the General asked.

Thorn pulled out three files and handed them to the General. "Each of these files must be completed before we will be ready to proceed with initial VR testing. The first file is a checklist to make absolutely certain that the computer systems you've built meet my specifications. The second file gives biological data so that we can form facilities capable of holding the subjects and keeping them healthy and fed while they are immersed in virtual reality. The third file covers the parameters that need to be selected. It might look complex, but it's very basic. The computer mainframe will fill in most of the blanks when we get subjects into the simulations. If everything goes quickly and efficiently, then I expect we should have your first people inside the system within the next three weeks."

"That is excellent news, Mr. Thorn. I would like to ramp up the simulations, starting first with simple drills and building in complexity as we go."

"That sounds easy enough to accomplish," Thorn said.

"Is it possible to record everything that goes on inside the simulation, and measure each individual's vital scores and functions?"

"Absolutely," Thorn said. "We can start with as many as twenty individuals on the first run. I thought you might want to send in an entire General's Avatar?"

"I will likely only send in one individual to begin with," The General said. "I would also like to formulate a special project, Mr. Thorn, using younger people."

"How young?" Thorn asked.

"Ten-year-olds," the General said. "I have a new batch of Gamers in one of my feeder facilities. I'm thinking it might be best to start them immediately inside the virtual reality system. Then I can measure their results and scores against others who have experience in the traditional games that I've been running for years."

"It sounds like an interesting idea, General," Thorn said. "Of course we can try that out and see how it will work. Ten-year-olds will be no problem to integrate at all. I wouldn't go any younger than five, just to be safe."

"Funny you should mention that," the General said. "I was just reading a report from one of my prime facilities, the facility that produced Cooper. It seems that there is one remarkable five-year-old attempting to gain admission to the program. If he makes it, I would like to include him in this pilot project as well."

"That will be fine," Thorn assured him. "If the five-year-old makes it into your program, it will be no problem to include him in the VR program."

11

The Baggers waited in the hallway before their first class.

They were lined up single file, and the line extended far down the dimly lit hall. There were a lot more kids in line than there were on the train here. Brandon guessed that they must have come from different Centres. He waited patiently with the rest of the children; there was a girl in front of him and a boy behind him. Everyone towered over Brandon, which was no surprise to him, but it did cause many curious looks in his direction.

"Please tell me you're the five-year-old that everyone's been talking about," said the boy standing behind him. Brandon looked over his shoulder and saw a friendly looking boy with shaggy blonde hair smiling at him. His eyes were blue and his shoulders were wide for a young boy of ten. He looked stronger than the rest, and far friendlier than most of the kids he'd met so far.

"Yeah, that's me," Brandon said.

"Good, I thought maybe you were just really small, or else they'd been putting something in my food that made me really big!"

Brandon laughed. "My name's Brandon. What's yours?"

The boy tapped himself on the chest quickly three times, then held his hand out to Brandon who shook it. "My name's Tony. It's nice to meet you, Runt."

Brandon wasn't sure what to make of the nickname. Whenever he'd heard it before, there was always a negative flavour to it, but when Tony said it he didn't get that vibe.

Tony sensed Brandon's confusion, and he smiled reassuringly. "Hope you don't mind me calling you that. It just kinda came out," he said. "I know most people use that word in a bad way, but not me. At our Centre we had a dog. She had a litter of pups, and there was one that was smaller than the rest; you know, a runt. Well, the others all got snapped up real quick by people who worked there. No one wanted the runt, though, and so he stayed with us at the Centre. Most of us never thought we'd get a pet, and so we were really excited to get to keep him. We called him 'Killer' as a joke, you know, because he was so teeny. All of us would save bits from our meals and smuggle them to Killer, and it didn't take long for him to grow." Tony laughed. "By the time he was full grown, he was the biggest damn dog you ever laid eyes on. Our instructors would say to us that sometimes even a runt can surprise you if you give it what it needs."

Brandon smiled and nodded his head. He liked the story.

"When I saw you standing there looking smaller than all the rest of us, but not really worried about it, you reminded me of Killer," Tony said. "Calling you Runt just seemed to fit."

"It didn't seem like you were trying to be mean when you said it," Brandon said. "I think I like it. Feel free to call me Runt if you'd like, Tony."

Tony ruffled Brandon's hair playfully, "Thanks, Runt. I think I will."

"Are you nervous?" Brandon asked. "Any idea what goes on during the trials?"

"I have no clue," Tony said, "I'm not nervous, though. I'll do my best no matter what. That's usually good enough to keep me ahead of the pack, so I'm sure that's how it will go here too. What about you? Are you nervous?"

Before Brandon could answer, the line started to move forward slowly. "Looks like there's no time to worry now," Brandon said.

Brandon broke into a grin as he recognized the instructor at the door, it was Wesley! As the kids filed in, Wesley was repeating instructions to all of them. "Go in the room and gather along the walls. No one is to sit down until instructed to do so."

A few minutes later, all of them were inside and standing along the walls. There were desks in the centre of the room, looking as if they had been randomly thrown together.

Wesley called for silence and when the murmuring ceased, he began to speak. "The first game is a simple one, but for one of you it will be your last."

The group began to murmur with worry. Brandon looked up at Tony beside him, who winked down at Brandon and smiled.

"There are fifty applicants in this room. Can anyone tell me how many desks there are?"

"There are forty-nine," Brandon said.

Wesley smiled and nodded at Brandon. "That's right. There are only forty-nine. We will play music, and when it stops, each of you must sit at a desk. You cannot sit on the table portion of the desk. The one of you who winds up without a seat goes home. Let's begin."

The music started and everyone began to walk slowly around the room. Whenever anyone looked at Brandon they smirked, and he knew that they were all imagining the little one going home. He smiled back at them; he hadn't come this far just to wash out in the first half hour. He walked as calmly as the rest, trying to think how he would get a seat once the physical jostling began.

Suddenly the music stopped. Brandon was ready for it. He might not be big, but he was certainly fast. With a quick zip and dodge, he sat in a chair slightly ahead of a boy. The rest of the chairs quickly began to fill up as the kids started to shove each other and jockey for position. As the number of available chairs dwindled, the amount of pushing and shoving increased dramatically.

Finally there were three boys remaining and only two chairs. One of the boys was beside Brandon, and didn't appear to be focused on the remaining empty chairs. Brandon looked at him and realized too late what the boy intended to do.

With a quick grab and a shove, the boy pushed Brandon right out of his seat. Brandon landed on the floor with a heavy thud and the boy grinned as he sat down deliberately in the vacant seat.

Brandon knew there was no way he could shove the other boys out of their chairs even if he could get to that side of the room in time. He had to think fast, or he was going home.

"Runt!" Tony hissed at him from a few desks away. Brandon looked at Tony and it was almost as if he could read his mind. Brandon rushed over to Tony and slid down on his lap. He faced forward and sat there looking as calm as the others as the game ended.

No one spoke. A few of the kids close by laughed and pointed, but Tony and Brandon just sat at their desk normal as could be. Wesley walked towards the two and stopped in front of them.

"Time's up and I see no one standing," he said with a frown. "I swear we had one more kid than desk available, but every desk is filled properly. I don't see anyone spilling over into the aisle or sitting on the desk tops."

Wesley stood silently, waiting. Finally Brandon looked up at him. Wesley winked at him, and Brandon could tell he was proud of the creative solution the boys had found by working together.

"Every single one of you should thank Brandon and Tony sometime before lights out. One of you would have lost an all-out fight with another your size and likely gone home. Because of the two clever boys sitting in one desk, you all get to stay and play more interesting games than this one."

Wesley paused to let what he had just said sink in.

"There will be no more elimination games today," Wesley announced. "Everyone head to room 212. We will begin in ten minutes."

Brandon jumped off of Tony's lap and gave him a slap on the shoulder. "Thank you, Tony, you saved me today. How can I repay you?"

Tony laughed and tapped his chest quickly three times before touching Brandon on the shoulder. "I have a feeling you might repay the favour once or twice, Runt."

Brandon smiled. "You can count on it, friend."

12

"Well, it looks like your boy hasn't failed out of the trials yet, Wesley," the Administrator said.

"No, sir," Wesley said. "He made it through the admission process successfully."

"I've been monitoring the reports as they come in, but they aren't terribly detailed. How did Brandon truly do during the process?"

"Out of fifty applicants, twenty will be accepted," Wesley said. "Of the twenty who are accepted, Brandon was ranked number nine."

"Very positive results for the youngest applicant ever."

"He's very smart," Wesley said. "From everything I've witnessed he could have easily been ranked number one or two."

"Then why wasn't he?"

"He positioned himself to be number nine." Wesley said. "He knew how to place in each game so that he finished exactly where he wanted."

"How do you know that?"

Wesley laughed. "I watched him throw games. He would be in the lead of a particular game, and then for no reason he'd back off to finish worse than he should have."

"Ridiculous," the Administrator said.

"That's what the other instructors said," Wesley nodded. "I kept very close tabs on what he was doing, though. Most didn't notice what was going on, or they explained it away. 'He simply sprinted too soon and couldn't hold the pace until the end of the race,' or 'The first few puzzles were easy for him to see, but when it got tougher the others caught up and passed him'."

"But you disagreed?"

"Absolutely," Wesley said. "I began to wonder when his rankings hit a consistent target each time."

"What target was that?"

"During the entire trial process, Brandon was one rank higher than the elimination rank."

The Administrator laughed. "So when they were cutting kids at forty...?"

"Brandon was ranked 39," Wesley confirmed. "To confirm my suspicions I lied to them all one day. I told them we were eliminating to a false number."

"The boy ended up being one above that?" the Administrator guessed.

"Exactly," Wesley smiled. "When I announced I had made an error, Brandon laughed out loud and winked at me. The boy is in his element, sir."

"I'm glad to hear it," the Administrator said. "We couldn't challenge him here, and I didn't know what to do with him if he failed out. Any other interesting news not contained in the updates?"

"Yes," Wesley said. "He's forming his own Hand."

It wasn't uncommon for players to want to emulate their heroes; often player groups would form in an attempt to become dominant teams throughout their time in the game facility. Some of them even attempted to form a team of the entire 20 members, calling themselves the 'Junior General's Avatars.' The General's 'D' Avatar had been formed that way and they were a very effective team on the world stage.

"He's building a core team of five from his group before he even gets accepted," the administrator said. "Is it fully formed?"

"Not yet. He wants to keep one spot open for the thumb. The word is that Brandon expects to attract an exceptional

Sponsor to help guide him and his team. He's saving the last spot for that person."

"What are they saying about his chances, Wesley? A normal child lives inside the facility for eight years, and many burn out before graduation. Does anyone think he will make it the thirteen?"

"Most believe that he will do more than just make it, sir," Wesley said. "They know it's a longer shot than normal, but those who know the system are saying he could be another Cooper."

"Another Cooper..." the Administrator said. "That would be something."

===

"Wow, look who's come to watch us get accepted into the Facility!" Tony nudged Brandon lightly in the ribs and pointed.

Brandon glanced towards the front of the room where the instructors were sitting. Cooper and the rest of the A Hand were entering the room, smiling and waving as the newest group of facility applicants began to cheer and shout out calls of adoration. The chief instructor stood and approached the men to welcome them. Cooper leaned forward and whispered something to the instructor, causing him to smile and nod his head.

The five members of the Hand sat down in the chairs provided, and the chief instructor walked towards the front of the stage to begin the ceremony.

"It's been an exciting two weeks for all of us during these trials. I hope each one of you is happy to be sitting here instead of back in your home Centres." Some of the children called out in agreement. Everyone remaining was relieved to have made it through the trials. The kids who didn't make it could try out one more time next year, but they would lose a year in the game facility and never be as skilled as the ones who had made the cut today.

"Normal procedure during this ceremony is to call you up from rank twenty to one and give you your player pin. Before we get to that, we have a special treat for you all. We're fortunate today to have some very special guests with us. The Right Hand of the 'A's' join us to celebrate your acceptance into the facility." Again there was more cheering and applause. This was an exciting bonus for the children that they would never forget. Word of this honour would make its way around the rest of the facility, helping to increase their reputation among the entire gaming community.

"Before we get started, Cooper has asked to address you all. Cooper, if you would do us the honour?"

Cooper stood up and sauntered to the front of the stage. He smiled and looked out over the students, pausing periodically to make eye contact with some of them. His eyes met Brandon's and his grin became more sly. Brandon returned his smile and nodded slightly.

"I still remember my entrance ceremony," Cooper began. "The General wasn't as busy back then as he is today, and he was our guest speaker. He didn't stay long, or say much, but what he did say still occupies my thoughts, whether I'm out on a secret mission, or training other soldiers to fight for our country."

Cooper paused and the entire room seemed very quiet. "Don't save your best effort for later, because later never arrives."

Cooper walked back and forth across the stage as he continued to speak. "Today there are thirty children who might have been better than all of you at playing the Games. We will never know if that's true, because they weren't better than you yesterday, or the day before." He pointed to the doorway and shook his finger. "Out there are kids who have more practice, and training, and experience than you at the games you will now learn to play, but that doesn't matter. Any of you can beat them, on the right day, at the right moment, under the right set of conditions.

"Some of you are afraid to be number one too soon. Some of you didn't do your very best at each moment of competing. I know why you did it. You're planning strategies... you're afraid of having others come for you before you're ready to compete with them. There are many reasons, and although I understand these reasons, I do not accept them."

Cooper stopped walking and looked directly at Brandon. "If you were a member of my Hand, I would kick you from my squad and send you home." Brandon felt the force of those words as if he was being hit in the stomach. "You're playing games to learn how to play the real game; the game of life. Life wants your best effort every second, not some of the time... all the time. If I were to do less than my best for even one moment, then my brothers or sisters could die."

Cooper began to move along the stage again. "Many are afraid that if they use up everything they have now, then they won't have anything to use in the next game. I am here to tell you, kids, that you will always have more. The more you use, the more you make. I know most of you won't believe me, but it's true."

Cooper walked back to the middle of the stage and saluted the crowd. "I look forward to serving with some of you, and I'm honoured to know you all. Don't save your best effort for later, because later never arrives."

Cooper walked back to his seat and sat down. The crowd erupted in loud applause and shouting. Cooper smiled and nodded his head in thanks, graciously indicating his teammates, who also waved to the crowd. Brandon stood and applauded with the rest. Cooper glanced at Brandon and made eye contact with him, raising his eyebrow in a questioning manner.

Brandon smiled and nodded back, thinking to himself, Message received, Cooper.

Cooper nodded in satisfaction.

13

Brandon was standing in the bathroom again, not twitching a muscle as the three black rats waited for him to move and give up his position.

"They stay longer each time we are here," the sloth said. Brandon smiled slowly and looked to his right. The sloth sat in its tree surrounded by the golden tinged rain forest.

While you take longer to arrive each time we are here, Brandon thought. *I didn't think you would appear this time.*

The sloth chuckled softly. "I'm getting tired of this dream, Brandon. How many times have we sat here and waited for the rats to depart?"

Twelve, Brandon thought.

"I marvel at your patience," the sloth said. "Oh, wait — I use the wrong word. I marvel at your laziness. Yes, that is a more fitting word for this situation," the sloth nodded.

What do you mean, laziness? You told me to stand still the first time I came here.

"Yes, that is what I told you to do... the first time," the sloth said. "When you find yourself somewhere new and you don't know what's going on, the best thing to do is to stand still and try to figure out what's going on. I also recommend trying something, eventually. I would have tried something long ago," the sloth grinned at Brandon. "I'm a sloth, and this process has been too long and slow even for me."

Brandon felt his cheeks flushing with embarrassment. *What should I do, then?*

"Ahh, excellent!" the Sloth said. "I expect you to ask for help. When you find yourself in a new and possibly dangerous situation, first stand still, and next look for help. You may not always find it, but you should always look for it. The main reason for being stuck in one place is because we don't even bother to look for a different or better place to go."

That makes sense.

"Thank you," the sloth said. "You are lucky to be learning such lessons so early in your life. Now listen closely to what I tell you, Brandon. We are about to move to the next part of this dream."

Brandon listened while the sloth told him what to do. It wasn't truly listening, it was more like feeling and seeing what was to be done. He nodded and smiled confidently when the sloth finished communicating with him.

Brandon closed his eyes briefly, then opened them and took one step forward and clapped his hands together. As his hands met, a boom like a tremendous thunderclap filled the room, shaking the ground and walls. In perfect unison, the rats turned their heads to focus on Brandon. Their empty eye sockets appeared to glitter with blackness, and the corners of their mouths turned upwards in evil smiles.

In the blink of an eye they launched themselves towards Brandon, their jaws opening wide to tear the boy's flesh from his bones.

Brandon was faster. Their feet had barely left the ground when they froze, floating in midair. The rats began to scream in frustration, their teeth gnashing and paws reaching for their prey. Brandon smiled. His hands were shoulder width apart, his fingers stiff with tension as he used his will to hold the rats in place. Slowly he began to bring his hands together, curling his fingers so that one hand cupped the other. As his hands moved together the rats came closer to each other. They began to press into one another and then squeeze against each other.

Sensing what was happening, the rats began to scream in fear as they were crushed together until they were nothing but a tight, dead ball of disgusting fur.

Brandon released his concentration and the small ball of dead rats fell to the ground with a dull thud. Brandon sank to one knee; the effort had clearly weakened him.

"Very well done, Brandon." The sloth said. "Better than I would have guessed. Perhaps all that waiting helped you to store enough energy for the task."

"Stop it," Brandon laughed. He could talk out loud now that the rats were gone.

"How do you feel? Could you do it again if you had to?"

"Right now?" Brandon asked. He thought about it for a moment and stood up straight. "Yes, I think I could."

"Excellent," the sloth said. "Show me." The floor began to swirl again, and three more rats appeared.

This time Brandon reacted quickly. He repeated the entire process, and in seconds the three rats were dead.

"Good," the sloth said. "Now get ready, third time's the charm."

Three more rats appeared and were dead before they were even fully emerged from their holes. Brandon sank heavily to the ground. The effort had drained a significant amount of his energy. "I think that's all I can do right now," he said. "If you bring more they will have to eat me."

"That will be enough for this session," the sloth said. "When you leave this place try to remember what it felt like, to stop them and crush them. Think about it for a few minutes right away, and then again during the day."

"Okay," Brandon said.

"We will see you soon, Brandon," the sloth said. "Your next visit will be more fun."

"What do you mean, we?" Brandon asked. The rain forest began to fade. Behind the sloth, Brandon thought he could see a giant owl launch itself into the air and fly away.

Brandon woke up and stretched. He could still feel the power in his hands and body. If three ugly black rats suddenly jumped out at him now, Brandon was sure that he could grab them with invisible hands and crush them.

He quickly shook his head. That was only possible in his dream, wasn't it?

14

"If I could have everyone's attention, please," the head instructor said. He stood on the stage of the main gathering hall, the only room in the Game Facility large enough to accommodate the entire population. It was uncommon for unscheduled assemblies to occur, and everyone was excited to know the reason for it.

"The General is here. It's been some time since his last visit and I know that we are all excited to have him back. The General has come to make a very special announcement, so please join me in welcoming him to the stage."

The crowd launched into loud, animated cheering. Everyone loved the General. When these children had lost their parents, the world had abandoned them. It was the General who'd built facilities all over the country to take them in. It was the General who made certain they were fed and clothed and educated. It was the General who followed their progress, and wished each child a happy birthday with a personally handwritten card, or note, or video message on their special day. All the children of the Centres loved the General. He was their father, and they were fiercely loyal to him.

None of them realized that they were, in fact, carefully cultivated slaves. The Centres were a massive psychological experiment in control and manipulation. The General had spent billions of credits on every detail of the child rearing process to ensure that his military machine and agenda were provided with the best possible human resources. Teams of top psychologists from around the world had designed the Centres to raise and develop their wards. The children were conditioned to compete, excel, and worship the General. He was in the business of finding and training loyal soldiers who would live and die for him without thought for themselves, and the Children's Centres had proven extremely effective at delivering this goal.

The General walked onto the stage, smiling and pumping his fists with excitement. These were his children, and his smile conveyed the pride he felt at being in their midst. He moved to the edge of the stage and touched hands with the children as they pushed forward in an attempt to make physical contact with their hero. After a few moments, he went back to the microphone and smiled as the cheering continued. Finally, he raised his hands and the cheering quickly subsided.

"You are the best of my children," he said. This statement caused another round of cheering, and it took several minutes before they calmed down enough so that he could continue. The General smiled and waved during the applause, letting them build into a frenzy of excitement and adoration.

"I know, a parent isn't supposed to have favourites," the General said when they quieted down. "The cold hard truth is that when a Gamer turns eighteen, the world becomes a much better place for having the protection that you all bring to it."

Again the crowd of over 1500 gamers roared with pride and excitement. The General navigated the stage and worked the crowd until it quieted down.

"I'm here to share some very exciting news with you all today," he said. The crowd became silent; the few who continued to talk were hissed at by their neighbours. No one wanted to miss the General's announcement.

"I'm here to announce something truly exciting," the General said. "The face of Gaming is about to change forever, and you will be the first to lead the way."

The General waved his arm and the huge curtain on the wall opened to reveal a massive view screen. The lights dimmed and a program began to play. In the video, the General appeared and began to speak. Over the next fifteen minutes, the video told the crowd about virtual reality and how it worked. Then it cut to a scene of a young person putting on a headset and being immersed in a virtual reality simulation. The video was professionally produced; it was both informative and exciting. When the screen went blank and the lights came up, the room was completely silent.

The General looked out over his audience, and smiled inwardly. He could see the hunger in the children's eyes. They had been introduced to the future of playing games, and they wanted to play. "Some of you will be playing in virtual reality before the year is over," he said.

The crowd cheered loudly. The General grinned.

Standing in the middle of the crowd, surrounded by kids much larger than himself, Brandon stood quietly. No matter what it took, he knew that he would be one of those kids.

Deep down, Brandon knew this was his destiny.

15

"**There must** be a way to immerse an individual into VR without putting them onto a table and inducing a coma," the General said.

"Why?" Thorn asked.

"It's too... invasive," the General said. "Why not just put a helmet on and sit still in a chair? I've seen prototypes like that."

"Failed prototypes," Thorn said. "The reason is complicated, General, but valid. The subconscious mind is more complex and aware than we realize. If you are able to move around, even in the slightest capacity, the subconscious part of the brain detects it and prevents a successful virtual reality experience."

The General looked at Thorn, his jaw twitching slowly. "Have you ever experienced it?" he asked. "Have you gone into the VR simulation?"

Thorn flashed the General a sly smile. "Maybe I'm in a simulation right now," he said.

The General laughed, and then stopped as he considered what Thorn was implying. His face became thoughtful; what if life itself was nothing more than a computer generated reality? As the implications of the thought sank in, the General scowled, causing Thorn to laugh.

"I'm just fooling with you, General. Of course we aren't in a simulation right now; that would be too incredible to believe. To answer your question, I have entered the VR matrix multiple times."

"I wish I could experience it," the General said. He looked like a young boy daydreaming about a far off fantasy world.

"I could arrange it," Thorn suggested.

"Absolutely not!" the General snapped. "Such a thing would be out of the question. If I were to die, or be harmed, or lost... this world needs me here."

"Perhaps we can come up with a method for using a headset," Thorn said.

"You said it's impossible."

"I said we can't do it that way at the present time, General. I agree with you that it would be better if we could use a headset and avoid the complicated process we currently employ. Thanks to you, I now have the funds and resources to work on developing better methods to put a subject into VR."

"Let me know when you succeed," the General said. "I want to try it out. This whole idea is fascinating to me, Mr. Thorn, I'd really love to give it a spin."

"You know," Thorn said, "I would be willing to let you call me Samson, if you feel this whole 'General' and "Mr. Thorn' name calling is too formal..."

The General made a sour face, but then smiled at Thorn. "I would like that, Mr. Thorn, but I'm afraid our country needs the General more than they do Donovan. The decisions and choices that I must make daily are too much of a burden for a simple man. If I was Donovan during those times, I don't think I'd still be here. The General is a strong and capable creature. As much as I would like to be Donovan, I must remain the General."

"I understand," Thorn said. "I won't bring it up again."

"Thank you," the General said. "Now tell me how things are progressing with our primary project."

"The new rooms are complete," Thorn said. "There are enough tables and medical equipment in place to insert one hundred children."

"And the adult facility?"

"Another hundred can be accommodated," Thorn confirmed.

"I'm ready to put my best people into VR now, Mr. Thorn." The General said. "I know the kids are going to take to this like insects to honey. Please begin to work with my soldiers to get them comfortable with the technology as well."

"Absolutely, General," Thorn said. "Who would you like me to start with?"

The General answered immediately, "Start with my best and see how their skills translate to the simulation. Start with Cooper. I'll have him report to you right away."

===

Cooper lie on the table and breathed calmly. He looked around and cracked the odd joke as technicians and doctors got him prepared for his first trip into virtual reality.

The room was white and well lit. Banks of complex machines and medical equipment surrounded him. An intravenous line was inserted into his arm, and sensor pads were glued to various parts of his body to deliver feedback. They had explained the process to him thoroughly, laughing when he'd nodded and said, "It sounds like a regular old coma to me, kids. I've been on that ride a couple of times. I'm happy you're all confident that you can bring me out of this one."

He'd met Samson Thorn and been instructed on the objectives for his first experience.

It was go time, and Cooper was excited.

"All right, Cooper, please count backwards from ten. Have fun in there."

Cooper grinned behind the mask that covered his face and began to count backwards.

16

Brandon and his group entered the mess hall. They were laughing and joking with one another as they approached their table, and didn't notice that it was already occupied until they were standing right at it.

Normally, anyone sitting at this table would get up and move for them. In the Game Facility there was one thing that earned respect more than anything else: rank in the games. Highly ranked players were lords of the facility, and Brandon's Hand had earned a tremendous amount of respect in the short time since they'd been playing. As a team they were a dominating force in the 10 to 12-year-old division. In the individual games, the four of them (they hadn't filled their last spot yet) all floated at the top of the rankings. Each would hold top ranking for a while and then allow one of the others in their group to claim it. This had been Brandon's idea, and they accomplished it by playing as a team even in the individual games. For example, Brandon would be in the lead of a race and suddenly slow down to let Tony pass him for the win. Brandon knew it wasn't exactly in the spirit of the games, but they all enjoyed top status, which was what friends should do for each other.

"Sorry guys and gal, I think we're at your table. We can get up and leave if you'd like?"

Brandon's group stood and gaped. Brandon smiled and addressed the man reclining in his seat. "Thanks, Cooper, but

I'm pretty sure you can sit anywhere you want in this mess hall."

Cooper flashed a smile and spread his arm to indicate the free seats around the table. The A's had positioned themselves so that there was an empty seat between each of them. Brandon and the others exchanged excited looks as they sat down.

The kids smiled and shook hands with the A's as Cooper made the introductions. They wouldn't have guessed a few weeks ago that they'd be sitting with the most popular celebrities in the free world.

"Your turn," Cooper said to Brandon. "Introduce us to your Hand."

Brandon smiled and pointed to his group, one by one. "The one with the wide shoulders that looks — and is — strong as a bull is Tony. The shortest and the fastest of our group is Alan. I'm Brandon, and this pretty girl is Kay. She's as fast as any of us, and definitely the most clever when it comes to solving the puzzle games."

"Ahh, yes," Cooper said. "Kay is the number one ranked player in your age group. Congratulations, young lady. That is no small accomplishment."

"She's number one at the moment," Brandon said. "Tomorrow or the next day it will be someone else in our Hand."

Cooper's mouth twitched at the corners and his eyebrows rose in confusion. "I don't understand," Cooper looked around the table. "Kay is the leader of the group, and therefore the best of your group when it comes to Gaming. She should have the number one spot at all times."

"We're all equally important in the group," Brandon explained. "We take turns being number one so each of us can enjoy the perks that come with that spot."

"Really?" Cooper asked with wide eyes. His team mates smiled and shook their heads. "Tell me, who came up with this idea? All of you at the same time?"

"Well... no."

"Who, then? Who had this idea to share the number one spot?"

Brandon looked at his group uncertainly. Then he looked at each member of the A's in turn. They looked at him with both interest and amusement. "It was my idea," he admitted.

Cooper nodded. He chuckled and folded his arms as he leaned back in his chair. "We've been watching you all since day one. Very impressive, for the most part." The members of Brandon's Hand grinned with pride. "There's one flaw that I see, however, and it will soon destroy you if you don't take care of it."

"What's that?" Brandon asked.

"This," Cooper motioned to the group spread out around the table. "No one knows their place. Sharing all the spots will confuse everyone, and ruin the group."

Brandon opened his mouth to defend his idea, but Cooper held up his hand to stop him. "Look, I know that you're trying to make everyone happy, but let me tell you from experience, kid, it won't work." He stood up and walked to the head of the table where there was an empty seat. "Who is leader of the A Hand?" he asked.

Everyone at the table replied instantly. "You are!"

Cooper nodded and sat down at the head seat. "You kids are forming a Hand. What happens if you wear a ring on the third finger of your hand and the next day you try to wear it on your pinkie finger? It doesn't work. Everyone has a place and there's nothing wrong with that. There are members of my hand that are better at me than some things. Hell, when you add it all up, they're better at me than most things." Cooper's teammates laughed and nodded in agreement. "I'm the leader, though, and all of us agree on that. When things get bad, there is never any confusion about where to look for directions." He tapped his chest. "I make the call, and when I do, the rest are looking at me and ready for orders. Each and every one of us plays a specific role which makes us the best at what we do."

Cooper stopped talking to let his point sink in. After a few moments, he stood up and placed his hand on his chair. "Now," he said, "who is the leader of your group?"

In unison everyone at the table, the A's included, said, "Brandon!"

Cooper nodded and motioned for Brandon to come forward and take his seat. "Your leader is your number one, and should always be ranked number one among you. Enough of this sharing nonsense. When you're in single competition games, all of you work together to have Brandon finish on top. It's very obvious that you can do it. If you have a problem with that, then you have a problem with his leadership, which must be dealt with if it happens. And do it outside of the games. If you can't solve the problem, then either you or Brandon must leave the group. Do we all understand each other?"

The children nodded seriously.

"Let me assure you, kids, if you run your Hand the way I am advising you to, then you will be the best of the best. If you don't, then you'll fail — like so many others have done in the past."

"Thanks for the advice, Cooper," Brandon said.

Cooper nodded. "No problem. One more piece of advice, then we can all eat."

"Sure."

"Get your final member, and do it soon."

17

"**I can't believe** how many applications we got," Brandon said.

"I can," Alan said. "Like Cooper said, we're the team to beat right now. It also helps that the A's come sit with us once in a while. Now everyone wants to be part of our group."

"Not everyone," Kay said. She nodded towards another table but no one bothered to look; they all knew who she was referring to.

Lohkam and his crew sat three tables away. They were ranked number one in the 12-14 group which was just above Brandon's. The lords of each age group were notorious for harassing the top ranked leaders in the group just below them. It was a nasty hierarchy of torment, and Brandon's Hand had learned that being number one did come with one or two drawbacks.

Knowing that Lohkam and his group were mistreated by the kids above them helped deal with the sting to a degree. It wasn't right, but there was nothing Brandon could do from his position as rank leader of the youngest group. He vowed to treat the leaders below him better when he moved up in the ranks... after he kicked Lohkam out of his position.

"Ignore them," Brandon said. "They're scared. Once we move into their category they'll lose their place. It must be terrible for them to know their days are numbered."

Tony laughed, "One more year and we'll own them. I can't wait."

Brandon smiled and nodded. "Who's next, Kay?"

Kay swiped a finger across her tablet and pulled up the next profile. "His name is Easton, and he looks real good on paper, guys. If he interviews well, he might be the one we want."

"Okay, let's hope so," Tony said. "I don't know about the rest of you, but I'm getting bored. We've interviewed, what, eleven kids so far?"

"Yeah," Brandon said. "Some good kids, but I agree. Hopefully we find the right one soon."

"There he is," Kay said.

Easton was of average height for a kid their age, with the athletic build that everyone in the game facility developed. His hair was such a dark black that it gave off an almost bluish sheen in the light. His eyes were dark blue, and he walked with an easy, confident grace. Brandon held out his hand as Easton approached, and Kay silently placed her tablet in his palm.

"Hi, Brandon," Easton said. "Thanks for seeing me."

Brandon stood up and the two boys shook hands. "Hello, Easton. Let me introduce you to everyone."

Brandon made the introductions and the others politely nodded to Easton, quietly listening and sizing him up. They would let Brandon do the interview; any member of the Hand could interrupt and ask a question at any time. After the candidate left, they would all discuss the interview and express their opinions, and if Brandon liked the applicant, they would take a vote. The vote would have to be unanimous for the candidate to be accepted.

"I have to admit," Easton said. "You seem older than five, Brandon. Not many five-year-olds in my Centre would be leading a group like this in the games."

Brandon smiled. "I get that a lot. We're all wondering why you want to join us. You're a year older than we are, and none of the other kids applying for this spot are. It makes more sense for you to get into a group your own age or even older. We've been watching videos of you in the games, and you're very good. Your rank in the individual games is high, too; a team should've snapped you up. What's wrong with you?"

Easton laughed and nodded his head. "You're right, I have a good rank, and others have asked me to join them. I always thought the best way to succeed was to do it on my own. I've spent all my time building a high solo rank."

"So what changed?" Alan asked.

"Someone suggested that I should consider trying out for your group."

"Really?" Kay asked.

"Yeah," Easton nodded. "So I thought about it, and asked around, and watched you guys play. I think you're going to do something big, and I want to be part of it. I can bring a lot to your team if you let me."

A half hour stretched into an hour. The average interview had taken only a few minutes, but the members of the Hand all seemed to hit it off with Easton. Finally, time was up because they had to go to class. Brandon ended the meeting by thanking Easton for his time and telling him they would be in touch by the end of the day to let him know what they'd decided.

After Easton left, Brandon looked around to gauge their reactions, and he saw that they were all smiling.

"Well," he said, "he is definitely worth a vote. Who wants him to join us?"

Everyone's hand shot up and they all laughed and nodded.

"There it is, then," Brandon nodded. "It looks like we have a full Hand. Now we can really get down to playing some games."

18

"**How did Cooper** do in the simulation?" the General asked.

"He did extremely well, General," Thorn said. An assortment of graphs and charts were displayed on the main viewer. The General scrutinized the data for the next few minutes while Thorn waited patiently.

"Yes, I see what you mean," the General said. "Although it doesn't look like he actually did anything productive."

"Entering the virtual reality matrix is similar to being born. The purpose of the first few sessions is to calibrate the system to his brain functions. Once the preliminary work is complete, you can expect more significant data. His results are above the normal scale."

The General nodded curtly. "It's your show, Mr. Thorn; I defer to your expertise in these matters. When does he go in again?"

"He's scheduled for another session tomorrow," Thorn said.

"Where do we stand with the Gamers?"

"I'm building a baseline with Cooper, and then the rest of his Hand. Once I have that all set up, we will begin to set benchmark readings for the students. I expect to start introducing them to the VR environment within the next few weeks. We are still working with the winners of your contest, is that correct?"

"Yes," the General confirmed. "The top ranked Gamers from each age group will enter the program first."

"Only the top ranked? I was hopeful that the five-year-old would be part of the first group."

"Oh, he will be."

"Really?" Thorn asked.

"The lad is skilled," the General said. "Against the ten and eleven year olds he leads in the individual rankings, and the group he formed is at the top of the team rankings."

"Interesting."

"Very," the General said. "The kid's a natural competitor and leader. I guess I shouldn't be surprised, considering who his parents are... or were."

"Who were they?"

The General paused, then shrugged his shoulders and told him.

Thorn's eyes widened in surprise and he sat forward in his seat. "Are you serious? Does the boy know? Isn't there an uncle who should be raising him?"

The General chuckled. "It was the uncle who gave him to us, and the boy doesn't know, nor will he ever."

Thorn nodded, "Of course, General, I understand. It was a terrible accident that claimed his parents. Some rumours claim that they were killed deliberately... I forget who ended up buying their company and acquiring the assets and technologies?"

The General's cold gaze matched the tone that crept into his voice. "Sensational rumours and lies are all that surround their untimely deaths, Mr. Thorn. Life isn't fair and sometimes terrible tragedies occur, which was what happened in their case. "

Thorn returned the General's gaze with a good natured smile. Both men knew the truth. Strayne Industries had been acquired quickly and cheaply by Infinite Solutions Division not long after the premature deaths of the young husband and wife. It was a surprising development, yet no news stations had reported on the story.

"Sometimes we have plans for life, but life has different plans for us," Thorn said.

"I don't understand," the General said.

"I mean life's not fair, General, although no one ever claimed that it was. Most of us think life owes us something, but the truth is that it's fragile and can end any time, which I understand better than most. I appreciate your confidence, and you can rest assured that no one will hear a breath of the boy's true identity from me."

The General smiled and nodded. "I knew that would be the case, Mr. Thorn."

As the two men continued their conversation regarding the timetables and logistics of the project, Thorn made a mental note to himself. He would be taking a very keen interest in young Brandon Strayne.

19

Brandon opened his eyes and realized he was inside the dream again. Black rats erupted from the stone floor and he wasted no time catching them in his invisible grip. He held them securely in the air until he sensed the familiar golden tingling to his right. The bathroom wall faded to reveal the gold-tinged forest with the giant sloth hanging from a branch of his tree.

"Good work," the sloth said. "Crush them and come to my tree."

Brandon crushed the squeaking rats and let them drop to the ground. He walked towards the sloth, lifting his foot slightly to step over the lip of the bathroom floor.

"I'm pleased to see that your skills are improving," the sloth said. "Did you capture the feeling and practice summoning it when you left last time?"

"Yes, I did," Brandon said. "A couple of times I think stuff actually moved. I made a pencil shake, and I'm pretty sure I knocked a book off of Tony's desk."

"Is that so?" the sloth asked. "You are ready for the next step, then."

A dark brown owl flew towards the sloth's tree and landed on the ground beside them. It stood a few inches taller than Brandon and its eyes were a deep gold colour.

"This is Owl," the sloth said. "She will deliver your next lesson."

Brandon looked at the owl in confusion. "How will I talk to her?" he asked.

The sloth laughed gently. "You will speak to her silently with your mind."

'That's right,' a voice replied inside Brandon's head.

'Hi,' Brandon said.

'Hello, young walker.' Owl said. 'Are you ready to learn your new lesson?'

'Yes, I am.' Brandon replied.

Owl stretched her wings and gave them a playful flap. 'I will be teaching you to fly.'

Brandon smiled with delight. 'Is it very difficult? To fly?' he asked.

Owl's rich laughter echoed in his skull. 'Flying is easy,' she said. 'It's landing that seems to be the tricky part.'

Brandon wasn't worried about getting hurt, so he nodded eagerly and waited for instructions.

'Flying is accomplished with your mind; the wings and body help you steer and adjust your speed,' Owl said. 'The power that you used to hold the rats in the air is the same force you will need to fly. Step one is to hold yourself so that you float in the air.'

'That's it?' Brandon was surprised, he thought it would be more difficult.

'Yes that's it,' Owl said. 'Birds don't have large brains. If it required too much effort to fly they would never get off the ground. Now go ahead and jump up into the air, and then hold yourself up there before you fall back to the ground.'

Brandon stuck his tongue out and bent his legs. Then he jumped upwards and tried to summon the glow to hold himself in the air.

He failed at his first and second attempts. On the third try, he got a slight grip, and hung in the air for a moment before he fell over and landed with a thud. After a few more attempts he was sweating and slightly frustrated. Owl nodded encouragingly while sloth sat watching him with an amused look on his face. After a few more unsuccessful attempts,

Brandon sat on the ground panting and looking seriously at Owl.

'How ya doing?' Owl asked.

Brandon grinned suddenly. 'Pretty good,' he said. 'I think I've almost got it.'

'I think so too,' Owl agreed. 'Once you're able to float we will fly around for a bit. It's much easier to fly than it is to float.'

'Really?'

'Oh, yes.'

Brandon stood up and dusted himself off. His brow knit together in concentration, he jumped straight up into the air as high as he could... and floated steadily in place, a foot or so above the ground. He let out a whoop of triumph and smiled at Owl.

The sloth nodded in satisfaction and moved its hand in a circular pattern. A tingling sensation began to spread over his body, and he transformed into a large owl. Brandon hooted and flapped his wings.

'That's much better,' Owl thought. 'Now we can fly. Follow me, youngling.'

Brandon flapped his wings hard and shot upwards into the sky close on the heels of Owl. She led him on a fast chase through the air, zipping left and right between the trees as they sprang up. Brandon didn't think; he let his body do the work and enjoyed the experience.

A short time later Owl flew up above the trees and waited for Brandon to catch up to her. Brandon came up beside her and stopped quickly. He used the energy of the glow to help hold him in place.

'What do you think of your new ability?' Owl asked.

'I love it!' Brandon replied. 'I don't want this to end.'

'All things end,' Owl said. 'This experience will last for a while, though. Let me know when you get tired.'

Brandon spotted a dark shape rising quickly towards them from the ground. Before he could ask Owl about it, the shape reached them. It was a man dressed in black garbage bags. He had a long black beard and even longer hair which were both windblown and uncombed. The man was dirty; it looked like he must live in a garbage dumpster. His feet were encased in heavy black army boots which didn't appear to have any laces to keep them on, and on his hands he wore shiny red gloves; Brandon could see they were made from metal bottle caps somehow strung together.

The man flashed a crooked smile, revealing yellow, jagged teeth. He raised a hand towards them and yelled out loudly. "Hi, Owl! Who's your friend? I can tell he's not a real owl... where did you find him?"

'He's a young student,' Owl projected and the man nodded his head.

"First day flying, boy?" the man shouted.

'Yes,' Brandon thought.

"You must be someone special to be so young and have them teaching you to fly." He did a back flip in the air, fell about ten feet, and then zoomed back up to their level. "No one taught me to fly; I learned how to do it all on my own."

'How did this man get into my dream?' Brandon thought to himself.

The man laughed loudly. "Who says this is your dream, boy? Maybe you somehow got into mine..."

'Don't confuse the child,' Owl said. *'Go play on your own; I will send him to you when he is ready.'*

"You mean if he's ready." The man said. "It's been a long time since you've brought anyone to me. I'm beginning to think people don't know how to dream big anymore."

'I think this one will make it,' Owl said.

"Well, I hope you do, boy," the man said. "It's been a long time since they sent anyone to learn my super power."

'You have a super power?' Brandon asked.

The man laughed loudly. "The boy who's been turned into an owl asks the old man floating in the sky if he has a super power. I like your sense of humour, young man. Good luck to you."

The man flew away quickly, and Owl started flying in the opposite direction. Brandon wanted to talk more with him but he was afraid of losing Owl, so he followed her.

They flew for what seemed like hours. Owl would stop every so often to let Brandon rest, but he would quickly regain his energy and they would be off again.

Finally they descended, and Brandon recognized the edge of the jungle with the bathroom wall. When Brandon's feet touched the ground, he became a boy again.

'That's all for this visit,' Owl said. 'Remember the feeling of flying. Practice feeling as if you're flying, and do it often.'

"I will," Brandon promised. "Thanks a lot. I'll see you again soon, I hope."

Owl shook her head. 'I don't think you will return for a long time, Brandon.'

"But you told the dirty flying man that I'd be back soon," he said. "I want to fly again, and I want to learn his super power."

'Most people live their whole lives and never get a chance to visit this place,' Owl said. 'Remember the feelings, and look for chances to use what you have learned.'

Brandon started to say more, but Owl jumped into the air and flew away. Looking towards the tree he saw the sloth raise its hand in farewell...

Suddenly he woke up.

<u>20</u>

"**Eight, nine, and... ten.**"

Cooper opened his eyes and sat up, swinging his legs over the side of the medical table.

He stood, looking around. His senses told him that he was still awake and the room appeared identical to the one in the Centre.

There were differences, though. There were no people here, and the whiteness of this room was more crisp and clean than it had been when he lie down on the table. The air smelled different, and the lights didn't flicker the same way they did before he closed his eyes.

He held his breath and counted. When he reached sixty and his lungs weren't burning from lack of oxygen, he knew for certain that he was in the computer program. Cooper nodded, opened his eyes, and sat back down on the table to wait for his guide.

Cooper referred to being inside the computer simulation as being "in the Vid." He liked the sound of it. He was certain that the kids would be saying it soon enough.

He grumbled at the thought of the kids playing in here. From what he'd seen so far, it wouldn't take them long to figure things out. Cooper was intrigued at the possibilities of this technology, though, and he was going to do his best to make sure he could compete with anyone and everyone in this new world.

The door to the room slid open and his guide walked in. The man was six foot four, with blonde hair and blue eyes. He had the physical build of a professional athlete or soldier; Cooper wondered if this is what the man really looked like outside of the Vid.

"Heya, Doc. Hope we're going to do more than walk around turning my head and doing knee bends today. I didn't even feel sore the next day from all the stuff you had me doing."

His guide smiled. "We will be more active today, Cooper. I'm glad you're up to the challenge."

Cooper snorted. "My whole life's been a challenge, Doc. I know I'm just lying on a table sleeping right now. I doubt there's much you can throw at me in here that can compare to real life."

"That could be a dangerous attitude, Cooper," the man warned. "Reality is simply your mind and body's interpretation of stimuli. It's possible to make things as real in here as it is outside. If your brain believes what's happening is real, then it is real, regardless of where your body is at the moment."

"Seriously?" Cooper asked.

"Absolutely."

"I didn't get your name the other day, Doc."

The two men shook hands. "My name is Thorn."

"Samson Thorn? This whole thing is your baby, right?"

"Just call me Thorn. Yeah, it's my baby."

"I can't wait to see what kind of things we can do, Doc."

"This simulation matches the real world in every way," Thorn said. "It's very realistic; I think you'll be impressed."

"Sounds interesting," Cooper said. "Is it possible to die in here?"

"Yes, it is. Your avatar — that's what we call the body you're inhabiting at the moment — mimics your real body exactly. If you were to be shot, or stabbed, or have a car dropped on you, the avatar would not be able to function and death would occur."

Cooper said nothing about his avatar not needing to breathe; maybe he'd found a glitch which he could use to his advantage later on. "What happens when my avatar dies?" he asked.

"You're ejected from the simulation," Thorn said. "You wake up, safe on your stasis table."

"So what's the plan? What am I supposed to do in here?"

"You'll learn how the environment works. I'm going to have you perform tasks and actions that you do in the real world so that I can make sure everything is working properly. I'll teach you how to operate inside the VR matrix, and in return, you help me identify the problems that need to be fixed. Once we have everything working properly, if you're interested, then you can help me test some of the modified game parameters that the students will compete in. Different gravity, breathable water, invulnerability to bullets, plus a whole list of other variables that I intend to alter."

Cooper smiled. "Sounds like fun."

"I think it will be," Thorn said. "The gun range is first on our list. Follow me."

"With pleasure.

21

Wesley stifled a yawn as he sat at his place near the centre of the long conference table, cupping his hands around his first hot drink of the day. Other instructors sat around the table sipping drinks or flipping through notes as they waited for the lead medical officer to arrive.

Each instructor kept detailed notes on his or her charges. Once a week they met to report on the ranking, mental states and physical concerns of their wards. Each instructor was responsible for closely tracking fifty students for three months. After that time, they would be assigned different players to ensure constant and fresh observation.

Basic training for civilians who enlisted in the armed forces lasted anywhere from three to six months depending on their unit. Basic training for the children of the Centres lasted until they turned eighteen. The average Centre child was in the General's program not for a few months, but for twelve to sixteen years. It was an incredible accomplishment to raise and train kids for that long without breaking them; the process required a lot of finesse.

Not every child became a soldier. Babies were raised as normally as possible; grouped together in nurseries, cared for by state workers, and continually observed by psychologists and medical doctors. As they became older, the results of their play, grades, and interactions enabled the administrators to assess and steer each individual towards their optimal vocation, thus maximizing their natural abilities and talents.

Wesley remembered a young woman named Jenny who worked in the South Western Children's Centre. She worked in the nursery with the babies and toddlers, and Wesley had dated her for a brief time. Jenny had been eager to share her memories of life growing up in the Centre with him over dinner and drinks. She was abandoned by her parents as a baby, and the Centre had been her home until she was eighteen. Her eyes lit up as she told him about life inside the Centre. From the sounds of it, her childhood had been what one would expect growing up in an orphanage; many kids the same age eating, sleeping, and going to school together. There'd been the occasional bully, but the adults who ran the Centre worked diligently to minimize this type of behaviour. Every few years the kids were given vigorous aptitude tests. Some of her friends qualified for special programs and were moved to other parts of the Centre, or even transferred to different locations altogether. Once they reached the age of ten, all children were fully profiled and regrouped with others who were similar to them in personality and interests. Jenny told him about one of her old childhood friends who was now one of the most famous movie stars in the world. As Wesley listened to Jenny talk, he'd gained a better understanding of how organized the Centres were.

Jenny admitted that she never showed any real talent. When she turned seventeen they had her spend time in the nursery, which she enjoyed and seemed to have a knack for. Turning eighteen was a stressful time for her; the closer a child came to their eighteenth birthday, the more the instructors spoke about the challenges and struggles of living in the real world. Jenny told him that most kids dreamt of obtaining work with the Centre to avoid exile from the comfort of a system that had been their entire lives. She had almost given up hope, but at the last moment the Centre had offered her a position working with the little ones. The pay wasn't great, but she knew the work and was able to afford a clean place to live in close by.

Listening to her story had disturbed Wesley. The Centre had taken a girl and raised her, looking for any talent that they could exploit along the way. They had programmed her to be afraid of the real world, and given her a job that no child would ever actively want to do. Rather than be disappointed with her lot in life, she was grateful.

Over the past few years, Wesley had spoken with many workers inside the Centres. Most had been raised within the system and groomed to perform specific duties when they became adults. Not everyone had been conditioned to fear leaving the Centres. Wesley guessed that they only did that to the kids that they wanted to keep as Centre staff. Wesley discovered that there were thousands of Centre graduates every year. Those who entered the workforce did so at every level in all facets of life, from common busboys and dishwashers in restaurants to brilliant business executives. Graduates of the Centres did share one common trait that had been carefully and systematically conditioned into them during their time inside; they were absolutely loyal to the person whom they believed had saved them from death and given them the best chance to excel at life... the General.

Putting together pieces of the puzzle had revealed a disturbing picture; the General was strategically placing loyal followers into every position in society, and he'd been doing it for years.

Wesley flipped through his notes, wondering where the kids he was currently tracking would end up when they turned eighteen. None of them were mediocre; the Game Facility was a high end division of the Centres. The kids he was working with would do more than change diapers or serve food.

Here in the Game Facility, everything was a game. Not just the actual games, but also patterns of sleep and mixed periods of activity. A gamer might sit around for days without being scheduled to play, and then be woken up at three in the morning to enter a game immediately. Sometimes a player would exit a physical contest and enter another one right away. Instructors monitored their players to make certain that no one was pushed past their breaking point. It was a system of controlled chaos designed to bring out the best in the students, stress testing them, but not pushing them so far that it broke them.

The lead medical officer entered the room and walked to his seat. "Okay, people, give it to me as quickly as you can. I have three other places to be at this exact moment."

Instructors began to speak in turn, each delivering normal reports that indicated their players were within acceptable parameters concerning mental and physical conditioning. The pace of the meeting moved quickly until one of the instructors reported an abnormal result.

"I think there might be a mental crack with one of my Alpha boys," the instructor announced.

The lead officer looked up from his clipboard with concern. "Which Alpha is it, and how big a crack?" he asked.

"Lohkam. I think it's very slight, if it exists at all."

The lead med officer typed Lohkam's name into his tablet, and read the information in his file. Every report, game score, altercation with other students, meal, game highlight, and a multitude of other details were documented. The lead officer spent a few moments scanning the information before nodding. "Okay, we'll take a closer look at him. Everything looks fine on the surface, but there could be something there. Good call, Instructor."

The rest of the reports continued uneventfully. The meeting concluded and everyone stood up to leave. The kids would be up in half an hour and there was work to do before then.

Wesley guessed that most instructors would be heading for a terminal to access Lohkam's file. If there was a chance he might be unstable everyone would keep an eye on him as he interacted with their charges.

Wesley knew the history between Brandon and Lohkam in just the few short months since Brandon had arrived. Wesley would be watching Lohkam for certain.

22

"**I don't recognize** any of these kids," Brandon said.

"Me neither," Alan said as he looked around the staging area.

"That's okay, guys," Easton said. He was sitting along the wall wrapping his hands with a length of blue cloth material that had been sitting on each chair when they came into the room. "They're older than you. We knew this would likely happen."

When they'd invited Easton to join, they understood that taking him into the group might mean competing in his age group instead of theirs. They had assured him that it didn't matter; many of the games they played contained kids who were a year older than them anyway.

What they hadn't fully taken into consideration was that some of the kids in here weren't one year older than them — they were two years older. Brandon inspected the other teams around them. Some of these twelve-year-olds were big.

"Don't worry about it," Kay said. "We can still clean their clocks. I don't recognize the game, Easton. What's it called, and how does it work?"

"It's called 'Monkey See, Monkey Don't,'" he said. "Pretty simple puzzle and action game, but tricky. We'll enter the field and see fake trees spread around the room. The room will have different coloured hand rungs all over the walls and ceiling. Red, blue, and green. You can touch each rung a certain number of times before it disappears. When you touch them with your wrap, they change to the next colour. Red turns to blue, blue turns to green, green turns grey and then disappears into the wall."

"How do we win?" Tony asked. The tank of the group, he was a fan of direct action. Many game tanks were big and they used their size and strength without bothering to think much about what they were doing. Tony was different. He was both strong and clever, a lethal combination against the competition. A smart tank was dangerous, and Tony was one of the most dangerous playing at their level. Despite that, he was still a fan of direct action.

"The team who captures the most trees, wins." Easton looked around. "I see five teams, so there will likely be fifteen trees. You capture a tree by climbing to the top and tapping a pad with both hands. Doing that wins the tree, but it deactivates your wraps."

"Putting you out of the game," Alan said.

"Exactly," Easton nodded. "Most teams can only get one tree, two if they are clever and have a good mix of talent. This game isn't about winning; the goal is to get points to retain standing. Ties are the norm; wins are rare and only happen when a total bunch of Baggers come in and can't figure out how to capture a tree on their first try."

"Why play a game just to tie?" Alan asked.

"As we move up in age and level, the games aren't just about winning." Easton said. "They're more about learning something. Sometimes you learn more from losing or a tie."

"Losing should teach you how not to do something." Brandon said. "Doing it differently might get you a win. You should always try to win."

"Even when it's impossible?" Easton asked.

Brandon flashed a grin. "*Especially* when it's impossible."

The rest of the group laughed and nodded. They followed Brandon because he knew how to win. He didn't seem to see the world the way most kids did.

"Each tree has four hand holds," Easton explained. "As soon as they are touched, a timer starts ticking, and when it runs out all of the hand holds disappear. Touching first the bottom, and then the next rung up with a different set of wraps, doubles the time they stay out. It takes two touches to get them to stay out long enough for a fast climber to reach the top."

"So it takes three people to climb a tree," Tony said. "Two to tap the rungs, and a third to rush to the top and capture it."

"Exactly," Easton confirmed.

"The person who captures the tree is then out of the game because their wraps no longer work," Kay said.

"Yep."

Alan looked around the room again, gauging the physical conditioning of the other teams. "That leaves four still on the ground. Some teams would have one more fast climber, so that's how they get a second tree and not a third?"

"One more thing happens to prevent a quick try from the ground for a second tree," Easton said. "Once our first tree is captured, we have one minute to get off the ground. Anyone still on the ground after a minute is kicked from the game and has to leave the area."

"That means it's very hard to get a second tree from the ground?" Brandon guessed.

Easton nodded. "If you want to stay in the game, you need to be on the rungs on the wall. Some very skilled kids can climb enough to take a chance on dropping on a tree from the ceiling. It's not a huge drop, but the hand rungs are really tricky and far apart up there. Most kids go for one tree, get their points, and call it a day."

"Anyone ever gotten three?" Brandon asked.

Easton laughed loudly. "No. Some kids tried at first, but it was just too difficult. Two is the best someone can do."

"Did you see the points you can get for winning this game?" Brandon asked. "A win today will lock up our first place position and get us into the VR simulations." He looked at the rest of his team seriously. "We're going for four, but we can still consider this a success if we get three."

Easton glanced at the others. No one laughed, and no one argued. They looked at each other briefly, then met Brandon's eyes and nodded. Easton sighed and nodded as well.

"Good," Brandon said. "Here's the plan..."

23

The door opened and the five groups entered the game area. The arena was just as Easton described it; fifteen tall trees were spread around the room. Each tree had four hand rungs on the trunk, and at the top was a flat, clear area with a glowing orb. Spread along the walls and on the ceiling were a myriad of random coloured red, blue, and green rungs.

Brandon's Hand spread out so they could see the entire room, but they didn't move toward a tree like the other groups did. Since there was no time limit for staying on the ground until their team captured a tree, they had decided to stand and watch for a few moments.

One of the other groups began to climb their tree. As soon as the first kid touched the bottom rung, Tony started counting slowly out loud. "One...two...three..." When the team captured their tree Tony stopped counting; he had reached twenty-one.

A second group began their attempt and Alan counted the seconds off as they made their capture. He stopped when they succeeded... at 26.

The third and fourth remaining teams began their climbs and Easton and Brandon made the counts, one for each team. The team Easton was tracking succeeded at 19, but the other team was too slow and the rungs disappeared before they could make it to the top.

"Thirty," Brandon said. "The rungs disappear at thirty seconds."

A buzzer went off and the members of the first three teams who were still on the ground began to walk towards the exit of the arena. Two of the groups had a few more seconds, but they didn't seem interested in using them. They all left at the same time.

The fourth group was busy attempting to climb another tree, but Brandon had seen enough. "The plan is good, let's get it done." He said.

Brandon dashed towards one tree. When he was halfway there he yelled out, "Now!" and Kay sprinted towards him as fast as she could. When she was halfway to him, Tony then began to run towards the both of them.

Brandon jumped and hit the bottom rung of the tree and he started counting the seconds out loudly. "One...two...three..." As soon as he landed, he began to run towards another tree.

Kay hit the rung of the first tree and reached up for the second rung. She dropped down and began to count as well. Once Brandon heard her counting he stopped his count but continued to head for his new tree. Kay got out of the way and headed toward the wall. When she got there, she stopped counting and put her head between her knees, panting to get her breath back.

Tony reached the tree just after Kay had dropped down. He knew that the two touches had gained him more than thirty seconds to make his climb, which should be enough for him to make it. He hit the bottom rung and climbed as fast as he possibly could towards the top. The other kids sitting at the tops of their trees were watching with interest. Tony made it to the top of his tree. Seconds later he heard a clunking as the hand rungs disappeared below him along the trunk. He lay on his back breathing deeply and smiling in triumph; most tanks couldn't climb so fast.

Brandon was almost at the next tree and he looked quickly to his right. Easton was barreling towards him at a fast sprint. Brandon smiled and jumped up on the trunk, grabbing the first rung and quickly dropping back to the ground to get out of Easton's way. Kay started calling out the seconds for Easton as Brandon trotted over to stand beside Kay and catch his breath.

The timing was perfect. If Brandon had been another second slower they would have collided. Easton was a fast climber but he knew he would need every second if he was going to make it to the top of the tree. There had been just one touch which meant he only had 15 seconds to do it.

"Nine..." Kay called out. Easton was already on the third rung and smiling. This was going to be cake.

"Twelve..." Kay called said as Easton climbed to the platform on the top of the tree. He grinned wearily as the others cheered loudly for his success.

After a few moments Easton stood up to view the rest of the field. Somehow the fourth team had captured two trees. That left them tied once Brandon's group captured their two trees. The kids from the other team had activated their tree and their minute on the ground had already expired. They walked off the field, looking curiously at Brandon, Kay, and Alan standing near the wall.

Brandon nodded to Kay and she jumped up to grab a rung. She swung from one to the next and the colours changed as she did so. A Red one became blue and then she grabbed a green and jumped back down to the ground. All the rungs changed colour like Easton said they would, the green one turned grey and the rung disappeared into the wall when Kay let go of it.

"The walls and rungs aren't slippery." She reported to the others.

"Good," Alan said. He turned around and nodded to the two in the tree tops. Both Tony and Easton touched their wraps to the glowing orb and a chime sounded, announcing their trees were captured.

Alan, Kay, and Brandon jumped up onto the rungs and began to climb.

Kay pulled ahead of the boys, zipping along the rungs like a monkey as she headed away from them in the direction of the closest tree. It took her only a few moments until she was hanging as close as she could get to an unclaimed tree. She gauged the distance and started to swing back and forth. When her swinging feet almost touched the ceiling she let go and sailed outwards. It looked like she wouldn't make the edge of the tree, but at the last moment she pumped her legs and arms and managed to somehow grab onto the lip of the platform. Everyone, including the other teams sitting in their tree tops, cheered as she stood up and waved with a grin on her face. Kay put both hands on the globe and the chime sounded again. They had three trees!

Everyone now focused on Brandon and Alan. Alan was in the lead and climbing carefully; picking rungs that would not disappear when he touched them so that Brandon could follow him. They made their way slowly to another tree. Alan was too big to swing onto a tree like Kay; she had barely made it and she was the best acrobat on the team. Brandon was simply too short to get the needed distance.

Alan got as close as he could to a tree and he called out to Brandon to hold on a second. Then he made certain his grip was as tight as it could be and he nodded to Brandon. "Okay, let's do this," he said.

"All right," Brandon said. He began to swing like Kay had done. When he was swinging as hard as he could he launched himself towards Alan. There was no way he could have made it to the tree, but he managed to make it to Alan and grab hold of his legs tightly. Alan grunted from the added weight but he managed to hold on to the rungs. "Damn, you're heavier than you look," he said to Brandon. "Don't take too long for the next swing, or we'll fall."

The boys were about fifteen feet in the air. The floors were padded, but they would most likely get hurt if they fell on top of each other.

Brandon used the momentum from his jump to keep swinging. Alan helped by rocking his legs to match the motion. Three quick pumps and Brandon let go of Alan's legs and sailed towards the closest tree. His speed was perfect.

Brandon landed lightly in the centre of the platform, bending his legs slightly and touching one hand on the platform to stop himself from falling forward.

The kids cheered as he stood up and looked around the arena.

With a large smile on his face, Brandon raised his arms in triumph before placing them on the orb.

The chime sounded for the fourth time.

Brandon looked at Easton and nodded with satisfaction.

24

Cooper sometimes wished he could be a normal, ordinary person.

Normal people woke up late, strolled through life accomplishing very little, came home every night and ate a boring meal. They sat in front of a view screen and watched the news or some other mindless program, and then went to sleep safe and sound in their beds.

A normal person didn't catch whatever snippets of sleep they could while lying in the cold, wet dark in hostile enemy territory. Normal people weren't crammed into the back of a packed transport plane for twenty-three hours and then dropped from 60,000 feet in a pressure suit, in the dead of night, with no ground support or direction. No stress or pressure... how lucky normal people were to be ignorant of how the world really worked.

Millions dreamed of being as brave, strong, and popular as Cooper. Yet Cooper dreamed of being a dishwasher in a restaurant, working eight hour days and living in a small apartment above a store.

Cooper smiled as he shook his head and slowly rolled it around his shoulders in an effort to loosen the tight muscles. He stood, jumped up and down lightly half a dozen times, and shook his arms and hands to get the blood flowing. By the time he opened his eyes his silly little dream was tucked safely away into a small corner of his psyche. He knew the truth of the matter… mediocrity wasn't for someone like him, and if he ever did find himself in that dream place he would quickly go insane. Cooper was exactly who he wanted to be.

He closed his eyes and summoned his glow, the golden tingling sensation he'd discovered years ago through meditation training as a student in the Game Facility. Cooper closed his eyes and envisioned a white office. He felt a slight movement, and when he opened his eyes he was standing in it.

"Thanks, Doc," he said. "I needed that little bit of alone time."

Thorn smiled from behind the desk and nodded. "No problem, Cooper. You seem to have gotten the hang of travel mode inside the simulation."

"It's simple," Cooper shrugged. "I feel like I've been training my whole life to be inside this simulation."

Thorn nodded. "You pay attention to my instructions and complete every task easily. I've never seen someone take to the VR environment so quickly. It took me two months to master teleportation in here, and I invented the technology."

Cooper smiled at the compliment. "What's next on the agenda, Thorn?" he asked.

"A confession," Thorn said.

"I have nothing to confess," Cooper said.

"I was talking about me," Thorn said.

"Okay…?"

"I've been building a profile on you, since you came here. The computer recreates you exactly to make this as realistic as possible. It's not just physical, Cooper, it's also psychological."

Cooper shrugged, "That's fine, Thorn, I take psych evaluations frequently. I'm as crazy as I have to be and as sane as is required to walk the paths that I do."

Thorn chuckled. "Yes, I'm fascinated by the contrasts inside that head of yours. I see a troubled area, however."

Cooper frowned. "What area is that?" he asked.

"Your loyalty to the General is… questionable." Thorn said.

Cooper laughed. "No. It isn't. The General is the father and mother I never had. Without him I'd be dead, or worse." Cooper stood up and walked to the bookshelf against the wall. "If there's one area in my life where I'm crystal clear, Thorn, it's my loyalty to the General. I would do anything for him."

Thorn nodded and looked at Cooper for a moment. Then he shook his head in sympathy. "I'm sorry, Cooper, but the General has lied to you."

"About what?" Cooper asked.

"About everything," Thorn said.

Cooper picked a book off the shelf and looked at it. Then he placed it back on the shelf and looked at Thorn. His eyes were flat and cold as he spoke. "I don't know you very well, Doc, but I like you. This is a line you don't want to cross with me; not now, not ever. I won't believe anything bad about the General, and there's no room in my brain to stand by and listen to it. Us orphans get pretty fired up when you start talking trash about our father... so don't bring it up again. We understand each other?"

"How are there so many orphans these days?" Thorn asked.

"Come again?"

"The Centres are full of orphans. Tens of thousands of kids without parents all over the country. Do you have any idea how many there are?"

"Times are tough, Thorn," Cooper said. "People can't afford to keep their kids. Lots of children have kids, and they just can't give them a life. I doubt the volume of orphans has increased significantly, the General has simply put a system in place to save them."

"Inside this simulation we have access to every memory from your life." Thorn said.

"What? That could be dangerous for you, Doc. There's knowledge in my brain that could get you killed."

"I've got maximum clearance," Thorn assured him.

"There's no way in hell you have that kind of clearance."

"Some of your memories are blocked. I don't know how, but they are. I'm guessing they taught you how to do that."

Cooper nodded.

"I want to show you a memory that you've repressed. Let me show it to you. You do that, and I'll never bring the General up again. Deal?"

Cooper hesitated and Thorn held up his hand. "I promise it won't be anything compromising from your career as part of the General's Avatar. It goes back much farther."

Cooper nodded. "Fine. If that's what it takes to shut you up."

Thorn nodded and pulled out his tablet. "This memory is an old one. You were less than two years old."

The white office shimmered and was replaced by another scene. The two men stood in front of a large mansion. The lawn was immaculate and there were four very expensive cars sitting in the large driveway. Thorn led Cooper into the house and walked upstairs to the hallway. He stopped outside a door; they could hear voices in the next room.

"They won't see us," Thorn said. They walked into a children's bedroom decorated in blue and white. The walls were decorated with cartoon animals and other happy scenes. A beautiful woman sat on the bed holding a small blonde boy tightly in her arms. He had his face buried in her shoulder. A good looking man stood over the two of them protectively, glaring at a man standing in front of them. Cooper and Thorn couldn't see the face of the man who was facing the parents, but they could see that he had a gun pointed at them.

"My parents?" Cooper asked.

Thorn nodded. "Two loyal and wealthy citizens of the state who recently spoke out against a young man in public, challenging his ideas and criticizing his plans."

"The man holding the gun on them?"

"Yes," Thorn said. "An aggressive and newly appointed General Donovan."

"You didn't need to come into our house and start waving around a gun, Donovan," Cooper's father said. He appeared relaxed despite the dangerous situation; Cooper could tell that his father had military training. "If our support is so important to you, then I'm sure we can come to an arrangement."

"That's good to hear," the General said. "But I don't require your public support, Charles, although you can help me in another area. You and Genevieve are both remarkable people... mentally and physically superior specimens."

"What are you talking about?" Cooper's father asked.

"I can see that no matter how hard we try, the three of us will never be friends," the General said. "There's only one acceptable solution to this problem."

"You're going to kill us in cold blood."

"Yes," the General admitted. "The news tomorrow will report the tragic story of your untimely assassination. Your deaths will be a great loss for our people, and another act of aggression from our warlike neighbours to the west."

"You're a monster," Genevieve said. She hugged her boy tightly, and her eyes blazed with defiance and hatred.

"I'm more of a visionary," the General said. "But I can see you will never understand that."

"Is there no way I can persuade you to spare our son?" Cooper's father asked.

"Officially, no, but I'm not a monster, Charles. I won't kill the boy; he will come to live at one of our new orphan facilities where he will receive the best training and education. Knowing the genetic stock he comes from, I'm certain in a few years' time he will be one of my best soldiers."

Cooper's father sprang at the General. Cooper was surprised by his speed, but unfortunately he wasn't quick enough. There was a quiet spitting sound from the silenced gun and Charles fell heavily to the ground. Genevieve opened her mouth to scream but a second bullet pierced her skull before she could make a sound. Her head sank to the bed, the momentum pulling the boy from her grasp.

The General tucked the gun into a holster behind his back and walked towards the boy.

"There, there, little fella, don't cry. It's okay, you're safe now."

The boy said nothing. He was in shock, and too young to really understand what was happening. The General lifted him into his arms and walked towards the door. "I'll take good care of you, son," the General said, closing the door behind him.

Thorn and Cooper stood in the room with the two bodies for a moment, then Thorn ended the scene and returned them to his virtual office.

Cooper stood in the middle of the room and said nothing. Finally he looked at Thorn. "Why did you do that?" he asked.

"It's important to know the truth," Thorn said. "If you are controlled and manipulated for years then you are not to blame for the actions you commit. Once you see the truth, you are responsible for whatever you do from that point forward."

"The General didn't save me at all."

"No."

"How many others are there?"

"I don't know yet," Thorn said, "but I think there are thousands."

"What do you expect me to do?" Cooper asked.

"Help me free them."

"How?" Cooper asked.

Thorn chewed the corner of his lip. "I have no idea."

25

"**Um, guys…**"

"Hush, Kay," Alan whispered. "We're supposed to meditate til the timer goes off."

"Yeah… I think we can all stop meditating now. Open your eyes, boys, now."

Brandon was reluctant to end the session; he'd felt a deep sense of calm settle over him. Every day they meditated for ten minutes in the mess hall before they ate. Today he felt so focused that even the noises from the hundreds of other children had seemed to melt away. Kay's tone was insistent, though, so he opened his eyes… and found himself staring at the General!

Brandon and his group quickly pushed their chairs back and stood at attention. Thoughts raced through Brandon's mind; what was the General doing here in the mess hall? Were they in trouble? Brandon took a deep breath and saluted with the rest of his group. A quick glance left and right revealed that everyone in the mess hall was standing at attention. Everyone was quietly looking at the General. Brandon smiled as he realized why the busy sounds of the room had disappeared during his meditation.

The General returned their salute. "At ease, everyone," he said. "Please go about your business. I'll be here for a short visit with Brandon, Kay, Alan, Easton, and Tony. Then I must be off."

The General sat down at the table and waved his hand for the kids to do the same. The mess hall slowly returned to as normal a state as it could, although other children continued to steal glances in their direction as often as they felt they could get away with it.

The General smiled and winked at the group. He knew exactly what this visit would do for their reputation. He took a moment to make sincere eye contact with each of them. He looked at Brandon last, and after a serious moment he let out his trademark booming laugh and slapped his hand lightly on the table.

The General opened his mouth to say something, but stopped himself and turned to look at the table behind him where the neighbouring children were watching intently. "Hey, Bob, Trudy, Jen, Keith, Michael, Brian, and Shandi? I know it's a bit of a pain, but I really need to talk to these kids alone. How 'bout you give us some space and run along, please." The kids nodded and got up from their table to leave. Then the General spoke loudly but to no one in particular. "If you can hear my voice right now but you're not sitting at my table... then go ahead and excuse yourselves, please. Thanks, everyone." Kids at four surrounding tables stood up and quickly left the area.

The General looked around one more time then he nodded and smiled at Brandon's team. "There," he said. "That will help build a bit more mystery. Everyone will be wondering what the old man said to all of you. You're going to gain popularity points today."

The team nodded in agreement. No one knew what to say. A visit from the General was very rare, and it usually involved a visit to address the entire facility. To have the General come sit at your table during lunch in the mess hall... well, it just didn't happen. They sat quietly and waited for the General to speak. They didn't have to wait long.

"All I can say is wow. I've seen the video; watched it at least a dozen times. No one has ever captured four trees. It was impossible to accomplish, we made sure of that when we set it up. Brilliant teamwork, people, just incredible playing. I'm very proud of all of you."

Kay, Alan, and Tony beamed with pride. Easton's face became slightly flushed from excitement. Brandon smiled politely and nodded as he looked at each of his teammates with a pleased expression on his face.

"I have to make one tiny request," the General said. "I know it probably won't sound fair, but it's important that you agree with what I'm about to ask you."

"We will do our best, General," Brandon said.

The General smiled. "I knew I could count on you all. Thank you very much." He leaned forward and lowered his voice. "I need you to keep the details of that game top secret," he said.

"We spent a lot of time, money, and effort to create that game. Your team did exactly what we wanted someone to come forward and do; you beat it through teamwork and strategy. If you were to tell the rest of the Gamers how you did it, then there are other teams who could soon replicate your performance. It wouldn't be fair, and it goes against what we're trying to do here."

"You want more teams to figure out how to beat it on their own," Brandon said. "So you get as many great players as possible."

The General tilted his head to look at Brandon and nodded. "You're absolutely right, Brandon. It would do us no good to have everyone beat the game the same way you did. All that would prove is that others can do what they see. We aren't here for that; we're here to create independent thinkers who can win many different ways."

Brandon looked around the table. Each of the children nodded in answer to his unspoken question. After a moment, Brandon looked back at the General. "We won't tell anyone how we did it, General," Brandon assured him.

"Excellent!" the General said. "Neither will the other kids who saw how you did it from their tree tops. I also want to talk to you about the contest."

"To win a spot in the VR trials?" Alan asked.

"Yes," the General said. "I realize there's another three weeks left to compete, but with the points you just won from 'Monkey See, Monkey Don't,' you have enough points to do nothing from now until the end of the competition and still win your age class."

"Maybe that's true, General, but that's not how we do things," Tony said. "This team plays, and we play to win."

"I know that's true, Tony," the General said. "I had something in mind that I think you might enjoy more than playing the same games you already seemed to have mastered."

"Oh, I hope you say what I think you're going to say," Kay said.

The General smiled. "How would you like to enter the VR training a bit earlier than the rest of the kids? You're obviously the best in your age group, and I see no reason to hold you back."

Kay squealed with excitement and shook clenched fists above her head. Alan held his hand out, and Tony tapped his chest three times before slapping Alan's hand in a high five. Easton patted Brandon on the shoulder and laughed happily, while Brandon grinned back.

"Can I take this response as a yes?" the General asked.

"Yes, sir!" Brandon said. "We can't wait to get started."

26

In an isolated underground office, Samson Thorn exited the virtual reality simulation. He lifted a complex looking helmet from his head and rested it on the desk.

Thorn walked over to the small refrigerator, grabbed a bottle of water, and drained it dry in one long pull as he walked back to his desk. He looked at the VR headset and nodded with satisfaction. Thorn's most trustworthy and intelligent employees had finally developed a headset that worked. With this apparatus Thorn could quickly enter and leave the simulations, bypassing the cumbersome process of being put under by medical staff. At the moment Thorn possessed the only working unit and he intended to make certain it stayed that way for some time. If the General found out about this, Thorn guessed that he might be considered no longer necessary to have Thorn around.

Thorn glanced at his computer monitor and saw that Cooper was still inside the simulation. The computer showed Cooper walking towards the exit gate, a room inside the simulation with special chairs that allowed the subject to leave their avatar and return to the real world.

Cooper had done very well during his session. Thorn would report everything to the General.

Well, not quite everything.

He wasn't sure if Cooper believed the scene with his parents or not. It was genuine, but Cooper might be too wary to believe the truth about what the General had done... especially when presented with the evidence inside a computer generated simulation.

Thorn pressed a button on his desk and waited a few moments. Soon there was a knock on his door.

"Come in," he said.

The door opened and a middle aged man wearing glasses and a white lab coat walked in. He was the lead designer who had developed the headset which sat on Thorn's desk.

"How did it perform?" Thorn asked.

The tech smiled. "It worked great, sir."

Thorn nodded. "It felt good. I don't have a headache or anything this time," he said.

"There was just one small glitch, but I believe I can make a few adjustments to correct it."

"What glitch?"

"It seems that time passed at a slightly different rate for you inside the Sim, but it's nothing to worry about. An hour passed out here, while an hour and fifteen minutes passed inside the Sim for you."

Thorn frowned. "What do you mean time passed at a different rate? How is such a thing possible?"

The tech shrugged his shoulders. "I'm not certain how it happened, Sir. It's nothing to worry about. I expect some fine tuning will be required as we perfect the headset."

"Do you think you can extend the time difference?" he asked.

The tech frowned. "Maybe, but I don't understand why you would want to do that."

Thorn smiled. How could he not understand why that would be desirable? Until this point every minute spent in the Sim equaled one minute of real time. One of Thorn's great disappointments was that customers would only be able to play inside for limited amounts of time. It would be slow going and difficult for advancement of the technology if people could only spare a few hours to play before having to get back to their real life chores.

His biggest customer at the moment was the military, but Thorn planned to quickly take the product to market and offer it to the civilian population.

With a time-scaled effect, it would be possible for a customer to spend more time inside the simulation. They could spend one hour of real time while enjoying hours, days, maybe even years, inside the VR world. It would be much easier to get people hooked on — and consuming — his product if they spent more time with it. Visions of billing not by real time played, but by virtual years spent, began to flash in Thorn's head. It would be an excellent money making opportunity. But even more important than that, his Sim world would grow and evolve quicker with customers spending more time inside it.

"Just see what you can do, please. The larger the time variance, the happier I will be. I also want to know if you can replicate this effect for subjects entering the Sim through the traditional method. I want everyone inside the simulations to experience time the same way."

"They will, Sir. It wouldn't work any different from..."

Brandon held up his hand to silence the man. "I don't care how it works, I just care that it works. Get to work and bring me the best results you can."

The man nodded and left the room.

27

Lohkam sat with his back to the wall and watched his teammates move around the ready room. His boys were making their way to each of the other teams and speaking with the leaders. One of the leaders looked at Lohkam with a questioning face. Lohkam gave her an intimidating look and nodded slowly. Lohkam knew how unsettling his look was, it could make your skin crawl. It made you want to be anywhere other than on the receiving end of it. Lohkam's flat stare and aggressive body language said that he didn't care about you or what happened to you. The bored look and piercing gaze assured you that something bad could happen. He'd been practicing this look for years; even before he came to the Game Facility. By the time he was ten, Lohkam had a reputation with the others. No one could prove anything, but Lohkam's smile conveyed that he was a kid who would punish you if you crossed him, and he would enjoy it.

A few moments later his team returned and sat down. Lohkam looked slowly around the room. He knew where the issue was before his crew even announced it. He sighed and rubbed the bridge of his nose with his thumb and forefinger. Then he rolled his neck slowly back and forth and closed his eyes. "Billy's the problem, right?" he asked.

"Yeah," one teammate said. "Billy and his crew aren't in the mood to cut a deal today, Lock."

"Why not?" Lohkam asked. He opened his eyes and saw that Billy was watching him with a grim expression on his face.

"He knows if we win this game today then we lock our division for the VR contest."

"Billy isn't gonna beat us for the spot. Trying to do that during this game is plain stupid."

"That's what I told him, Lock. He said he didn't care. He said it's a tie for sure. It's too embarrassing for them to lose this game. Brandon and his team just broke the high score on it a couple days ago. Billy says for a crew to not capture at least one tree would be shameful for them."

Lohkam spread his arm to point at the other three teams in the ready room; they weren't even bothering to put on their wraps. "They aren't worried about being shamed. It's a stupid game anyway. They can get us out of their hair and try for the wildcard spot."

Lohkam's crew just nodded in agreement and looked at him quietly.

"Fine. I'll talk to him," Lohkam said. He stood up and sauntered over to Billy.

"Need a minute, Billy," Lohkam said.

"Sure, what's up?"

"I hear you're gonna go ahead and capture a tree."

"Yeah, sorry, but we gotta get one."

Lohkam nodded. "Sounds like a great plan." He said. "The price seems a bit steep, but I'm sure you can do something else once you're out of the Facility."

Billy frowned. "What are you talking about?"

Lohkam pointed towards his team. "See my crew over there?"

"Yeah."

"You notice the tank isn't our regular one?"

"I do," Billy said.

"The one joining us today is sick of games," Lohkam said. "He can't wait to get out of here. So I told him I could help him out."

"How you gonna do that?"

"He wants to enter Weapons Facility. It's violent and physical, not something I would want to sign up for, but some kids just like to go that way."

"Yeah, I guess." Billy said.

"If he busts someone up bad, and I mean real bad, then he'll use up his last warning here and get kicked from the facility. Then he can go ahead and apply to Weapons."

Billy didn't say anything. He was sizing up the tank, who was smiling in Billy's direction with a cruel look on his face.

"Anyone who walks onto that field today with wraps on their hands and isn't on my team... well, they're gonna be his main target. He'll be kicked from the facility, but before he is, it's gonna get violent. This is his third strike. First strike was because he beat someone so bad the kid had to drop out. His second strike involved paralyzing some poor guy in an accident. They couldn't prove it was done on purpose, so they could only give him a strike, but I'm here to tell you that he did do it on purpose."

Billy looked pale and his eyes were wide.

"This is just one stupid little game, Billy, not worth getting hurt over. Definitely not worth losing the use of your legs... or maybe your life, if he gets a bit too carried away."

Lohkam turned around and began to walk back to his group. "Or maybe it is," he called back over his shoulder. "I guess that's just gonna have to be up to you."

Lohkam got back to his group and stopped, keeping his back to Billy. "What's he doing?" Lohkam asked.

"He's taking his wraps off, Lock. Same with the rest of his team. What the hell'd you say to him?"

"Same thing you did," Lohkam said with a smile. "I just said it better."

===

Five minutes later, the door opened for the game 'Monkey See, Monkey Don't.' Of the five teams, only one entered the field.

Lohkam and his crew captured one tree, then exited the arena. They walked back into the ready room, which was now empty. They boys laughed at their victory.

"Not as fancy as Brandon's win," one of the teammates said.

Lohkam laughed harshly. "It's a win. No one gets to see how they did it, so maybe our win was more skillful than theirs. That's the proper way to spin the story."

"I doubt it. I heard they took four trees," another said.

"Doesn't matter," Lohkam snapped. "They won early and we won early. Pretty soon we'll see who the real winner is. I'd put my money on us, boys.

<u>28</u>

Mr. Thorn will see you now."

Wesley stood up and followed the secretary down the hallway. The door at the end of the hall was open, and the attractive young woman walked to it and entered without knocking. Samson Thorn was sitting at a large, dark wooden desk talking to someone on the phone. He smiled and waved his hand, motioning for Wesley to take a seat across from him. Thorn held up one finger to indicate he would be only another minute, and Wesley nodded.

"I understand, General. Yes, I absolutely agree with that. I'm glad you feel that way. Wesley just walked in for his initial consultation with me, actually. Really? I'll be sure to tell him."

Thorn hung up the phone and stood up to reach across the desk. The two men shook hands and sat back down. "Hi, Wesley, I'm Mr. Thorn. I'd prefer to be called Samson, but the General wants it kept formal."

"Nice to meet you, Mr. Thorn," Wesley said. "I'm honoured to have been selected as one of your VR instructors."

"We're referring to the virtual reality program as 'the Sim'." Thorn said. "I'm glad to have you join us. The General said you've been doing a remarkable job with your kids since joining the Game Facility."

"It was mostly luck on my part," Wesley said. "I was fortunate enough to get Brandon in my group of kids. He and his team have become very successful."

"Yes, that's why you're able to join the Sim so early," Thorn confirmed. "The General wants to keep everything in place for Brandon's Hand. In order for that to happen, we'll need you to be in there with them."

"Why not just put a simulation of me in there?" Wesley joked.

Thorn nodded thoughtfully. "Perhaps we can work towards that, Wesley. Yes, I bet we could learn enough about you over time to build a very convincing NPC avatar. That's a great idea, thanks."

"What's an NPC?" Wesley asked.

"A Non Player Character," Thorn said. "A construct that looks like a regular person inside the Sim, but it's not controlled by a real person outside of the program."

"You can do that?"

Thorn nodded. "My vision is that someday you won't be able to distinguish between a player controlled avatar and a computer operated NPC. We aren't even close to that yet, but it's a new technology at the moment and there's always a rapid growth curve in the world of computers." Thorn stood up and walked to the door. "I hope you don't mind, but the rest of this meeting will be private and confidential. I'll be asking some sensitive questions to make certain you're worthy of the security clearance required to work in the Sim."

Wesley nodded. "Of course, sir."

Thorn closed the door and walked back to his desk. He opened the top right drawer of his desk and flipped a small black switch. Then he typed a command on his keyboard and the monitor showed a view of the hallway directly outside his door. He looked up and nodded to Wesley.

"All right, the room is secure from listening devices and I can see any approach to the office. This may be the most secure talk we've ever had."

Wesley let out a sigh and slumped slightly in his chair. "That's a relief," he said. "It's strange to walk right into your office. Much better than our normal meeting spots over the years of back alleys and greasy spoon restaurants."

"We play a dangerous game, Wesley, and it's a true testament to our skills that we haven't been found out. When I hired you to infiltrate the Centres I never thought you would get so deep into the organization."

"I'm sorry I haven't been able to contact you since being assigned to the Game Facility, but they have me living there now, and security is extremely tight."

Thorn waved his hand dismissively. "Don't worry about it. I'm glad things are going smoothly for you. It would appear that Brandon is everything we hoped he would be."

"The kid's remarkable," Wesley said. "He's a natural leader, and I can't get over how creative and swift his mind is."

"It's in his genes," Thorn said. "Everything has gone according to plan. Once we get him inside the Sim, I'll finally be able to start working with him myself."

"And the others?"

"Yes, the others as well, although they are likely too old to be of use. My best chance for success is with Brandon."

"The others aren't that much older," Wesley said.

"There are laws in our universe that exist and work even though the average person doesn't know about them," Thorn said. "Laws like gravity and the generally known laws of physics which we all know about. One of the little known, yet very powerful, laws is called The Law of Imprinting."

"Never heard of it."

"Most haven't, but that doesn't make it any less real," Thorn said. "The Law of Imprinting states that whatever a child has become by the time they are ten years of age, is how they will remain for the rest of their lives."

"I don't understand what you mean," Wesley said.

"You can imprint characteristics onto the psyche of a child between the ages of zero and ten. Manners, cultural preferences, loyalties, traits of all types and sorts."

"Are you serious?"

"Absolutely," Thorn said.

"That sounds a lot like brainwashing."

Thorn shrugged. "A nicer term is conditioning. To make it sound even less harmless, it's referred to as 'raising.' The primary role of a parent is to raise a healthy, responsible child to follow the laws and rules of the society they live in."

"Okay, I see what you're getting at," Wesley nodded.

"The General understands this law and he's spent considerable time, money, and effort to raise his orphans in specific ways. By the time each child turns ten they behave exactly how the General wants them to. Children raised by the Centres are not eligible to participate in advanced programs until that age to ensure their complete loyalty to him before they are distracted with any other tasks or training."

"Wow."

"Yeah," Thorn said. "So the odds of me being able to influence the ten-year-olds in the VR programs is slim, because they are already fully conditioned to be loyal to the General."

"Brandon is only five."

"Yes," Thorn smiled. "The General must be so confident in the program by now that he's allowed the boy to advance before he should."

"Dangerous if someone else can take over his imprinting."

"Who would be so bold?" Thorn asked. "The law is not well known. I'm guessing the General wouldn't expect someone to infiltrate his secure and protected program to make such an attempt. After so many years of success they must be confident in the security of the entire system. His confidence has merit. It would take a skilled opponent to come along and turn one of his children."

"Yet that's exactly what you intend to do." Wesley said.

Thorn smiled. "I do. The General may be father to thousands, perhaps tens of thousands. If my plan works properly, then I will show him the power that can be gained from being a parent to one special individual."

29

"**Don't worry, kids**, we won't stick you with lots of needles or other nasty things," the technician said.

Brandon looked around the room. They'd learned that there were two other teams and ten single kids who had also qualified to win their divisions earlier than the rest. The twenty-five kids sat in the room while a technician explained the basics of VR technology to them. Alan looked at Brandon with a grin. They'd talked about getting poked with needles before they got here, and none of them were afraid; a little pain was worth the price of getting to play in the Sim. Besides, it looked like their biggest pain wouldn't be a needle. Lohkam's crew had won their age group early too. Brandon had been looking forward to a small break from the bully, but it looked like that wasn't going to happen. Brandon hoped that inside the Sim they would have an opportunity to face each other.

"At first, we'll only put you into the Sim for a few hours at a time. All we need to do for that is put one tiny intravenous needle into you. We'll also put sensors on your head and chest, but that doesn't hurt. The better you do inside the Sim, the longer you get to stay there. Over time there will be a few more things that we need to hook you up to, but by the time that happens I think most of you will be used to the process."

"When do we get started?" one of the kids asked.

"Right now," the technician said. "When I call out your names please go stand by the door. An instructor will take you to your table and send you into the Sim for your orientation and alignment session. All questions from now on will be answered inside the Sim by your instructor. If there are any of you who've changed your mind and don't want to play in the Sim, now is the time to speak up."

The room remained silent as the kids looked at each other with grins on their faces. Everyone wanted to try this.

The technician nodded and began to call out names. The group was broken into three smaller clusters made up of one team and a couple of solo players. Brandon's group was called first. They stood up together and walked to the door.

The door opened and Brandon smiled when he saw who his instructor was. "Welcome to the Sim, kids," Wesley said with a grin. "Follow me and we'll get you hooked up and inside as quickly as possible."

The eight children followed Wesley down a long white hallway. They entered a room with ten silver metal tables positioned inside. Wires and cables extended from the white ceiling to a metal pole standing beside each table. In addition to the wires, there was a bag of clear liquid hanging from each pole.

"Everybody pick a table," Wesley said. "They look cold and hard but are quite comfortable to lie on."

The tables were positioned in two groups of five, with one table surrounded by four others. Brandon's Hand moved to one table cluster. Another kid was standing beside the middle table and one at another, but Tony smiled and waved them away, sweeping his arm towards it and smiling at Brandon as he did so. Brandon nodded and stood beside the centre table. His team mates chose tables surrounding him and they waited for further instructions.

"Everyone lie down on your tables now, please," Wesley instructed.

Brandon was surprised that the table felt warm and soft. Wesley was right; they were very comfortable.

"Today we'll be inside the Sim for only a couple of hours. Technicians are coming around now to put the monitors on and stick you with a small needle. Things seem a bit strange at first when you get inside. You will be asked to close your eyes and count backwards from 10. When you get to zero and open your eyes it will seem like nothing has happened, but in fact, you will be in the Sim, in a room that looks exactly like this one — well, not quite exactly. Each of you will be in your own room. Wait there until I come to get you. It won't take that long, but make sure you just sit there and wait. If any of you have a question, raise your hand and ask it now."

A moment of silence passed. "All right, then," he said. "See you in the Sim."

Brandon looked straight up at the ceiling for a few moments and then he heard someone approach his right side and gently take hold of his bare arm. He felt a slight pinch and guessed that he'd just been stuck with a needle. He breathed a sigh of relief; it wasn't as bad as he'd thought it would be. A technician leaned in front of Brandon, obstructing his view of the ceiling. The man was wearing a surgical mask, but Brandon could tell he had a pleasant smile on his face from the way his eyes were slightly squinted. "Okay, young man, I'm going to place a small mask on your face in just a moment. When I do that, I want you to close your eyes and start counting backwards from ten down to zero. When you reach zero you can open your eyes. If the transfer works properly there will be no wires attached to you, and I will have disappeared. Good luck, and enjoy your time in the Sim."

Brandon nodded his head and the mask slowly lowered over his mouth and nose. He closed his eyes and slowly began to count backwards.

He reached zero and waited for another brief moment... then he opened his eyes.

The mask over his face was gone. He turned his head and the technician was no longer in the room. He sat up slowly and looked around. The room was small; it contained only the table that he'd been lying on and a chair close by. There was a man sitting in the chair looking at him with interest. It wasn't Wesley.

"Hi," Brandon said.

"Hello, Brandon," the man smiled. "Welcome to the Sim."

"Thanks," Brandon said. "It looks the same as real life."

The man nodded. "We built it to look that way. After we get your avatar aligned and running properly, we will show you many new and interesting games. Some will seem like real life, but many will be much more fun than that."

"Where's the rest of my team?" Brandon asked.

"They are in rooms like this one. Don't worry, you'll see them shortly."

"What's your name?"

"My name is Thorn," the man said. "I created the Sim."

"Wow, that's great," Brandon said. "Do you meet everyone when they come in here?"

Thorn shook his head. "I don't meet many souls at all inside the Sim," he said. "Only a special few get to meet me in here."

"Oh," Brandon said. "Well, thanks, then. It's nice to meet you."

Thorn stood and walked over to the side of the table. He shook Brandon's hand. "Of all the people I've ever met, Brandon, you are the most powerful one that I've seen."

Brandon wasn't sure how to reply to such a comment, so he said nothing. Thorn nodded his head and continued. "I know the others won their contests to get inside the Sim early, but you did it better than anyone else. How would you like special training and tips from me during your play in here?"

Brandon couldn't believe his luck. He didn't need to think about it, he simply blurted out his answer. "Yes, please, Mr. Thorn, I would like to learn as much as you can teach about the Sim."

Thorn smiled and touched Brandon's shoulder lightly. "It will be my pleasure, Brandon. And don't call me Mr. Thorn. It doesn't seem right for you to call me that."

"What should I call you, then?" Brandon asked.

Thorn shook his head slightly. "I don't know. When you think of something, feel free to give it a try."

30

"**Good morning, sir,**"

"Morning, Harold," Thorn said from behind his desk. "What have you got for me today?"

"An update on the time variance issue."

"Ah, yes — I hope it's good news?"

"It is," Harold said. "Looks like we can stretch the time difference between the Sim and reality significantly."

"How much?" Thorn asked.

"That's up to you, really. We'll encounter one significant problem as we go out of synch in time with the Sim, though. It will impede or eliminate our ability to have two-way communication."

Thorn nodded and considered the implications. With no time variation he could sit at his desk and talk with subjects inside the Sim, which was very handy during development of the virtual world. To lose the real time communication would be a serious factor from a design and control perspective.

"Thanks, Harold. You've done a great job on this. Keep it quiet and let me think on it for a bit. I know we'll be experimenting with it for sure, but I'm not quite certain how or when to do so."

As Harold left, Thorn's attention returned to his monitor. The children were inside the Sim for their second session. Their avatars had been calibrated and now they were ready to begin learning how things worked in the VR world. Currently the group was sitting in a classroom, listening to Wesley tell them about the basics.

Thorn's gaze kept drifting to Brandon. He sat near the front of the room surrounded by his teammates. Brandon's Hand looked more like Cooper's Hand than a group of ten-year-olds. They possessed the poise and confidence of a mature unit. Thorn couldn't wait to watch them work together in some of the games he'd designed.

Thorn reached for his VR helmet and put it on. With the flip of a switch he entered the Sim.

He stood up, closed his eyes, and pulsed a thought. Thorn opened his eyes and saw that Cooper was already here.

"We ready to meet with our boy then, Doc?" Cooper asked.

"In a few moments," Thorn confirmed.

"You scanned them all the same way you did me?"

"Yes."

"How many of them are true orphans?" Cooper asked.

"Of the twenty-five, all of them are General orphans," Thorn said.

Cooper made a grim face as he looked at Thorn. A true orphan was a child who'd lost their parents to natural causes. General orphans were kids that had no parents because the General had killed them for his own purpose.

"Even the little one?" Cooper asked.

"Especially the little one," Thorn said.

"Who were his parents?" Cooper asked.

"If you were one hundred percent with me on this project, Cooper, then you would already have that information."

Cooper looked at Thorn for a few moments and then shook his head. He still wasn't entirely sure Thorn was telling him the truth. He'd agreed not to reveal this line of discussion with the General quite yet, because he still hadn't made up his mind about who or what to believe.

Thorn chuckled. "Well, then, perhaps soon."

===

Brandon stood up with the others. So far his experience inside the Sim was the most boring thing he'd had to put up with for months. Everyone had grumbled yesterday when they exited the Sim. Although they were told to expect a boring time, they'd all hoped to do or see something exciting. Brandon was certain today would be much more entertaining, but so far it had involved listening to Wesley talk about how the Sim was exactly like real life.

"Make a line in front of that door and I'll take us all to the basic exercise room now," Wesley said.

The kids stood up and quickly formed a line. When everyone was ready, Wesley opened the door. The doorway was bathed in bright white light; it was impossible to see what lay on the other side.

"You're all about to experience your first bit of fun in the Sim," Wesley said with a smile. "The exercise room isn't close to us, but this doorway will act as a portal. Step through it and you will come out in the exercise room, which actually lies many kilometers from here. When you find yourself in the exercise room, get out of the way for the next kid to come through, please. I'm going first. First in line count to three then step through, followed by each of you until we're all there. Any questions?"

Wesley looked around but none of the children raised their hands. He nodded and stepped through the portal and disappeared.

When it was Brandon's turn, he walked calmly into the light. He felt a slight sensation of movement which was followed by another feeling of thudding to a stop. He looked around curiously. Instead of being in an exercise room with the others, he was standing in a hallway with a white door at the end of it. Brandon shrugged his shoulders and walked towards the door. He knocked lightly then opened it and walked in.

"Hey, guys," he said.

Cooper laughed and looked over at Thorn. "Heya, Brandon, how are things for you inside the Sim so far?" Cooper asked.

"Boring," Brandon admitted. "Do we get to play some new games soon?"

"Yes, you'll be playing soon," Thorn said. "We have to make sure everyone knows the rules of the Sim first."

"Wesley said the Sim is like real life," Brandon said. "All of us know the rules of real life, so why make us listen to them again?"

Cooper looked at Thorn's face and chuckled. "He makes a good point."

Thorn grabbed a pen from his desk and held it in his hand. After a moment the pen floated upwards into the air.

"The Sim is mostly like real life, but there are some ways that it's different. That's why it's important to go through the training and learn the basics."

"Okay," Brandon watched the pen float with excitement in his eyes. "What am I doing here, then? Shouldn't I be with the others in the exercise room?"

"I've decided to give you some private lessons," Thorn said. "Cooper and I will be teaching you things that the others won't get a chance to learn right away."

Brandon smiled at the idea of learning secret things that the other kids might not, but then he frowned. "Why teach me stuff and not the others?" he asked.

"Because you're special," Thorn said. "You're going to do things that others can't figure out anyway, so it's best to guide you and make sure you don't hurt anyone by accident."

Brandon thought about it for a moment and decided not to argue. He shrugged and nodded his head. "Sounds good to me," he said.

Thorn laughed at how easily the boy accepted the news. "I'm going to send you back with the others now, Brandon. I'll see you again very soon, though. Go through the door and you'll come out in the exercise room with the group."

Brandon waved and walked back to the door. He opened it and stepped into the white light.

When he was gone, Cooper chuckled. "The boy seems much older than he is. "He's so calm and sure of himself."

"Much like you are, compared to others your age," Thorn said.

"Yes," Cooper admitted.

Thorn walked to the doorway which was still a brilliant white. "Come with me," he said. "I think the boy will learn very quickly. If you're going to teach him secret skills, then I guess I'd better make sure you know how they work first."

"That would help," Cooper laughed as he walked to join Thorn.

<u>31</u>

"**What is it** that I'm looking at, Mr. Thorn?"

The General sat at the head of the table with a mug of coffee in his hand. He'd just spent the last few minutes flipping through the detailed report that Thorn had compiled for him. It was obvious from the way he skimmed through it that the General wasn't impressed with the information he was reading. He looked at Thorn with flat eyes and a bored expression on his face as he waited for a reply to his question.

"You're looking at the details of the project so far, General," Thorn said.

"It's thin."

Thorn smiled and reached for the remote control. He turned the monitor on and both men gazed at the scene. The camera appeared to be placed high above a field covered by trees and brush separated in the middle by a small river, about fifteen feet across. In the middle of the gently flowing water, floating about two feet above the surface, was a ruby coloured globe the size of an orange. The camera view showed two groups of students kids making their way towards the river from opposite sides of the field. The three on the left were closer, and they jumped over brush and batted tree branches out of the way as they raced to reach the shore first.

"They have begun to play simple simulations," Thorn said. "This one is a straight race to the centre where the goal is to avoid all obstacles as they appear."

"We can do the same types of things in our gaming facility," the General said.

Thorn arched his eyebrow and pointed to the screen. "Really?" he asked.

As if on cue, the earth in front of the lead player erupted forcefully into a solid column. The runner wasn't quick enough to avoid it and collided against the surface with a heavy thud. After a brief moment of leaning dumbly against the earthen wall, she crumpled raggedly to the ground.

The General chuckled. "Ouch."

Thorn smiled. "A benefit of being inside the Sim," he said. "We can quickly fix any damage to her avatar to minimize downtime."

"When can we step it up?"

"When we work out all the bugs," Thorn said. "I also think it's prudent to allow each new player to become accustomed to the Sim. There's no benefit from going to high intensity overnight, General. We need to ramp them up gently."

The General sat and watched the screen until the game was concluded. The winner jumped into the middle of the stream and grabbed the ruby. Instead of landing in the water, the girl floated above its surface and smiled as the others made it to the edge of the stream.

"I agree, Mr. Thorn," the General said. "But I want updates at more regular intervals."

Thorn nodded. "That's fine, General. Whatever you want."

"Yes." The General looked from the monitor and met Thorn's gaze. "Whatever I want..."

32

"**This is starting** to get confusing."

Brandon took a bite of cereal and looked at Alan from the corner of his eye. "What is?" he asked.

Alan pointed around him with his spoon. "All this in-and-out stuff. We come out of the Sim, then we go back in. Then we go in again and fall asleep inside. Then we wake up and come out. It's all messed up."

"Yeah, I agree," Easton said. "Sometimes I don't know if we're in or out of the Sim."

"We're out," Kay announced, nodding her head confidently.

"I know we're out right now," Alan said. "I'm just saying that it's getting hard to tell sometimes. We eat inside the Sim, too, and the food tastes the same as it does in real life."

"They're doing it on purpose," Brandon said. He bent over his bowl and continued to shove the cereal into his mouth. Sometimes they didn't get enough time to finish meals, but Brandon made certain to eat fast. He never went hungry.

"Why would they be doing it on purpose?" Alan asked.

"To get us fully into the Sim so they can study us when we don't realize we're inside of it," Brandon said.

"Why?" Alan asked again.

Brandon shrugged and drank the milk from his bowl, emptying it and putting it back down on the table. "Don't know. Don't care. Doesn't matter." He looked at Easton's bowl with focused interest until Easton chuckled and pushed it towards him.

"Of course it matters," Alan said. "There are lots of answers we need to know."

"Why only matters if you can use the answer to change the now," Brandon said. "We can't change what they're doing to us. So just be where you're at and do the best you can when they give us a job to do."

"You make it sound so simple," Easton said.

"It is," Tony agreed.

"We've barely done anything inside the Sim," Kay said.

"That's gonna change soon," Brandon said. "I think we're all aligned and tested now. It's been, what... three days inside there?"

"That's what I'm saying!" Alan laughed. "I'm not sure how long it's been." They all laughed.

"There's one thing I know for sure," Brandon said, putting down his second empty bowl of cereal. "The Sim isn't exactly like the real world."

"It seems that way to me," Tony said.

"Then you need to look harder," Brandon said. "It's a computer generated program."

"Maybe this reality is, too,"

Brandon made a sour face. "That's weak, Tony. Trust me, guys, we can't believe what they told us. The Sim is different, and we all need to believe it if we want to be number one. Accepting this fact is gonna be our biggest advantage in there."

"It's hard to believe you, Brandon, when we've seen it for ourselves," Easton said.

"You've only seen what they want you to see," Brandon said. "Next time we go in I'll show you something. They're lying to us all, and I can prove it."

"How?" Alan asked.

Brandon shook his head. "You wouldn't believe me if I told you. Just start telling yourselves that the Sim isn't like real life at all. We can do whatever we want to do inside the Sim — if we believe we can."

"I don't know..." Kay said.

"When we get back inside, I'm gonna show you something," Brandon said. "If you don't believe me after that, then we're doomed to be as crappy as the other teams."

"Okay, everyone," Wesley announced. "Breakfast is over. Time to get back into the Sim."

Brandon smiled at the group and stood up. "Let's go, kids."

===

They opened their eyes and got out of bed. The players had begun to 'park' their avatars in beds when they exited the Sim. One kid had joked that it made real life seem like a dream, and the idea had quickly been accepted. Most of them now referred to real life as 'the Dream.'

"Follow me, guys and gals," Wesley said. "We're done with the boring stuff. Now the games can begin."

Brandon nodded and the others applauded quietly. His instincts were often right, and the team was always proud when one of his hunches came true.

As they were walking, Brandon's group slowed their pace to lag behind. When the main group went around a corner, Brandon stopped and his team gathered around him.

He reached into his pocket and pulled out a small coin. He flipped it in the air a couple times then handed it to Easton. Easton inspected it then handed it back to Brandon with a nod. Brandon held his palm out flat and dropped the coin onto it, then he closed his eyes and squinted slightly in concentration. The coin floated up into the air and hung suspended above Brandon's open palm. The others exclaimed in hushed tones of surprise.

"That's unreal!" Alan said. He snatched the coin from the air and Brandon opened his eyes.

"It some kind of trick?" Tony asked.

"Yeah," Brandon said and tapped his head. "That's what I'm telling ya, guys. It's different inside the Sim. All of us can use our minds to do this kind of stuff. But we have to be careful others don't find out about it."

"What kind of stuff can we do by floating a small coin in the air?" Kay asked. "I don't think there'll be a game of coin toss, but I guess if there is, we'll win."

Brandon grinned at them. "Stop it," he said. "Stop thinking small. If someone told you that anything is possible in here, what would you do? Would you laugh and call them crazy? Or would you agree with them and start to think of ways to use your powers to beat everyone else at the games?"

"We'd use it to win, Brandon, you know that." Eason said.

Brandon nodded and pushed his way out of the circle that they'd formed around him. He pulled back his arm and threw the coin as hard as he could. It raced a few feet and then, suddenly, it stopped to hang in mid-air. Faster than any of them could see, the coin zipped to land with a loud slap into Brandon's hand. He smiled and tossed the coin up again. This time it did a lazy figure eight in the air, increasing in speed along its path as Brandon waved his fingers below it. Finally he snatched the coin out of the air and looked at them with an excited grin.

"Anything is possible in here," he said.

The rest of them nodded in agreement.

33

Brandon's Hand huddled together to stay warm while they waited for the game to begin.

It was cold, they were outside, and the ground was covered with deep snow all around them. Tall stone cliffs were on both sides of the area, and a single path wound its way through a dark pine forest.

Both groups had entered the field at midpoint through the silvery white doorway that opened and closed as they traveled inside the Sim.

They had been told this game would be cold, but they really had no idea what cold meant. Life in the Centres hadn't exposed them to the harsh temperature fluctuations of either hot or cold. They'd also been sheltered from rainstorms and winds and all other types of weather that regular people took for granted. Centre children began to experience outside weather conditions at the age of fourteen through field trips. The older kids in the Sim would have a distinct advantage because of their experience with temperature in this game.

"I feel like my face is going to fall off," Alan said.

"I can barely move wearing all these clothes," Tony complained.

"It's not that bad," Easton said, although his lips were blue and his teeth chattered when he thought no one was paying attention to him.

Brandon said nothing. His eyes scanned the cliffs to either side for a few moments before stepping off the path to explore.

He didn't seem to be bothered by the cold; he took off his outer jacket to allow for better movement.

"What are you doing?" Alan asked. "You're gonna freeze."

Brandon glanced at Alan with an annoyed look. "Be quiet and help me figure out a strategy." He said.

"But —" Alan said.

"No," Brandon hissed. He gave the group a serious look. "What's this game about?" he asked them.

"We need to capture the flag at their start point without being shot by the other team and immobilized." Easton said.

"Wrong," Brandon shook his head. "What's this game about?"

"It's not wrong," Kay said. "That's the game Wesley explained to us."

Brandon looked slowly at each of them and then returned to scanning the surrounding area. He took four steps away from the path and sank down into the snow up to his knees. "Tony, come here, please." He said.

Tony took a breath to complain about the cold, but Brandon's body language and facial expression commanded silent obedience. With a sigh he walked towards Brandon, sinking down to his waist as he reached the younger boy's side.

Brandon nodded and helped Tony out of the snow. The two moved back to the path with the others. Brandon tapped Easton lightly on the shoulder and they walked away from the centre of the path in the opposite direction from before. The same thing happened; Brandon sunk down to his knees and the heavier Easton sank to just above his waist.

Brandon chuckled as they came back to join the others. "My small size really does give me the advantage sometimes." He said. "Kay you should be almost as light as I am, so you and I can go off the path farther than the others."

Kay nodded.

Brandon's expression changed from concentration to a more relaxed look.

"Here's what this game is really about," he said. He reached down and grabbed a handful of snow and made it into a ball. "It's about how we deal with the cold, and the snow, and the different ground conditions."

He unslung the plastic rifle from behind his back. It looked like a real weapon, but instead of bullets they fired small plastic balls. When one of the balls hit the target pad located on either the front or back of a player's uniform, a thin layer of material underneath their clothes stiffened, causing that player to become frozen in place until the game was over and the instructor unfroze them.

"If we're cold and buried, then we can't shoot as well as we normally do," Brandon said. "The other team is full of kids our age or a bit older. I don't think any of us have played in snow before. Our fight isn't with the other team, it's with the cold. If we beat the cold, then we win."

"It's so cold," Tony complained. "If we wait much longer I don't think I'll be able to move at all."

Brandon sighed and removed another layer of clothes, carefully sliding off his coat but allowing the target harness to remain in place. "It's not cold," he said. "Right now we're lying on a bed in a warm room; only these avatars are feeling the cold."

"Yes, but these bodies we're in are feeling it as if it's real," Easton said. "These avatars are exactly like real bodies in here, Brandon. We can't control what cold does to our bodies in the Sim any more than we can in the Dream."

Brandon laughed and nodded his head with excitement. "You're exactly right, Easton! Which is so exciting, don't you think?"

Easton shook his head. "I don't see what you mean," he said.

"Okay, that's it," Brandon shook his head. "We start meditating during our down time. We can control how the cold affects us, both here and also in the Dream. If I don't accept the cold, then my body will produce more heat and I'll be okay. I'll make my glow warmer and it'll keep me warm."

"Well, it does seem to be working for you," Alan said. "You haven't frozen yet, and you're barely wearing anything."

"Thank you," Brandon said.

"I'm not sure it will work the same way in the Dream," Kay said.

Brandon smiled. He thought it was great that they were all referring to real life as a dream. He knew what could be achieved in dreams better than most, thanks to the sloth and owl.

A loud blast of sound erupted from both nowhere and everywhere simultaneously, indicating that the game had begun. Immediately the ground they were standing on became soft and they all sank down to the point where the snow was chest deep. Thanks to Brandon's exploring before the game started, they knew to move toward the sides. Each found the proper distance where they were barely submerged in snow at all, with Brandon closest to the outside.

"Don't worry about the Dream right now," he said. "Just worry about this game. Now take off your outer coats and let's move into the woods. There's less snow in there for us to have to deal with. I'll tell you the plan as we go."

34

The plan was simple, yet it turned out to be very effective.

Because they had figured out how the snow depth worked, Brandon's team was able to race to the woods and secure positions ahead of the other group. Kay and Brandon climbed into the trees while Alan, Tony, and Easton secured positions on the ground.

Ten minutes later three figures appeared, crawling and stumbling toward the woods. They'd figured out how to walk on the snow, but looked tired, as if the learning cycle and the cold had sapped their energy. As they got within firing distance, they instinctively sank low and aimed at the trees.

At Brandon's signal, Tony and Alan fired their weapons, and plastic bullets flew at their opponents with sharp crisp spitting sounds.

Tony hit his target after just six shots. He grinned and stopped firing once he realized he'd been successful. Alan fired a couple more shots and tagged his target as well, stopping to watch the third target run for cover while the first two remained frozen in place.

With a spit from his weapon, Easton fired a single bullet. His target was moving and should have been impossible to hit, but as the plastic bullet started its flight, Easton squinted his eyes and began to concentrate. The team collectively held their breath as the bullet altered course as if by magic and streaked at an impossible angle, directly towards the girl on the run. With a distinctive click, the pellet tapped the centre of her back target, freezing her suit in mid-stride and sending her sprawling into the snow.

The team waited another few minutes, but no one else appeared. Brandon and Kay dropped from their perches in the trees and the group gathered in a tight huddle.

"Ideas?" Brandon asked.

"Two of us move left and two move right, hugging the outer edges of the path," Kay suggested. "It looks like there's some tree coverage on the left. Fifth person hugs the trees and moves ahead of the others on point."

Brandon nodded and scanned the group. "Any other suggestions?"

"It's a good plan," Alan said. The others nodded.

"Okay," Brandon nodded. "Whose turn for point?"

Tony made a sour face. "Mine, but that's not gonna work for this map. I'm gonna pass, if you all agree."

Most groups consisted of players who didn't like taking point, but not Brandon's Hand. They all wanted to play point; it was where the best moves, stories, and wins came from. The group looked at Tony proudly; it was smart teamwork to know your limitations and let someone else step forward. They would remember his call and reward him for it later.

Everyone else's hand shot out in unison, each showing a different combination of fingers splayed and clenched. They'd developed a quick hand game to decide votes and sudden role changes during play. Kay smiled victoriously; she would be point this time.

===

Two on one side, two on the other, and Kay somewhere hiding in the tree line. It appeared that even with proper focus and attention the cold could eventually affect everyone's avatar, even Brandon's. The others had put their jackets on before they left the trees. They were almost in sight of the enemy start point, and Brandon was just now beginning to feel the gnawing tickle of the cold against his skin.

Everyone moved purposefully and in formation until the enemy start point came into view. A flag was planted in the ground and waved slightly in the breeze. Brandon had hoped to see the remaining two enemies huddled together against the cold or stuck up to their waists in the snow, but they were nowhere in sight.

Brandon raised a hand to indicate caution, and at that very moment they heard the sound of bullets spitting from rifles to their left. Brandon hit the ground as a spray of plastic bullets sped past him; a second slower and he would've been tagged.

The bullets stopped firing. It wasn't possible to hit the chest or back targets when an opponent was lying on the ground, so there was no point in firing. It was also against the rules for anyone to fire if their target plate was covered. Their opponents were waiting for them to stand, walking slowly toward them in order to get a closer shot. The enemy had the advantage.

Brandon looked up to see the two figures walking towards them with weapons drawn. Both were grinning confidently, no doubt thinking that they were about to win the game.

Brandon smiled back, waving his hand as they approached. From the corner of his eye he saw Kay make her way out of her hiding place in the trees and toward the flag. She was safely behind the enemy, and out of their view.

To draw their attention, Brandon jumped up and began to run. The enemy immediately started firing, but Brandon zigzagged as he ran to present a difficult target. He'd run only about twenty steps when the siren blared, indicating that the game was over. He turned back to face his opponents.

Their expressions had changed from triumph to confusion as they looked first at Brandon, and then back towards their flag. Kay waved at them with a big smile on her face, the enemy flag resting on her shoulder.

Tony, Alan, and Easton were dusting the snow off themselves as they approached.

"They didn't manage to get even one of you?" one of their opponents asked with disappointment.

"Next time for sure," Brandon said encouragingly.

"How are you not cold?" the other kid asked, shivering.

Brandon looked at his team and smiled. "Long story," he said, "and not very interesting."

35

"**How many dead?**" Thorn asked.

Cooper flipped through the papers in front of him. "Fifteen," he replied.

"Decent figures."

"Acceptable numbers," Cooper agreed, "considering the complexity of the exercise. The first three times it was a total wipe, killing all forty people."

"Avatars," Thorn corrected him. "When you call them people it makes their deaths sound more... tragic."

"Yeah, well they are tragic, Doc," Cooper said. "I've died twice in here, and although I haven't experienced the real thing, Sim death is extremely painful and traumatic."

"Yes, it is," Thorn said.

Cooper looked at him seriously for a moment. "Why?" he asked. "Couldn't you have made the process a bit less... realistic?"

Thorn grinned. "Everything has a price, Cooper. If it cost you nothing to be ejected from the Sim, then individuals would play an entirely different way, wouldn't they?"

"I suppose they would, yes," Cooper said.

"Of course they would," Thorn said. "When a child touches fire, they learn very quickly not to do so again. Sometimes the price for self-sacrifice is worth it, but the pain built into the process makes a player think about the consequences. I think it's a brilliant addition to the program."

If Cooper had an opinion he chose to keep it to himself. He flipped through the rest of his notes and pushed them towards Thorn. "All the statistics are here, Doc. I think that's everything I have for you today."

Thorn nodded and took the sheets. He would have the documents scanned and filed later by an NPC secretary. Cooper stood up and walked toward the door, pausing before he opened it.

"If you have a minute, I'd like to talk about the General and what you showed me a few days ago."

Inwardly Thorn smiled. Keeping his outward appearance calm and expressionless, he nodded. "Of course." He gestured to the couches at one side of the office where less formal discussions took place. Cooper took a seat while Thorn went to the refrigerator and grabbed two bottles of water. He handed one to Cooper, then sat down across from him. Thorn took a drink and waited for Cooper to speak.

"I've done some asking around," Cooper said. "No one can confirm the details surrounding the death of my parents."

Thorn nodded. "I'm not surprised. There would have been no video or record of foul play. No news stations would have reported any suspicion of murder. The General's control is comprehensive."

Cooper made a wry face. No one understood the General's control over media and other sources better than him. Many times he'd used it to his advantage when performing covert operations. It was one of the main reasons that he was leaning towards believing Thorn. The entire operation sounded exactly like the General.

"One of my closest friends is a psychotherapist," Cooper said.

Thorn froze with the bottle raised to his lips. Slowly he lowered the drink and looked at Cooper. His expression was as flat as his voice. "Do not tell me you've mentioned this to someone else."

Cooper shook his head quickly. "Of course not," he said. "That's why I'm talking to you now. I want to get your permission to have them hypnotize me. If what you showed me came from my mind, then his process will confirm the truth."

Thorn leaned back and considered Cooper's request. He thought long and hard about how crucial Cooper was to his cause. This was a deadly and intricate game he was playing; one small misstep or a bad moment of luck could end it all. Thorn sighed and nodded. He'd risked much by showing Cooper the truth, and he would see it through to the end.

"Fine, you may approach this... friend, but it must be done in the most clandestine and secure way possible. They tell me you're the best at this sort of thing, which is the only reason I'm willing to give you the opportunity to do it. But that's it, Cooper. When this has been done you must decide one way or the other where your true loyalties lie. I need to begin the next phase of my plan, and if you aren't going to be a part of it, I have to know."

Cooper nodded and stood up. "Thanks, Doc. If my friend confirms what you showed me, then I'm yours. If not, then I forget it happened and remain the General's man."

Thorn nodded grimly. Both of them knew what would happen if Cooper didn't join him. One of them would die, and each was confident it would be the other.

"Bring your friend to my facility to do the hypnosis, please," Thorn said.

Cooper hesitated, but Thorn held his hand up placatingly. "I assure you I won't interfere, Cooper, but my building is one of the few places that is safe from the General's ears and eyes." Thorn got up and went to his desk. He wrote a name on a piece of paper and held it up for Cooper to see. "This is the friend you're talking about, right?" he asked.

"Yes..." Cooper nodded grimly, not happy that Thorn knew the name of his friend.

"He's on my list of people to interview for possible recruitment to the Sim project," Thorn explained. "There will be no suspicion if he comes to my facility for a few hours. It's the only way I will permit it."

Cooper was silent for a few moments, then nodded. "How does later today work for you?" he asked.

Thorn smiled. "It sounds perfect."

Cooper left the room and Thorn walked to his desk, leaned back in his chair, and disconnected from the Sim. In his real world office, he removed his headset and put it on its pedestal. He sat at his desk for the next fifteen minutes, reviewing the discussion with Cooper in his mind. Finally he nodded and picked up the phone and dialed a number. There were arrangements to be made before Cooper's friend arrived. No matter how the hypnosis turned out for Cooper, his friend would not be leaving the facility alive; Thorn simply couldn't leave a loose end like that in the wind.

Cooper had unwittingly signed his friend's death warrant.

36

The door knocked and Thorn finished reading the last paragraph of the material he was studying before he placed the tablet on his desk and looked up.

"Come in."

Cooper entered and sat down. He said nothing; Thorn remained silent as well.

"It's confirmed," Cooper finally announced.

Thorn nodded. He'd watched the entire session, thanks to a hidden camera in the interview room. If things had gone unfavourably, Thorn knew that the traps in the room would have proven effective at killing Cooper. Thankfully that wouldn't be required. He still had to deal with Cooper's friend, but that would be easy enough.

"So what does this mean?" Thorn asked.

"It means I'm now your game piece instead of the General's."

Thorn shook his head. "That's not how I work," he said. "I don't want blind followers. Your life should have always been yours. I would like to help you get back as much of it as you can."

"That's not possible, Doc," Cooper said. "Maybe we can help some of these boys and girls out, though, or at the very least try to stop the General from doing it to any more of them."

"You know better than I do how powerful he is," Thorn said. "The General is the safest man in the world... at the moment."

Cooper looked at Thorn and suddenly wondered how powerful Thorn actually was. His security checks had come back textbook clean — perhaps too clean. Something about his demeanour suggested that the General might have seriously underestimated this man. There was definitely a game going on between the two men, but Cooper knew it was way out of his league. He shrugged his shoulders. "I'm not going to even ask what you're up to, Doc," he said. "As far as everyone else in the world is concerned, I belong to the General. Within the Sim, I can communicate with you safely and I'll follow your instructions, as long as it doesn't endanger myself or my Hand."

"Are you still performing operations for the General?" Thorn asked.

"Not since he had me come in here to spy on you," Cooper said with a wink.

"What have you told him, about me?" Thorn asked.

"My reports have been boring and uneventful," Cooper said. "You only showed me one thing that I should have reported, and now that I know it's true, I'm glad I didn't."

Thorn looked at Cooper shrewdly. This was the moment when he either stepped off the cliff and committed to bringing Cooper in as far as he dared, or decided to hold back and look for other avenues to work. Thorn took a deep breath and decided to take the step.

"I'm going to teach you about the Sim," he said.

"I think you already covered the Sim."

"There are many little tips and tricks that I held back. In fact, I'm holding a significant amount of technology back from the General."

"Why?"

Thorn smiled, but it wasn't a friendly smile. "Why is not a question you will want to ask me too often, Cooper. The answers you'll get from asking me why will only cause you to lose sleep."

"I've seen some crazy stuff, Doc. I doubt you can tell me anything that'll make me have trouble sleeping."

"How old are you?"

"24," Cooper said.

"Trust me, son, there are things I know which would chill you to your very core."

Cooper looked at Thorn and shrugged. "Okay, Doc," he said. "What else do you need from me?"

"I need you to make Brandon your best student."

Cooper laughed, "That won't take much. He's likely the best already."

"Together, you and I will need to see that he stays that way," Thorn said. "This program is designed to be a long one, but it might not be long enough. We have ten years to get Brandon into top shape. We also need to bring as many of the others along as we can. The Sim will break many of them. It will be an extreme struggle to keep half of them from going insane, and the ones that don't succumb will need to be incredibly talented at all aspects of the Sim."

"Ten years? Why ten years, Doc?"

"The specifics are too complicated to get into," Thorn said. "There is a group of very intelligent people who feel that we will face extinction no more than ten to fifteen years from now."

"By we you mean...?"

"I mean everyone. Something is going to happen that could destroy all of us."

Cooper was stunned. "Do you know what it is?"

"Not specifically," Thorn answered. "The pattern of economics and agriculture, and the ecology of the planet are all rapidly deteriorating. The two superpowers are more interested in destroying each other than addressing the real problems. Some of us believe we've spotted the situation early enough, and it's their intricate and complex equations that are allowing us some small window of opportunity to prevent the catastrophe. Everything will end, and we have to do our best to stop it."

"Have you thought about informing the General?" Cooper asked. "If he knew, then maybe…"

"Oh, the General knows," Thorn said with disgust.

"What do you mean?" Cooper asked.

"I mean," Thorn said. "That the General's ultimate goal is to destroy our planet."

37

The General's smiling face appeared on the large video monitor at the front of the room, and the crowd became quiet as they waited for him to speak.

"Good morning, everyone," he said. "I want to welcome you all to the Sim; my creation that will be a training centre for you to learn and grow in so many new ways. I'm sorry that I can't be with you today, but important business has called me away. I wouldn't miss the chance to address you, though, so I'm taking the next few moments to tell you what's in store as you begin this grand new adventure."

The General's face faded and was replaced by video footage of Cooper and the other members of the General's A Hand. Scenes of many different scenarios flashed by as the General's number one team ran, swam, climbed, fired their weapons, and performed a myriad of other activities on diverse and interesting looking playing fields.

"Cooper and the other elite groups have been busy field testing hundreds of simulations over the past few weeks, while most of you have been getting acclimated to the Sim. I'm confident that you'll all have great fun over the weeks, months, and, for some of you, years to come during your time in the Sim."

Thorn's smiling face appeared on the screen opposite the General's. "I want to introduce you to the genius who created this incredible virtual reality world that you'll be living and playing in. This is Mr. Thorn. From here forward, many of your interactions from me will come through him. He speaks with my complete authority and has a much better understanding of how all of this works than I. Please join me in giving him a big welcome."

The students all began to applaud wildly and Thorn nodded graciously on the huge monitor.

"Thank you, General, and hello, everyone. I've had the pleasure to meet many of you already, and I look forward to getting to know each of you as we embark on this journey together. It's been over a month since the first players began to enter the Sim. Many of you have competed in a number of games, which has helped us to fine tune the Sim and come up with a very comprehensive scoring system. As of today, the earlier scores have been wiped clean, and we will begin keeping permanent score. This means we will rank and award points based on variables such as your time inside the Sim, games won and lost, achievements from new projects, skills you will be able to learn, and much, much, more. All of this information will be tracked, and you can view your scores at any of the main computer centres outside of the Sim. The Centre will be the main area inside the VR world to find all major updates, announcements, and track your rank against all the other players. There is a wide range of ages, sizes and skill sets among you. If you're an older kid thinking you'll automatically rank higher than the younger children, I think you might be in for a surprise. The younger players among you are more fearless and will likely score better than many of those of you who are older, at least in the beginning."

"Our imaginations have been extremely busy which means no one should ever run out of new games to play, or challenges to experience. It's my hope that some of you will display an ability to develop new games for others to play. A new job class is opening up for graduates of the Facility: that of Game Designer."

Thorn smiled at his audience. "I know it's confusing and quite a lot to understand at the moment. We will all learn as we go, and if you have any questions you can send them to me from the Centre. "

"There are only one hundred beds available for use at the moment, but there are one hundred and forty-five students in this room today. The way to get more play time inside the Sim is simple; win. Some of you will not be able to get a table as often as you would like, while others might end up living inside the Sim for very long periods of time. I encourage all of you to learn from your experiences and make the most of every opportunity when you're in there. You never know what will get you the best score. Sometimes it will be winning against all your competition, and other times it might be for helping the entire team to win even though you might not cross the finish line at all."

"We intend to keep you on your toes. The General selected you because you are the best of his children. If you get to stay, then you will become the very best."

Thorn smiled and nodded to the group as his face faded and was replaced by the General's.

"I wish you all luck and success," the General said. "Now, who wants to play?"

The crowd erupted in a roar of cheering and applause.

38

"**Still no luck** producing a functioning headset VR unit?" the General asked with a frown.

Thorn shook his head sadly, careful to convey severe disappointment through his body language, lending credibility to the lie as he sat across the table with the General. "I'm afraid not, sir," he said.

The General shifted in his chair and leaned forward to shuffle through reports lying in front of him on the table. "It's been just over two years since we began this project, Mr. Thorn. I would have thought by now that a headset would be available. I'm anxious to enter the Sim and experience it for myself."

"The process is extremely safe and easy to perform, General. We've done the entry process hundreds of thousands of times now, and we haven't experienced significant complications at all."

"I know," the General said. "For some reason it just doesn't feel right, though. I refuse to be put under and hooked up to wires and medical sensors."

Thorn and the General had gone over this point countless times and it never led anywhere pleasant. Thorn quickly changed the subject. "I do have excellent news to report, however. We've added new programming so that in complex games and scenarios involving more than five players, they no longer go up against only computer generated opponents. In the next few days, teams will be able to directly compete against each other in larger simulations."

"What?" the General asked, "What are you talking about? I've seen thousands of games and simulations being played. I always thought they were two teams of real players going up against each other."

Thorn chuckled and nodded. "Thank you for the compliment, Sir, but until now it has been against NPC opponents. There's been exceptional improvement in NPC development, and for the most part they now appear and act very realistically. They are indeed excellent if you've thought they were real players."

"If it's been non-player characters facing off against my players until now, " the General said, "then it has been very convincing indeed. Tell me the benefits of players now being able to face each other."

"They could face each other in numbers of ten versus ten or less. For the larger games, there are many benefits to players facing off against computer generated opponents," he said. "We could put each team into the same situation as the others and get a true sense of how they might look for, and come up with, different solutions to the same initial problem or challenge. Many of our simulations will continue to be run this way, because the opportunities for diversity are so promising."

"That makes sense," the General agreed.

"There are also many scenarios which will become more challenging, and therefore more rewarding," Thorn said. "Playing against computers provides a limited amount of challenge to the professional, which our players are rapidly becoming. The real progress comes from facing the ever-adaptive and always strangely creative real mind."

"Have the players always known they were facing digital opponents?" the General asked.

"Of course, sir. It was the only way to slowly and methodically desensitize them to the more martial and fatal aspects of their training. They see a target, they shoot it, or stab it, or snap its neck, or blow it up. They don't feel any remorse or guilt because it isn't real. They've done this so many times that violence is just a response to specific stimuli."

"How will they handle facing live opponents?" the General asked.

Thorn's mouth quirked into a slight smile. "They won't be facing 'live' opponents, General. They'll be facing digital avatars the same as always. The only difference is that the avatars will be controlled by other players. It should present no challenges with the conditioning."

"They will recognize the avatars they face now."

"I'm sure they will adapt to that," Thorn assured him.

The General smiled. "Excellent, Mr. Thorn. You really are doing a wonderful job with all of this."

"Thank you, sir. We're building so many layers to this training program... I'm pleased that everything is going smoothly."

"I'm also intrigued by the Longevity and Blurring projects. How long can we keep them inside the Sim now?"

"We can keep them safely inside for three months at a time," Thorn said. "Many of the top ranked players are inside that long before we pull them out. I think we could stretch it out longer, but their muscles atrophy and then it requires too long a break to get their physical condition back to normal, which causes them to lose too much time from the Sim overall."

The General shook his head. "There are ways to fix that. We'll bring in more medical staff to monitor and physically manipulate them to prevent the muscular atrophy. This is one envelope I want to keep pushing, Mr. Thorn. I also have another project going on where we place subjects in cryo stasis. I would like to see if we can immerse them in the Sim."

Thorn nodded his head. "Sounds interesting, General. Of course we would be willing to try that."

"Good," the General nodded. "What about the Blurring?"

"It's working very well. We put a subject to sleep here and secretly immerse them in the Sim. They wake up thinking they are still in reality and live normally inside the VR world until we bring them out. When we do bring them out, we are careful not to let them know what we did."

"Are you able to do the opposite?"

"Have someone think they are still inside the Sim when, in fact, they are in reality?" Thorn asked. "We haven't bothered to try. I can't imagine why something like that would be of interest."

"Something like that is of extreme interest to me, Mr. Thorn. I don't imagine it will be too difficult to Blurr the subjects into thinking they are still inside the Sim, will it?"

"I don't think so, no," Thorn replied.

"Then let's get to work on it," the General said.

39

This wasn't a fun game.

Brandon took large gulps of air, gasping for breath as quietly as he could with his back pressed tightly against a cold, dark wall. Less than twenty feet away, he could hear angry, armed men moving towards him. When they found him they would kill him as quickly as they'd slaughtered the rest of his Hand.

Brandon glanced around for a hiding place. He spotted a rusted steel grate across the street from him. It looked like a sewer shaft; dark green stones surrounded it, covered with foul water that trickled downwards out of sight. A brief glance around the corner told him the men were almost on top of him; the sewer shaft was his best hope.

Brandon let his eyelids droop slightly as he summoned his glow. Years of repeated practice, both inside the Sim and out, allowed him to summon the energy field without having to fully close his eyes. With a powerful push, he sent a wave of energy at the grate, watching with satisfaction as the rusted bars bent to either side. He wasted no time deciding if the opening was big enough for him to fit through; if it wasn't, he would be shot trying to get into the shaft, but he had no other choice. Besides, he'd died worse ways. He sprinted silently across the street and, at the last moment, leapt feet first into the opening.

With a heavy grunt he passed through the opening, scraping his back in the process. He controlled his descent by pressing his elbows against the sides of the shaft. He turned onto his belly, mentally pushed the bars closed again, and froze in place, waiting to see if anyone had spotted him.

Almost immediately the first hunter came around the corner. His eyes scanned the street and buildings, but he failed to note the sewer grate. As the next man came into view, Brandon looked down to see if he could sink further out of sight until the men had passed.

He was surprised to see the shimmering glow of a fire below him and what looked like a small stone room. He could see a man hunched over the fire, his hands stretched out to gather warmth. Brandon smiled as he recognized the white shock of hair standing up on the man's head, even from this distance.

Brandon slowly began to shimmy downwards, no longer worried that the men on the street would hear or see him. A few seconds later he dropped gracefully from the shaft and landed lightly on the floor, just a few feet from the man sitting at the fire.

The man continued to warm his hands with his back to Brandon. "Just you, boy?" he asked.

Brandon walked to the fire and squatted down, stretching out his hands towards the flames. "Yeah, the rest didn't make it," he said.

Cooper turned his head to look at Brandon with a grim frown. "Well, that can't make you very happy," he said.

Brandon nodded. "It's been a while since we've paid such a price. None of them wasted their sacrifice, though. You should have seen Alan — he took out five of them before they cut him down, and Tony had to have gained serious points from the way he went out. It was amazing."

Cooper nodded. "Can't wait to see the footage," he said. "You ready for the last stage, then?"

Brandon nodded. "I'll try my best, but we were told it would take at least two of us to get this done."

"That's right, but everyone knows you're much more skilled than two regular players. Don't worry, Brandon, you still have a shot at it."

Brandon smiled and stood up. He jumped lightly on his feet and rotated his head from right to left. "Can you tell me anything?" he asked.

Cooper shook his head. "That's not allowed, I'm only here to give you this." He reached behind him and pulled out a blade. It was about two feet long and slim with a sharp, tapered edge on one side. The large knife was silvery with gold shapes etched into the blade.

The handle looked plain but as soon as Brandon gripped it he smiled, the hilt was sharkskin, wrapped with fine silver wire to ensure solid contact with the wielder's hand. He hefted the blade, feeling its perfect balance and lightness. "Thanks," he said.

Cooper nodded. "Down that hallway and first door on the left," he said. "Good luck, boy."

Brandon ran silently down the hall, warily listening for hints of a surprise ambush or trap as he moved. He saw the doorway Cooper had described, and moved to it. Just as his hand touched the doorknob, he heard a small voice behind him.

"Please... help me..."

Brandon looked over his shoulder and saw a small, cramped cell cut into the wall. There was a small boy sitting inside; he wore filthy rags and his hair was damp and matted against the side of his head. A cut on his forehead was black with dried blood, and his nose was swollen and red. Dirty clothes hung from the boy's gaunt frame, and his filthy hands gripped the bars tightly, cracked fingernails jagged and broken.

Brandon turned away from the door and took a step towards the boy. "What are you doing here?" he asked the boy. "Who put you in that cage?"

"A horrible man beat me and threw me in here. I don't know how long ago... but he hasn't fed me and I'm very hungry," The boy said. His eyes looked both sad and hopeful as he watched Brandon intently. He tried to smile, but his cracked lips revealed a broken tooth and bloody mouth. Someone really put a hurt on this kid, Brandon thought to himself angrily.

"Okay, hold on a second. I have to do something in this room," Brandon told the boy, "then I'll come right back for you."

"But what if you don't come back?" the boy's eyes started to water. He was terrified of being left in the cage. "Other people have said the same thing, but they never come back out of that room!"

Brandon shook his head. "Listen, kid, I can't help you first. I have really important business to get done. Believe it or not, you're actually safer inside that cage at the moment."

The boy started to rock back and forth slowly, and a small whine began to build in his chest. "Please, sir," the boy said. "If you open that door before letting me out, I'm gonna die!"

"Why do you say that?" Brandon looked closely at the cage and then back at the door. Sure enough, there was an intricate group of wires running from the door to the cage.

"That's what he told me," the boy was rocking back and forth more forcefully. Brandon could tell the kid was going to become hysterical soon if he didn't do something.

"Okay, okay, calm down for a second," Brandon stood and considered his options. The game instructions had been clear. They were to infiltrate the lair and kill the boss. No one had told them how brutal the fight to get this far would end up being, or how high the cost in lives. There wasn't any mention of freeing a prisoner, but this could be a random bonus. He tapped the blade thoughtfully against his shoulder for a moment. Then he nodded.

"Okay, get back from the bars," he said. "I'll let you out now."

The boy smiled in relief and backed away. "Thank you so much, sir, you've saved my life."

Brandon nodded and smiled back as he approached the bars. His hand touched the lock and he bent closer to examine it.

Suddenly, Brandon felt a tiny scratch. He looked up and saw the boy's filthy hand on top of his own. The kid's nails were sunk deep into Brandon's hand, and he could feel liquid fire beginning to spread into it. He jerked his hand back and stepped away as the boy grinned viciously at him. Immediately Brandon knew he'd made a mistake. The instructions had been clear and he hadn't followed them. Now he was going to pay the price.

Brandon sank to the ground as the fiery poison quickly spread from his arms and into his legs. He slumped against the wall and looked at the boy silently.

"Not very smart, Mister," the boy said with mock sympathy. "You shouldn't have helped me. Being a nice guy just cost you the win."

Before he could reply, Brandon toppled over onto the floor. He was dead before his head hit the ground.

40

Tony and Easton were the final team members to arrive. Kay opened the door to Brandon's room and let them in. It wasn't possible to lock the door — that would never be allowed in the Centre — but with Tony leaning against it, no one would suddenly burst in on them.

Brandon sat down on his bed and looked at them with a pleased smile. "We've finally got enough points," he announced.

"For all of us?" Alan asked.

"That was the deal," Brandon nodded. "No one buys the perk until we can all afford it."

Easton whistled slowly. "Is there another crew out there who all have it?"

"Not a single one," Brandon said. "The perk is so expensive, no one else has done it yet."

When the Sim had reached its first year anniversary, Thorn had announced a new point system. From that day forward, players earned points by playing games that could be spent to acquire a myriad of things inside the Sim. A staggering number of perks were added to the Sim, and players immediately began to make purchases from a list of abilities, skills, and power ups that could be equipped and used. Examples of simple and low cost perks included cosmetic things such as changing an avatar's eye colour or gaining the ability to make its hair glow for a short period of time. More expensive perks were things like adding to an avatar's strength, growing in height by an inch or more, or gaining better lung capacity in order to be able to run for a longer period of time before tiring. The list of perks was extensive, and it continued to grow as the years passed.

Brandon and his crew had stood before the master list on that first day and scanned the entire menu. Almost in unison, their eyes had settled on one perk. Brandon had whispered, "I want that one," while the rest murmured in agreement. They had met in Brandon's room, which was their command centre, and unanimously agreed to work towards saving for it. The five of them had sworn to wait until everyone could buy it at the same time.

After two years of playing and saving small amounts of points from every game, they finally had enough to make their purchase.

All of them would soon be flying inside the Sim.

"How does it work, again?" Kay asked. "It's been a while since I've read the perk description."

"Here, I think I have it," Easton said, pulling up the info on his tablet. "Flying Perk: Once activated, it can be used in special flying zones inside the Sim. Players with the flying perk will have access to brand new games and contests. Team play will be allowed in most flying games; as always, check details on each game before signing up to play."

"It still gives us wings, right?" Tony asked.

"Oh, yeah," Brandon said. He'd grown considerably over the past three years, which was no surprise since he was the youngest of the bunch. His face had become slightly longer, his height had shot up, and he'd lost the button nose and smaller mouth that young children all seemed to have. Although he was a veteran of the games like the rest of them, he was still only eight years old. If he was a normal child, he'd still have another two years to wait to even have the chance to apply to come here. Brandon hadn't been a normal kid at five, and he was definitely not a normal kid at eight. "If we don't get actual wings, I don't even want the perk."

Easton looked at his tablet for details and nodded. "Yep, we still get the wings graphic, but now we can modify them in colour and texture and even make them ghostlike or invisible if we want to."

"Awesome," Alan said. The rest nodded in agreement. "When are we going to go and buy them?" he asked.

"I want us to vote one more time that we actually want them," Brandon said.

The rest of the kids laughed, but they stopped when it became obvious Brandon wasn't joking.

"I'm serious," he said. "We've been saving a portion of our points for a long time now, and it's a very expensive perk. We need to decide if we should spend the points in another area or if we go ahead and treat ourselves to what is likely just a vanity perk."

Everyone knew he was right. Getting your wings was a status symbol first and a strategic purchase second. There weren't many games to play inside the Sim that involved flying. There also weren't many areas inside where you could use your wings. The General had vehemently demanded that the Sim remain realistic. 'Magical' or non-realistic occurrences inside the Sim functioned only in special zones or parks reserved for special conditions, and all of these areas were expensive. The General made it that way to encourage serious play in the Sim.

"Well, I vote yes," Tony said. "We've wanted this forever. There were times I died inside a Sim game and the only thing that made the pain and misery bearable was knowing that someday soon I was gonna be able to fly. Now that day is here and I want to do it. I don't care if we could buy a different perk that might allow us to do something better. I want it. I vote yes."

"Anyone gonna vote no?" Brandon asked. If everyone agreed, there was no point in wasting time. Brandon never wasted time needlessly.

Easton raised his hand slowly. "I'd vote no, I guess."

"Anyone else?"

Kay raised her hand also.

"Okay, then," Brandon said. "It has to be unanimous, so let's hear it."

Easton shook his head. "I want to fly badly, but it's such a huge amount of points. There are better perks we could buy that would really help us compete."

"We already compete," Tony said, "we compete and win most times."

The group chuckled at the understatement. Their ratio of wins versus losses was unmatched by anyone. All groups and ages competed against each other, and Thorn had been right when he said the young ones would do well against the older groups. Of the top 20 teams, 14 were young, and Brandon's Hand was number one on many scoreboards. They were formidable and they didn't even have some of the best perks available.

"So you say no because we could use the points to buy a better perk that will help us in areas where we don't really need help?" Brandon asked.

"I guess," Easton said. "I'd like to fly… it's just that I think maybe we should be more responsible."

Kay laughed and shook her head. Brandon raised his eyebrows at her.

"I was thinking the same thing," she said. "But it sounds ridiculous when I hear it out loud. I think we should go for it. It's been our goal forever, and we can afford it, both points-wise and from a competitive point of view." Kay nudged Easton and smiled. "Come on, old man, let's kick loose for a change and go flying."

Easton looked at the others for a moment, then smiled and nodded his head. "All right, let's do it."

Brandon stood up. "Okay, then… let's go get our wings."

The group let out cheers of excitement as they filed out of the room.

41

Thorn stared at the monitor and watched the scene unfold.

Brandon and his Hand were smiling as they entered the beginners' area. Jostling and pushing each other playfully, the five of them stood at the top of the hill and looked down.

Resembling the bunny slope at a ski resort, it was more of a long ramp than a hill; the perfect place for new fliers to learn and hone their skills. The kids watched an instructional video, then nodded and spread out to give each other wing space. In unison, they gently tapped a spot just behind their right shoulder and smiled in delight as ghostlike wings sprang from their backs. The wings all had the same faint gold tinge to them.

Brandon went first, beginning by walking slowly down the hill. The air caught his wings, gently lifting him a foot or so off the ground. He laughed and tried to position his wings to steer himself back to the ground. A few moments later he succeeded and thudded into the grass, rolling and laughing at his first semi-successful attempt. The others joined him and began to jump, glide and land with varying degrees of success.

Thorn watched them for a few more minutes, scanning the entire scene as if searching for something specific. Finally he looked away from the screen and raised his eyes questioningly at the computer designer sitting beside him. "Did it happen while I was watching?" Thorn asked.

The designer smiled and nodded. "About a dozen times, sir. You didn't see it?"

Thorn shook his head with a frown. "I saw nothing. Have others noticed this, too, or just you?"

"Others have noticed it as well, sir. If you'll allow me to work with the settings, perhaps I can slow the frame rate down to help you spot it."

Thorn stood to allow the designer access to his keyboard. The scene inside the Sim froze and then rewound. The designer began to play the recording, and after a few moments he suddenly he hit the pause button.

"Okay, there was one. Let me just back it up slightly and then run it in slow motion..." Thorn watched as the next few frames advanced slowly. He saw nothing... until suddenly he gasped.

"Whoa!" Thorn exclaimed, "What the hell was that?"

The designer smiled and rewound the scene to play it again. After a couple of times rewinding it and playing it slowly, he played it a final time on regular speed.

"Yes, I saw it that time," Thorn said. "Now that I know what I'm looking for it's impossible not to see it."

"Excellent, sir. We were hoping you could tell us exactly what it is."

"You mean, who it is," Thorn said.

The designer frowned in confusion. "I don't understand what you mean. We all see a smoky shape," the designer said. "None of us can tell what it is, but it looks like a ball of dark smoke that just appears for a brief instant and then disappears. At first we thought it was something wrong with the circuitry, which prompted us to conduct thorough diagnostics of every circuit, every chip, every processor. The inspections all proved clean. Then we guessed it might be caused by a glitch in the recording software, but we found nothing there either. We've tested every system and component of the Sim exhaustively, Mr. Thorn, and we can't come up with a reason for the smudge to be there."

Thorn considered the information for a few moments, then shook his head. "I'm not certain what it is," he admitted. "Does it appear to have any pattern?"

"Initially we thought no, but after we tracked and observed it for a while, it does indeed appear to have a pattern," the designer admitted.

The two men sat looking at each other. Thorn waited for the designer to give him an answer, but the other man said nothing.

Finally Thorn snapped at him. "Stop sitting there like an idiot. What's the pattern?"

The designer pointed to the screen and lightly tapped the live image of Brandon. He was now gliding smoothly down the hill as if he'd been flying forever. "Brandon is the pattern," he said.

Thorn stopped breathing for a second as he watched the monitor again. Sure enough, the smudge appeared again right beside Brandon. "Are you telling me that this is only occurring near Brandon, and nowhere else inside the Sim?"

The designer nodded. "That's exactly what I'm saying, sir. We've looked for it everywhere else for the past three weeks since we first observed it near the boy. The only time we see this smudge is when Brandon is inside the Sim, and it's always found very close to him."

Thorn watched the monitor and said nothing. Finally the designer spoke up. "Would you like us to bring everyone out and do a complete reboot of the system? That will likely eliminate the smudge."

"No!" Thorn blurted. Realizing how that must have sounded, he smiled and took a deep breath before he replied in a much calmer tone, "That won't be necessary yet. Leave the issue with me and I'll see what I can learn about it. We might need to do a complete reboot, but I want to try a few things first."

The designer nodded. "That's fine, sir. Let me know if you require any assistance."

"I assume you've isolated and compiled a complete video of its appearances?"

The man frowned. "No, we didn't do that," he said.

Thorn waved his hand absently. "Don't bother. It's a small and insignificant issue; leave it with me and I'll take care of it."

The designer nodded and left the office.

Thorn slowed down the playback and when he saw the smudge again he hit the pause command. He looked at it for a long time, trying to think of what to do.

The designer said everyone saw a smoky, round shape.

Thorn, on the other hand, saw the clear and distinct image of a man standing near Brandon. Thorn had no idea who the man was or what he was doing hidden inside the Sim, but he meant to find out.

42

"**The Sim program** has grown significantly, Mr. Thorn, " the General took a sip of his coffee, placed the cup back on the table with deliberation, and smiled pleasantly as he met Thorn's eyes.

"It has," Thorn agreed. "Over fifteen hundred Centre students and three thousand enlisted adults."

"I think we can begin to integrate them."

"To have children face adults inside the Sim?" Thorn asked.

The General nodded as he took another sip from his cup. Thorn considered the logistics and nodded positively. "It's not a difficult merge to make," he said. "You don't think such a thing is a bit... premature?"

The General's face tightened slightly and he shook his head. "We are in year three of the Sim, and approaching the four year anniversary. Both groups have had adequate time to become accustomed to the VR technology. Most spend more time in the Sim than they do in reality, according to the reports that cross my desk."

"That is true," Thorn admitted. The General's players spent so much time inside the Sim that reality was truly turning into the dream they all referred to it as. There were enough tables now to accommodate all players, and those who could mentally handle the simulations were so addicted to it that they spent only as much time out of the Sim as they had to. Those who couldn't handle the Sim..."What about the dropouts?" Thorn asked.

"What about them?" the General asked.

"As you instructed, those who have cracked are being held in stasis, but they can't remain that way forever, sir. What do you want us to do with them?"

The General nodded curtly. "Dispose of them."

Thorn felt a cold wave spread over him. "Kill them," he said flatly.

"If they are of no use to us, then they're already dead," the General spoke as if he was telling a waiter to take away the remains of his dinner.

Thorn nodded.

"Hold on a second," the General said. "Are they completely empty?"

"No," Thorn said. "They simply can't determine what is real from what isn't. They have moments of lucidity, but most of the time they are dangerous and unstable to both themselves and others around them." Thorn remembered the first few who had cracked. It had begun only a few months ago when, over the course of three weeks, forty-two children and twenty-seven adults had suddenly started to kill their friends and team members. It had occurred both within the Sim and out. Innocent people had died painful and permanent deaths. Thorn and the lead designers had quickly developed a test inside the Sim to determine if players were about to snap. Those that failed were kept inside the Sim, their bodies put in stasis. So far one hundred and thirty-four had failed the profile testing.

"They are still inside the Sim, right?"

"Yes,"

"Let's see if we can put these poor soldiers to use then. I'm sure they would like to make their lives count for something in the long run."

"What did you have in mind, General?"

"Since they are Blurred, I suggest we have them play a game or two. Let's see how effective the project has been so far."

43

"What does 'Blurred' mean?"

Cooper stopped what he was doing and gave Brandon his full attention. "Where did you hear that term?" he asked.

Brandon shrugged. "When those kids went nuts and started stabbing each other a few weeks ago. Someone said they were 'Blurred'."

Cooper sat down and leaned against the wall, motioning for Brandon to do the same. The two had spent a lot of time together over the years and gotten pretty close; not as close as Thorn and Brandon, but almost.

Cooper ran his hand through his hair and looked at Brandon. "Your eyes ever get tired? You know, blurry vision?"

"Yeah, sure," Brandon said. "It's tough to see straight. Things get blurry and you can't tell exactly how it all looks. If someone is a bit too far away and you're seeing blurry you can't tell if they are friend or enemy, or if they have a weapon on you or not."

"Exactly," Cooper said. "It can get the same jumping back and forth between Sim and the Dream. Sometimes if you get tired, or weak, or just super stressed out, it's tough to tell if you're in the Sim, or back in reality. Blurred."

"Oh," Brandon said. "They want us all Blurred."

"Why do you think that?"

"Since the beginning they've made a real mess of how we come in and go out of the Sim." Brandon said. "I remember early on some of the team was confused about if we were inside the Sim or out. I told them that's what the General wants...for us to get so confused we don't know where we are."

Cooper was impressed. "Why would he want that?"

Brandon shrugged. "I can think of a couple reasons," he smiled at Cooper, "You think I'm right?"

Cooper chuckled and gave Brandon a playful shove with his shoulder. "You could be," he said. "How are you doing with it? You get blurred much?"

Brandon laughed. "I've never been blurry, and they've tried real hard to get me that way."

"Really?" Cooper looked doubtful. "You've never once been confused? Hell, I've been blurry myself once or twice."

"Nope. I always know where I am," Brandon said. "So what's the difference between blurry... and Blurred?"

"Control," Cooper said. "If you're blurry, then you aren't sure where you are, but after a bit you can figure it out. It might take a while, but you can get it worked out. If you're Blurred... well, then you've lost your way and can't figure out where you are no matter what happens. It makes you go a bit crazy."

"That why they started stabbing people?"

"Yeah. They panicked and thought they could figure out where they were by stabbing a person and seeing if it was an avatar."

The two sat quietly for a few moments. Finally Brandon asked another question.

"What's gonna happen to them?"

"They'll be taken out of the Sim when it's safe," Cooper said. "They'll send them back to the regular Centre and get them some help. Eventually everything will be fine."

Brandon knew Cooper was lying, but he decided not to press the issue. "That's good," he said.

===

"Good morning." The General stood at the head of the command centre where a large screen covered the entire front wall. Seven people sat around a large table and watched him All of them wore crisp uniforms decorated with various medals and ribbons signifying the top ranks from each division of the General's impressive military machine.

"I've brought you here to observe the first of many operations involving recruits from our Game Facilities. Please keep in mind that this program is very young, at less than four years old. There will be many improvements over time as we learn from our efforts, but I think you'll all be impressed by what you see in the next few hours. Feel free to ask as many questions as you like."

The General motioned for everyone to look at the main viewer and the lights dimmed. A first person perspective camera view appeared on the screen, apparently from someone wearing a helmet cam. The person appeared to be inside an airborne carrier, along with a team of both male and female soldiers.

"The fifteen individuals you see on the screen have been equipped with equipment appropriate for their mission. They are flying into enemy territory, where they will be air dropped under cover of darkness. Their job is to work as a team to infiltrate a particularly well defended encampment, eliminate all defence, and assassinate the camp leader who is currently number three on our most wanted list."

"This mission has been tried before," a woman said from the left side of the table. "It was a horrible failure, as I recall. The enemy position is deeply fortified and protected."

"That's true," the General agreed.

"This is a suicide mission," she stated.

"Perhaps."

"Are some of the people on that carrier children?" a Major asked.

"All fifteen people are products of PROJECT SIM," the General said.

"Ah," the woman nodded, "the virtual reality simulator. I've been curious about its progress."

Others around the table nodded their heads and murmured in agreement. The General smiled confidently as he sat down, swiveling his seat to watch the scene on the front monitor with the rest of them. "I think you'll be pleased with the results. One of our goals inside the Sim is to induce a state where subjects are no longer able to distinguish reality from the simulation. We've coined the term 'Blurred' to describe this condition, and are working patiently to attain it with our players. It will take years of gradual and subtle manipulation to allow us to bring subjects in and out of this state, but we're seeing incredible results in just the short time we've been at it."

"The subjects we are viewing have achieved a stable Blurred state?" an older commander asked.

"Blurred," the General said, "but not stable. These subjects weren't able to handle the stresses involved. The fifteen you see have lost their grasp on reality and cannot be brought out of the Blurred state."

The crew began to parachute out of the plane.

Finally the woman spoke up. "What is it we're supposed to see?"

"The power that comes from soldiers who are convinced that they're playing a game," the General said. "These children and adults have hundreds of hours of real combat experience; they've died countless times and learned from each failure. As they attempt to destroy this fortification, I want all of you to see how effective the Sim program can be."

For the next three hours, the military leaders watched with rapt attention as the fifteen players fared better than trained and hardened veterans had done in past attempts. With impressive precision and skill, the motley looking crew managed to destroy over three quarters of the base. Of particular note was the point group which consisted of four children that the General confirmed were each no older than 15. They communicated perfectly, entering and securing buildings with the confidence and accuracy of a veteran special ops team.

It looked as if they might actually accomplish their impossible mission, but a bad streak of luck caused the General to swear loudly as the group was surrounded by enemy forces and quickly dispatched.

"What just happened?" a Major asked. "They were doing so well, then everything just fell apart."

The General shook his head angrily, "Rewind the footage back three minutes," he said.

As they began to watch the playback, the General said, "Watch the lead point step on that mine and tap his right leg." Everyone watched as the boy did exactly as the General described.

"Why did he tap his leg and then continue to walk forward?" the woman asked. "He obviously knew he'd just stepped on a land mine, yet he kept going as if it wouldn't hurt him."

"Perks," the General said with disgust. "Inside the Sim, players have the opportunity to purchase extended abilities with points that they accumulate. This group was specifically told that no perks would function in this scenario, but that one appears to have forgotten. If he'd been inside the Sim, tapping his leg would have frozen the mine and allowed him five seconds to get safely out of the blast radius. He should have yelled at the others about the mine and just fallen on it once they'd moved away to safety."

"But instead he said nothing and all four of them walked right into its path."

"Exactly," the General said. He pointed at the other three groups who had quickly perished after the point group was taken out. "See that one right there?" He pointed to an adult who appeared to be leading the others in coordination with the point team. "Once he learned the point team was down, he signaled for a wipe."

"He did what?" the oldest commander at the table asked.

"He signaled for them to all die quickly."

"Why would he do that?"

The General sighed. "So they could respawn and try the scenario again with the point kids back in play."

"They'll be surprised when they don't respawn," a Colonel said. Others shook their heads at the dark joke and the General made a sour face.

"Thoughts?" the General asked.

"Remarkable," the woman said. Everyone else at the table nodded in agreement.

"Admittedly, there are bugs to work out," the General said. "But did any of you expect to see a performance like this from such an ordinary looking group of people?"

"The Sim is producing better results than we could have predicted," the woman said with a smile. She stood up and everyone else in the room followed suit.

She approached the General and shook his hand. "Excellent start, Donovan, keep up the good work."

The General smiled. "Thank you, Madame President."

44

One recreational program that a player could buy was a simple, solo flying program.

The player paid the required amount of points — an extremely large number of points — stepped through a doorway and immediately began to fall thousands of feet towards the blue ocean surface below.

Brandon smiled and enjoyed the free fall. When he was just a few hundred feet away from the water's surface, he tapped a spot behind his shoulder and a pair of beautiful golden wings sprang from his back, catching the air smoothly and lifting him upwards. Letting out a shout of joy, he sailed through the air, spiraling lazily for a few moments before banking right to catch a warm thermal current which would lift him higher.

Time seemed to melt away.

After what seemed like hours of relaxing flight and peaceful exploration, Brandon summoned the glow and visualized a small island. Within minutes he spotted the island off in the distance, surrounded by water in every other direction as far as his eyes could see. When he got close enough he saw a small white cabin with two chairs and a table in front of it. There was a figure sitting in one of the chairs, lifting a glass of cold drink to his mouth. This simulation was supposed to be private, but for Brandon it was an excellent place to meet with one of his favourite people.

Brandon sped towards the table, fully extending his wings to grab as much air as he could at the last instant, causing him to flare slightly upwards. At that exact moment he tapped his shoulder and deactivated his wings, dropping from a height of seven feet to land softly on the ground. He smiled as he walked the last few paces to join his visitor.

"Impressive flying," Thorn said. He smiled and raised his glass in a salute to Brandon before taking another sip.

"Thank you," Brandon poured his own drink from the pitcher and sat down. The two spent a few quiet moments enjoying the perfect weather as the soothing sounds of the ocean washed over them.

Thorn was first to break the silence. "I see you let the little boy in the cage kill you again."

Brandon sipped his drink and looked towards the horizon.

Thorn chuckled. "How many times is that, now? Ten?"

"Eleven."

"You're supposed to leave him."

"Yeah, I know."

Thorn looked at Brandon with amusement in his eyes. "Want any hints?"

Brandon's head didn't move, but his eyes shifted to gaze in Thorn's direction. "Has anyone ever saved him?" he asked.

Thorn shook his head.

"Then no thanks, I'll see what I can come up with on my own."

"Your father added that to the game," Thorn said. "He wanted to make sure that everyone understands there are times when orders must be followed, regardless of the cost."

Brandon laughed harshly. "My father?" he asked.

"The General," Thorn said. "That's how you all refer to him, isn't it?"

"Not me," Brandon said. "He's not my father. He's just an old man who has everyone else fooled into believing that he cares about them, when really he uses us all like game pieces on a board."

"Perhaps."

"There's no perhaps about it. He's never even entered the Sim. For the last five years, we hear from him every once in a while on the vid screen, but he's pretty much useless," Brandon shook his head. "The General hasn't been a father to any of us. If I had to pick a father, someone who cares about me, and helps me, and looks out for me... well, there's only one man I can think of who fits that description."

"Who?" Thorn asked.

"It would be you," Brandon said.

Thorn looked at Brandon to gauge his sincerity. This was the first time the boy had uttered such a thought out loud. He had alluded to it with Cooper, but he'd never told Thorn that he considered him to be like a father.

Thorn smiled and clapped Brandon on the back. In his mind he felt a rush of triumph. It had taken years of carefully calculated planning and nurturing to get to this point. Brandon was almost ten years old, and Thorn had painstakingly given the boy his time and attention ever since they'd first met. The law of imprinting was simply too strong with the others, but Brandon had been very receptive at his young age. The special treatment and extensive periods of personal one-on-one time with Thorn had been the perfect mix.

"It would be dangerous for you to think of me in that way," Thorn said.

"Maybe." Brandon thought about the implications. Not quite ten years old, but he'd always been very mature. "It's the truth, though. Is it okay...? If I call you Father?"

Thorn felt a warm tear form in his eye, and as it trickled down his cheek, he wondered if it was genuine. It was too difficult to tell after playing games for all these years. He allowed himself to pretend the extraordinary young man sitting beside him was the kind of son he would be destined to have, if he'd ever decided to have children.

"Brandon," Thorn said, "when we're alone, I would be honoured to have you call me Father."

45

The lights turn on in the dorm but my eyes are already open. I wasn't sleeping anyway.

I lay in my bunk and look around. The other kids are sitting up in their bunks; some of them stretching and yawning, others getting up and walking towards the bathroom. Many form tiny groups and begin to talk with each other, joking or asking questions. They group up and start to get ready for the day. No one bothers to talk to me; I guess that's how they deal with new kids here, or maybe they've decided not to like me already. I get that a lot.

It doesn't matter, this is my first day at the Game Facility and I can't wait to get playing.

I walk to the bathroom and get looks. Then I hear whispers.

"He's a tank if I ever saw one."

The other kid laughs. "Too soon to say that. Maybe he plays his first day in the Sim and goes back crying to his old Centre. He's too young to even be here."

I pretend not to hear them and walk over to a sink. I splash water on my face and brush my teeth. Kids come in and stand at the sink beside me, and they still haven't shut up about me. "That's not so young," the kid says. "Brandon was a lot younger when he came here, and look at him."

"Oh, please," the other kid laughs. "You saying this one's another Brandon?" He addresses me directly. "Hey, kid."

I keep looking into the mirror and continue to brush my teeth.

"Kid," the boy says. "Okay, fine then, don't answer me." He goes back to talking to his friend. "I doubt the kid's another Brandon, and he's not that much younger. I think he's nine."

Yeah, I'm nine. I was so excited to get here early, start playing games in the Sim like my hero. All of us know the name Brandon. The little kid who came to the Sim early and is one of the best players they have. Whenever there was a whisper about him, we'd all get together and listen to the stories. It made us play our games harder. We all wanted to get to the Sim early and be like him. Maybe even meet him. I was so excited when they told me I'd be coming here early. Was.

I spit into the sink, turn away from the other two, and walk quickly out of the bathroom. Everyone wants to ignore me? That's fine. I'll get into the Sim and show them what I can do. I'm excited to be here. When they see how well I do — when I start beating them at their own games — then I bet they'll want to talk to me. That's how it was for Brandon. That's how it's gonna be for me.

I follow a couple of kids, hoping that they're going to the mess hall. I don't get many looks on the way. No one is very friendly, but that's nothing new living in the Centres. New kids get ignored until someone is interested enough to say hi. I walk behind the kids as if I own the place. The kids who look like they belong get talked to sooner than quiet scared ones. I'm not a scared kid.

"You going to the birthday party today?" the girl ahead of me asks her friend.

"Wasn't invited."

She laughs at him. "It's gonna be a huge event. I don't think you need to be invited. I'm going."

"I guess I might go, then." The boy tries to sound like he doesn't care, but it's obvious that he does. I wonder who's having a birthday party? In the regular Centres we don't get birthday parties. A small chocolate and a taped message from the General is what most of us get. If you've done something special, then you might get a message where the General says your name, or a little note from him.

"Will the General be there?" the boy asks. That gets my attention. The General being at a birthday party must mean it's someone important.

The girl laughs. "Are you nuts? The General never goes inside the Sim."

That's interesting information. I'll tuck that into my memory in case I ever need it.

"Cooper will be there, and maybe Thorn," the girl says.

We enter the mess hall and the two walk towards a table filled with other kids. There's no way I can stay close to them and hear any more, so I look around for an empty table to sit at.

I see one table far from the other kids. There's one boy sitting at it, but no one else is at any of the tables nearby. Maybe I've found someone even more alone than me. I walk over and he looks up at me.

"Mind if I join you?" I ask.

He smiles at me and nods. "I don't mind at all." He spreads his hand to show the emptiness all around him. "Lots of room here; grab a seat."

"Thanks," I say and sit down a couple seats away from him. I look around and watch what's going on. That's how I like to work; look around first before I make any moves.

"Not hungry?" I look over at the boy and he's watching me as he takes a bite of his food.

"Yeah," I say. "Just getting an idea of how things work around here. First day."

The boy smiles and keeps eating. "Welcome to the Game Centre," he says. "Go get something to eat, and if you want, I'd be happy to show you around."

"Really?" I ask.

"Sure," he shrugs. "I don't have anything to do until this afternoon. Might as well show a Bagger around the place." He grins, "Maybe someday I'll need a favour in the Sim and you'll remember how kind I was to you."

"Likely," I say. "Can't wait to get in the Sim."

"They used to make us wait before they put us in," the boy says. "Now they throw you right in, don't they?"

"Yeah, I go in this afternoon. They gave me a couple of hours of free time to check the place out and try to meet some friends."

"How's that working out so far?"

"About as good as it ever does for a new kid coming into a group of orphans."

He laughs and I stand up to go get some food. "Be right back," I say and he nods.

I come back with a tray of food, and as we sit, he shares the basics about the Game Facility while I eat. When I finish eating, he stands. "Okay, let's take the quick tour and I'll show you the places you'll need to know."

We spend the next hour and a half exploring the different areas of the Centre. Turns out my life here will be about eating, sleeping, and playing in the Sim. When I ask him about books or videos to watch, he just smiles and tells me that's all inside the Sim. There's a big exercise room with kids working out. We stop and watch them from the hallway outside.

"You gotta make sure your body stays fit and healthy out here," he says. "The better you get at playing in the Sim, the longer you stay in it. Your body out here will lose muscle and so they kick you out to make sure you don't get all weak and sick in the Dream."

"The Dream?" I ask.

He points to the ground. "Yeah, we call this place — reality — 'the Dream'."

"Why?"

"Because after a while, the Sim seems more real than being here," he says. "Before long, you're gonna be spending so much time in there that this will seem more like what you call dreaming."

I nod, "So they make us work out here?"

"Yeah," he nods. "We all get that done as quickly as possible and get back inside. If you get really good, they will assign medical people to help kind of exercise your muscles a bit while you're out, which lets you stay in longer."

"Are you any good?" I ask.

He shrugs. "I'm not horrible." I can tell he's better than that, but I let it go. I'm sure I'll see him sometime in the Sim.

I tell him it's time for me to get into the Sim, and he walks me to the ready room.

At the entrance, I shake his hand again and he smiles. "I'll be going in a bit later. Maybe we'll run into each other."

"That would be great," I say.

He starts to walk away and I call out to him. He turns around and looks at me.

"I never got your name," I say.

"That's okay," he says as he turns around and walks away. "I didn't get yours, either."

===

"Three... two... one..." I open my eyes and look around. I'm in the same white room, but the doctor and nurse are gone.

I stand and walk to the door. I walk down the hallway like they told me to do and I see the big door at the end. There's a boy standing there. His name is Alan and I met him just before they put me in.

"How ya feeling?" he asks.

"The same as I always do," I answer. "You sure we're inside the Sim?"

He laughs and nods his head. "Yeah, but don't worry. Everyone doubts it when they first come in here. Over the next few weeks you'll play some cool games that'll prove we aren't in the Dream any more."

He pauses, likely waiting for me to ask him what he means by 'the Dream' but I just nod because I've already heard it.

He shrugs his shoulders and faces the door. "I'll take you on the big tour, don't worry, but first we have to make a stop somewhere."

He closes his eyes and suddenly a bright white light appears behind the doorway. This must be the 'travelling' I learned about from the prep info they gave me to read. Alan's eyes open and he grabs the door handle, turning it and swinging the door open. "After you," he says.

We walk through the doorway and find ourselves in a large, open field of green grass with big oak trees all around. Birds fly through the sky and the clouds are white and fluffy. It's a bit scary — I don't think I've been outside like this for quite a long time. It also feels very comfortable, though. Strange. There are a lot of people standing around and there's a big table in the middle of the area with wrapped gift boxes and streamers everywhere. A big banner that read, 'Happy Birthday!' is strung up in big colourful letters. I look back at Alan and he smiles.

"There's a birthday party today that I won't miss," he said. "We've been waiting a long time for this day, and it's time to celebrate."

I follow him as he walks towards the crowd, which parts as people recognize him and let him through. We work our way to the front table where there are three others standing there who wave and call him over.

"Thought you weren't gonna make it," the girl smiles.

Alan laughs and shakes his head. "You know there's no way any of us would miss this, Kay." Then he turns to me. "Guys, let me introduce you to the Bagger I had to show around today." He points to each of the people and introduces them. "This is Kay, and that's Tony, and Easton."

I nod and shake hands with each of them. Before I can tell them my name there's a commotion off to our right. A bright white light in the shape of a doorway appears, and three people walk through. I gasp in surprise as the last person comes through and the whole crowd screams, "Happy Birthday!"

I recognize them all. The first man is Mr. Thorn. The second is Cooper! I can't believe I'm standing so close to him! The third person I've seen before... I just spent the whole morning with him. I guess he's the birthday boy everyone's been talking about.

I stand to the side as the kids I'm with walk over and greet the boy with handshakes and hugs. He laughs and smiles as he returns their hugs warmly. A few moments pass and he waves at the cheering group, then he sees me and winks. After he hugs Kay, he walks over and pats me on the back.

"I'm surprised to see you so soon. How did you get here?" he asks me.

"He's my Bagger for the day," Alan says. "You know him?"

The boy grins and nods. "Met him this morning when you all exiled me to a lonely table. Obviously, you were planning this party!"

I stand there a little confused as everyone laughs. The boy is still looking at me. He extends his hand again.

"Looks like we should formally meet, Bagger. I'm Brandon."

I can't believe my luck! On my first day I get to meet my hero! I'm a little nervous but I grin back and shake his hand.

"Great to meet you, Brandon," I say. "My name's Carl."

46

"**Good place to** take a nap?"

Brandon jumped in surprise. "How do you always manage to do that?"

Carl smiled as he walked up behind him. "Do what?"

"Sneak up on me like that," Brandon said. "There are very few people who can sneak up on me. Cooper, Thorn, Kay... yeah, I think that's about it. Oh, and I guess you."

"I've just got a gift for moving quietly," Carl said. He squatted down beside Brandon and poked his head around the corner. Brandon quickly yanked him back; immediately a small feathered dart whizzed past the space where Carl's head had been.

"Whoa!" Carl exclaimed.

"Yeah," Brandon said with a grin. "Things are not going so well at the moment."

"Where's the rest of your Hand?"

"We split up. At first this seemed like an easy contest, so we decided to split up and meet at the goal."

"Then the pixies showed up?" Carl smiled.

"Yes... then the pixies showed up." Brandon nodded toward the far corner of the room. There were three tiny figures lying lifeless on the ground, tiny people about the size of Carl's hand, with wings and colourful clothes. Each one had a small bow in their hands. Tiny feathered arrows were scattered on the ground beside them. The wall above them had a dark stain on it — a combination of blast powder and blood.

"You catch 'em by surprise?" Carl asked.

Brandon nodded. "Surprise, followed by a blast," he patted a nasty looking shotgun lying on the ground beside him. "They had another group around the corner, though; almost returned the favour of surprising me, clever little buggers."

"It's clear where I just came from," Carl said.

"That's the wrong direction," Brandon said. He continued to scan the room as he spoke, his gaze freezing when he looked at the ceiling. Pointing towards the far corner, he said, "What do you think that is?"

Carl squinted to get a better look. "It's too far away, is what it is," he said. The ceilings were quite high in this particular game. If he had to guess, he'd estimate that it was at least forty feet above them.

"It's an air duct or something, right?"

"Yeah," Carl agreed.

Brandon nodded and carefully took a step backwards before standing up. "Okay, Carl, I need you to do something for me."

"I don't think I can throw you that far, Brandon."

Brandon chuckled. "I need you to turn away and close your eyes. Then count to ten before you open them."

"Why?" Carl asked.

Brandon looked at Carl silently. Carl remembered that Brandon was the leader of one of the best teams in the Sim, and he nodded his head obediently. "Okay, fine," he said, turning his back and closing his eyes.

Carl felt a disturbance in the air behind him and was sure he could hear wings beating. Carl frowned but kept counting. When he got to ten, he opened his eyes and looked behind him. Brandon was gone! Quickly looking upwards, Carl saw Brandon holding onto the grate and turning the screws to loosen it.

"Hey!" Carl whispered as loudly as he could. Brandon looked back at him. "How'd you get up there?"

Brandon held his finger to his lips as he smiled.

"Did you just *fly*?"

Brandon looked surprised. "Did you see me fly?"

Carl was confused. "This isn't a flying map."

"How do you know?"

"They would have told us." Carl said.

Brandon chuckled and shook his head. "Carl, you've been playing for a little over six months now and doing amazingly well. Don't make the mistake, or it will ruin you."

"Which mistake?"

"THE mistake," Brandon said. "There's one thing you have to remember above everything else."

"What's that?"

Brandon dropped down and quickly activated his wings, landing gently beside Carl.

"I like you, Carl. Every time we're in a game together, you help us out. I've never seen anyone become a ghost like you; it's a great talent. I hope you don't join another team and have to play against us very often, 'cause I think you would make life more difficult for us."

Carl swelled with pride at the compliment; to have one of the best in the Sim praise him was a big deal!

"So let me tell you something I don't tell many people," He leaned in close as if other people could hear them, then he whispered, "The biggest mistake you can ever make is to believe that anything they tell you is true."

Brandon leaned back and flashed a grin, waiting for Carl to react.

Carl nodded slowly, "Okay, I'll remember that. Thanks, Brandon."

Brandon turned back to face the grate. "No problem, Carl." With a tap he popped his wings again and said, "and as soon as you can, be sure to get yourself some wings. They come in handy a lot more than most people think."

"Maybe I don't even need them," Carl said. "Why believe they're required to fly inside the Sim, Brandon? That's something they tell you, isn't it?"

Brandon's body whipped around. Taking a quick step closer to Carl with squinted eyes, he raised his hand, but said nothing. Finally he smiled and wagged a finger at Carl. "Carl, I think you just blew my mind."

"Hey, what are you two doing standing here yipping at each other?"

The boys looked towards the front doorway. Tony stood there, a dead pixie dangling from each hand as he panted heavily. "It's clear up ahead," he said. "Let's move."

Brandon nodded and walked past Tony, slapping him on the back as he did. "Good stuff, Tank. Come on, boys, lets finish this. I'm getting hungry."

47

"**How long we** been in this time, Brandon?" Easton asked.

Brandon finished his set with the weights and placed the bar on the rack. He looked at Easton, then each of the other Hand members. They all watched him expectantly, but he shook his head.

"Are you kidding me?" Alan asked. "We're for sure in the Sim right now Brandon. It's been days since they put us inside."

"We're in the Dream," Brandon assured the group as he grabbed a towel and wiped his face.

"I'm not so sure, Brandon," Kay said. Brandon started to reprimand her but saw that she was serious and paused with concern. There was no joking when it came to calling out the Blurr; determining where they were was the key factor to everything they did. Brandon knew the controlling powers were trying to do something dangerous that depended on players losing their perception of reality. His group's primary concern was to always know which side of the veil they were on, and they'd never once been wrong. Kay and Brandon had always been able to tell the others exactly which reality they were in, but Brandon could tell from Kay's confused look that even she wasn't sure. He shook his head softly to confirm he was right and she swore under her breath.

"They must have brought us out while we were sleeping," Tony muttered. He accepted Brandon's call on this without question; they all did.

"I don't know," Easton said.

Brandon noticed Easton's demeanour was... different. He walked quickly towards the mat room. "Follow me. Now."

They got to the mat room and formed a circle with Brandon sitting cross-legged in the centre.

"Ten minutes," he said, "then we re-assess the call."

Everyone nodded and closed their eyes. Brandon examined them as they began to meditate; he wouldn't be meditating with them. He would be watching.

He'd recognized that look in Easton's eyes; knew the older boy was close to cracking. Brandon pursed his lips in concern. He wasn't going to lose one of them like this.

Brandon was now twelve, which meant the others were all close to their magic number of eighteen. Easton would hit it first, at the end of this year. By the old rules of the Centre, they would leave when they turned eighteen, but there was rumour of new rules allowing expert players to remain at the Centre and play in the Sim.

He shook his head and stopped thinking about the future; he couldn't change what was going to happen then. He just wanted to keep his team healthy and effective right now. That's all there ever was...right now.'

His watch chirped, announcing the ten minutes had passed. Slowly the team opened their eyes. Brandon watched, scanning them closely for signs of confusion.

Easton kept his eyes closed a moment longer than the rest, then took a deep breath in through his nose, and a long breath out. The corners of his mouth turned upwards into a smile and Brandon relaxed. Easton's eyes opened and he looked at Brandon. "You're right," he said. "The smell and background vibe is distinct. We're definitely in real life. How could we have missed it?"

Brandon shrugged and Alan answered. "We get used to stimuli, and soon can't sense the finer details, which is the only way to be sure. Slowing down our minds and giving them a break from all thought and perception is the best way to reset and help us sense where we really are."

"It's a tough battle," Kay said. "We know how to meditate and why, yet we still find reasons to put it off. What about all the others who don't have a clue that they should be doing it?"

"They get Blurred," Tony said. "I wonder what happens then?"

"Nothing, most of the time," Brandon said. "But I think every once in a while... something bad happens."

"How do we fight this when we're no longer together?" Kay asked.

"We don't know when that will be," Brandon said. "I think they're gonna let us stay together."

"That wouldn't be normal," Easton said doubtfully. He was worried about having to leave his friends behind.

Brandon smiled. "We aren't a normal group," he said. He shrugged his shoulders, "Don't worry about what might happen; we do our best by being in the moment. Let's just keep doing that and see how it goes."

"All right," Easton said. "So what do we do now? They think we believe we're in the Sim, right?"

Brandon shook his head. "When it comes to this particular game, we play the same way as always; we know where we are, and we act that way. If you were operating as if we were in the Sim, then change that mindset. We're in the Dream and we all know it now, right?" he looked around and everyone nodded confidently. "Then that's how we interact with everyone. Games within games won't help here, so we won't pretend we think we're in the Sim but really know that we're in the Dream... it's too confusing. Work out and get caught up on our fitness level so we can get back to the Sim as soon as possible."

The team nodded and began to walk towards the exit. Brandon stopped them to make one more point. "We should be proud that as a team we've been able to stay unBlurred all this time. I don't think there are many groups who can say the same thing. We continue to fight the Blurr. It would be very bad for our group if we lost our grip on reality. I think that would be the end of us, so let's keep working together to stay on top of it."

The group nodded and left the workout room.

In a room far from the facility, a technician watched them leave the room on a view screen. He made note of their activities and conversation in his log book.

48

"**I have a** new challenge for you and your team, Brandon."

Brandon sat across from Thorn in his office inside the Sim. They never spoke outside of the Sim in order to remain safe from the prying eyes of the General.

"What kind of challenge, Father?" Brandon asked. He'd been expecting a meeting like this for a while. Easton would turn eighteen the following week, and would be leaving the Centre.

"What I'm about to tell you must remain a secret," Thorn said.

"Between the three of us?" Brandon guessed. "I assume that what you're telling me, you've already told Cooper?"

Thorn shook his head. "Not yet. If you agree, then I'll talk to him next."

"Okay… what is it?"

Thorn brought an image up on his large monitor. It was a city, clean and bustling with people. "We're ready to release a civilian version of the Sim to the public," he said. "Regular people will subscribe and pay a fee to play. Preorders started a month ago, and the numbers are huge. Beta testing will last for two months, and will consist of a small number of lucky people selected to help us play inside to test the mechanics and systems of the game."

"How many testers will you have?" Brandon asked.

"Ten thousand," Thorn said.

"Are you kidding me?" Brandon's eyebrows raised at the thought of so many individuals inside a VR program. "What's the population of the Sim at any given time?" he asked, "a few hundred?"

Thorn grinned, "Two hundred thousand."

Brandon was stunned.

"Officially," Thorn said, "there are only three thousand players inside the Sim. I'm counting all the NPC's inside as well. Each non-player character is considered an individual by the computer."

"But they aren't real," Brandon said.

Thorn laughed out loud, and Brandon smiled at the humour behind his comment.

"The NPC programs have evolved like bacterium over the eight years that the Sim has been online," Thorn said. "We've instilled artificial intelligence into them and allowed NPC programs to live complete lifetimes. They have also been given the capacity to procreate, passing on their learning and traits to their offspring. Plus they have the ability to bond with each other and form relationships. In many respects, they are identical to us."

"You mean there are generations of NPC's inside the Sim that have lived and died and had families?" Brandon wasn't sure exactly what Thorn was saying to him, but it sounded complicated.

"Yes," Thorn nodded. "When you walk through a city in the Sim to play a game, the population exists before you get there and after you leave. If you stop to buy a newspaper at a store, or to eat at a restaurant inside the Sim, those NPC avatars are living their lives and you're just another customer in their day to day existence."

Brandon looked at Thorn seriously. "You've created a real world, full of thousands of real people."

Thorn began to shake his head, then paused and nodded as he shrugged his shoulders. "Yes, I guess you could argue that's what I've done. Unlike the real world, however, I could turn it all off and wipe them out with the flick of one switch."

Brandon decided to let this issue go. "What do you want us to do?" he asked.

"We now know from our experience in the Sim that we can populate a virtual world with realistic and richly interactive NPCs and accommodate a large number of player controlled avatars as well. What I need is experienced eyes and ears — veteran players inside the new world. I want to send groups of Sim players in to observe and give me feedback so that we can catch glitches and make improvements to the game before it goes fully live."

Brandon thought about it for a few moments. "Sounds boring," he said.

Thorn chuckled and shook his head. "It will be far from boring, my boy," he said. "There is a main area where the players and NPCs will be able to to interact and live, but there will also be a lot of player created areas — small islands, dimensions, and instances that subscribers will be able to buy, where they will be able to create their own content. It's my hope that these designers will attract other players to come mingle and interact."

"You're going to have people pay you to create their own adventures and rewards?" Brandon asked.

"In many cases, yes," Thorn smiled.

"Sounds like a powerful idea. Hackers will have a blast with it."

"There'll be very strict and specific rules governing the core functioning of the simulation," Thorn said. "That will keep it manageable and as simple as can be. But people don't like simple. They can't wait to complicate things, which we will allow them to do. The best designers will thrive, and the bad ones will disappear." Thorn smiled wickedly, "Hackers will regret trying to tamper with the system."

Brandon thought about it for a few moments, then nodded. "Sure, we'll give it a spin."

Thorn smiled. "That's great news. Before I put you into the Beta test I have one other new simulation that I want you to try for me. It's identical to the new game world in most ways, but very different in one aspect."

Brandon shook his head, looking puzzled. He was quick and adaptable, but Thorn seemed to be throwing many things at him today. "You want us to play in a new VR simulation, but before we do that, you want us to play in... a different new VR simulation?"

"Exactly. I want to put you and your team into a new simulation for three weeks. No coming out or going back in, you'll be in there solidly for three weeks."

"Are you going to try to Blurr us?" Brandon asked with concern. "I don't want to find out you've been switching us back and forth."

Thorn shook his head. "I don't agree with Blurring, Brandon, that's the General's project. This isn't his VR I'm putting you in, it will be mine. I won't try to Blurr you, I promise."

Brandon looked uncertain and Thorn could tell that he was doubtful.

"Listen to me carefully, son," Thorn said. "Until now the only VR simulation that you've been in is the General's Sim. That's because all of you belong to him, and that's the only VR program that I was given money and time to work on. I've learned valuable information from developing the Sim to his specifications over the years, and now I have enough money, experience, and time, to build my own programs. I don't have the same agenda that the General does, and I promise not to try to purposefully Blurr you."

Brandon thought about what Thorn was saying. "How will you be able to place us in other simulations without the General knowing?" he asked.

"The General has made false assumptions over the years. He doesn't understand that I control the game facility, and although he sees a lot of information, he sees only what I allow him to see. I've made the process so complicated and full of information that it's easy for me to lose players for a few weeks at a time. It's quite simple, since I can show them to him in simulations and deliver false reports that he can't verify."

Brandon nodded thoughtfully.

"Here's the major difference with the new simulation I want to put you in. Your avatar will age and you will only have a vague memory of this reality. Time will pass differently; you'll live thirty years during the three weeks that you're inside."

"What?"

"That's right," Thorn nodded. "You'll go in as you are now. You'll live for what feels like thirty years. Your body will grow and age, and you'll gain the life experience from thirty years of living. Then you'll come out of the simulation and wake up with thirty years of memories, but you'll still be inside your body as it looks now, and only three weeks will have passed."

Brandon considered what Thorn was asking him and his group to do. "Why would you do something like that?" he asked.

"There are many reasons," Thorn said. "Maybe when you come back you'll be able to give me some of them. It's an incredible opportunity to become experienced but keep your youth. Trust me, Brandon, if someone had offered this to me at your age, I would have jumped at the chance."

Brandon thought about the offer. "All right, Father. I'll ask my Hand if they want to try it. If they say yes, then we'll do it."

Thorn nodded. "You're not the first group to do it, if that makes you feel any better. Cooper has already done this process three times."

"So he's a thirty-something-year-old man with ninety extra years of memories and experiences?" Brandon asked.

"Yes."

"Well, that gives him a big head start on me," Brandon said. "What do you call this new VR simulation which the public will be playing in? Sim 2?"

Thorn shook his head. "I don't want it named after anything the General has had a hand in. The new simulation is called Tygon."

<u>49</u>

"**This seat taken?**"

I look up from reading my paper and smile.

"You're starting to tick me off, Cooper."

He slides into the seat across from me and flashes his familiar grin. Reaching across the table, he grabs a piece of muffin with one hand and pops it into his mouth. With his other hand he deftly snatches my coffee cup and takes a sip before putting it down in front of him. He looks the same as always, tanned face, white teeth, piercing eyes, and that white shock of hair standing up on his head. There's a smell about him, too, kind of like vanilla and candy apples. That combination should be strange, but it's pleasant.

"Why's that, boy?" he asks.

"Because you haven't aged. How old are you now?"

He looks down at his watch and smirks. "Here? I'm twenty-five minutes old." He taps his head. "Up here I'm about a hundred and ten." Then he points into the air and waves his finger around. "In the Dream, still holding at thirty-five." He takes another sip of coffee and makes a motion of wiping sweat from his brow. "Whew, that's a lot of different ages to keep track of."

I grab my coffee out of his hand and take a drink. "I'm older than you now." I try to keep the disappointment from my voice, but getting old isn't fun.

Cooper waves his hand dismissively. "Somewhere in there, yeah, you're older than me, but I think if we were to total it all up I'm still your elder, boy." He takes the coffee from my hand again and places it deliberately in front of himself. "So show some proper respect."

I chuckle and shake my head. I love it when Cooper shows up. He makes things exciting, and it's also a good sign that something significant is about to happen. "So what are you doing here, old man?" I ask.

"It's time for you to head back," he says with a wink.

"Thank God," I say.

Cooper chuckles. "God. You've bought into that story here, have you?" he asks.

"It's just a saying," I say with a shrug.

"Yeah, well there's always something happening that can't be explained, and our minds try to find a reason."

We sit for a moment, listening to the sounds of the coffee shop around us.

"Where are the others?" he asks.

"Gathering intel," I say.

Cooper squints at me. "Are you all still close?"

I look at him with a flat stare. "Thirty years is a long time to be together," I say.

He looks at me and drains the rest of the coffee. "That's not an answer, Brandon."

I flash him a smile. "Of course we're still close," I assure him. "There have been some bumps and hiccups along the way, but we're tight. Are you telling me you don't know this? I'm sure you've watched us from time to time."

"What about life? How's it been?"

I don't know how to answer him, so I just let it come out. "When I got here, I was twelve years old. I've lived thirty years in here. It's been a long play."

"Try it four times," Cooper snorted.

"I don't know if I could," I say. "I don't think I can."

Cooper stands up and moves his chair closer to mine. He puts his hand on my shoulder and gives it a squeeze. Then he taps my chest lightly. "I told them you were too young for this." He looks angry, but he shakes his head and smiles. "You're right, boy, I've been following you this whole time, and you've been amazing. All of you have been incredible. I'm proud of you, and don't worry, you won't have to do this again. At least not for a few 'real' years."

I laugh at his choice of words. "You've done this enough to know that these years are very real."

He nods thoughtfully, then stands up and claps me on the back. "Okay then, sport, time to get back to reality. I'll send you off, then go find the others."

I get up and follow him out the front door. He walks quickly and I hustle to keep up with him, turning into an alley and stopping halfway in.

He turns around and gives me a serious look. "Okay, let's get this over with. C'ya on the other side."

I frown in confusion, not sure how I'm going to leave the simulation from this alley. Cooper pulls a gun from within his jacket and fires it at me. My reflexes kick in and I manage to dodge the first two bullets, moving towards him as I avoid them, but his third and fourth shots hit me. I flop to the ground and look at Cooper in surprise.

"Why did you shoot me?" I whisper.

He shakes his head in annoyance. "Sorry, Brandon," he says, "but this is the only way to get you out. It's not pleasant, but I'm trying to make it quick. You're still spry and quick for a forty-something-year-old."

"I try," I smile. The pain is intense, but familiar. Years ago, when I was a kid, living in another place, I got killed many times in the Sim. I cough and wince, spitting blood as Cooper gets closer. "Come on, old man, finish me off, then. I'm gonna ask Thorn to find a better way to exit these simulations."

Cooper nods, pointing the gun at my head. "Good luck with that. I've asked him for the same thing, kid."

I nod and close my eyes. I hear the gun blast and then I'm gone.

50

"**Haven't seen you** in a few weeks, Brandon. How ya been?"

Brandon glanced to his left as Carl joined him in the hallway. "Some crazy games, Carl. Thought for sure I would have seen you in them."

"They kept me busy in mostly stealth games," Carl said. "A lot of single missions where I have to infiltrate and kill lots of targets."

"How are things?" Brandon asked.

"Not bad," Carl said. "It's good to be out of the Sim for a rest, though. I was in there last session for a long time. Everyone needs the Dream once in a while."

Brandon nodded slowly. "You ever meditate, Carl?"

Carl shook his head. "No time for that. I know you recommended I try it a while ago, but I just never seem to get around to it."

Brandon stopped at a doorway. "This is my stop. Listen to me very carefully, Carl. You want to go somewhere nice and quiet and have a good fifteen to twenty minute session of meditation right away. Promise you'll do that for me."

Carl nodded slowly. "Okay, man... I'll go do it right now."

Brandon slapped him on the arm lightly. "You'll be glad you did. After you're done you should come see me. I need your help with an upcoming game and I'd like to discuss it with you."

Carl walked away and Brandon watched him go with a look of concern.

Carl was Blurred, and from the looks of it, they'd had him in a bad way for a while. Brandon hoped he could get him to snap out of it.

===

Wesley walked into Thorn's office, went to the fridge to get himself a drink, and then sat down across from his boss. Thorn was watching Cooper bring Tony out of his thirty year simulation on the monitor.

"That was messy," Wesley observed.

"Indeed," Thorn said. "Apparently Tony doesn't like being ejected from the simulations."

"I don't think anyone does, sir," Wesley said. "It's not pleasant."

Thorn ignored the comment. He didn't acknowledge the complaint from very many people, and certainly not from Wesley right now. "I want you to be present when we debrief Brandon and his Hand," Thorn said.

"Of course. How long a rest will they get before we send them into the public prototype?"

"We can determine that after we speak with them and see how much this play affected their psyche."

Wesley nodded. "How did the other ten groups fare during their thirty-year sessions?"

"We knew it was an aggressive scenario when we came up with the idea," Thorn said. "Some of them were damaged during the process, but we won't know how severely until later on. We have to move forward with as many groups as we can. Thirty years allowed each child's natural tendencies and nature to manifest, so we know how to place them and where. Some will be very influential characters in the large production we're about to launch."

"I don't fully understand what it is exactly that you're launching, sir," Wesley admitted.

"That's okay... neither do I," Thorn said. "The nature of this new game is that players will shape most of the content as it happens inside. Soon this world will be obsessed with the new virtual reality game I'm going to release. 'Tygon version 3.0' will be played by everyone, and the public will line up to pay for the chance to play. Our Sim veterans will be heroes and villains, saints and sinners, leaders in the game for both forces of good and evil. NPC's could never deliver the types of thrills I want to give to the fans, but our boys and girls from the Centres will do the job nicely."

"The General will never allow it," Wesley said.

"By the time we get to that point," Thorn said, "the General will have no say in the matter."

51

"**The Enemy has** developed virtual reality technology," the General said.

"I know," Thorn replied. "They stole it from us."

The General stared at Thorn, his jaw clenching and eyes smouldering. "What are you going to do about it, Mr. Thorn?" he asked.

Thorn smiled, "I can assure you, General, that there is no one on this planet who understands this technology better than I do. Since day one of this project there have been extreme safety measures in place to control my programming."

A frown crossed the Generals face; faint, but Thorn saw it. "What kind of safety measures?"

Thorn waved his hand, "Tracking, reporting, viral self-protective capabilities, self-destructive protocols if need be... sir, I know exactly who took it, how they got it, who they gave it to, and what it's being used for at this very moment." Thorn fixed the General with a serious stare and stopped talking.

The two men quietly stared at each other.

"Who stole it?" the General asked.

"I think if I told you the answer to that question I would be dead within a few hours. My death would cause more problems than you can imagine, General, I hope that's not a surprising revelation to you by now."

The General said nothing.

"What do you want me to do about this, sir?" Thorn asked.

"You've kept too much from me over the years, Samson," the General said.

"As have you, Donovan."

"Yet our relationship has proven beneficial to both of us,"

"Indeed," Thorn agreed.

"You've done an outstanding job with the Sim project."

"Thank you. I have been following the first groups of graduates from the Sim. They are performing better than any of their peers in the field. I've also noticed some early departures from the Sim program for no apparent reason. During the past six months, over eighty Blurred children have been removed from the facility. I can't find any record of where they were transferred to."

"We've had this conversation before, Mr. Thorn. Centre resources belong to me. They are my property, and, once they leave the Game Facility, they are none of your concern."

Thorn nodded, "Of course, General."

"I understand you're finally about to launch the civilian version of the Sim."

"That's why I asked you here today," Thorn said. "I want to offer you a percentage of the profits from civilian revenues."

Both men knew such an offer wasn't required. They also knew it was an appropriate gesture and would ensure the two men stayed intertwined like a pair of poisonous snakes drifting in the ocean. If one let go to bite the other, then both would be destroyed. Fortunes intermingled would allow this thin stalemate to continue, which suited them both.

"Your offer is unexpected, and extremely generous," the General nodded.

"I'm also happy to announce that we've finally been able to make a fully functioning VR headset." Thorn bent and produced a headset from beneath his desk. He slid it across the desk towards the General, who picked it up and inspected it with a grin.

"If you're still up for it, you can now go into the Sim without any IV's, tubes or wires."

"Thank you, Mr. Thorn, but that won't be necessary," he pushed the headset back towards Thorn.

"You don't want to enter the Sim?" Thorn asked.

"Of course I do," the General said. "When we began this project and it seemed so difficult for you to accomplish, I started a division of my own to work on the challenge."

"Oh." The surprise was visible on Thorn's face which made the General smile. "That's great news."

"Yes," the General said. "In just a few days I'll be able to enter the Sim on my own and see all the marvelous things you've created with my very own eyes."

52

Brandon and the others entered his room and began their regular routine of scanning for listening devices and cameras. They each took a specific area and searched thoroughly. Kay completed her search first and stood facing the group with her thumb held up, waiting for the others to finish. When everyone had thumbs raised, Brandon nodded and the group sat down in the middle of the floor.

"Are we in the Sim, or the Dream?" Brandon asked the group.

As one they all answered, "The Dream,"

Brandon closed his eyes and took deep breaths, then he opened his eyes and nodded. "I agree," he said.

"Welcome back, everyone," Easton said. The group nodded somberly; they'd just lived thirty long, challenging years inside a virtual reality that still seemed more real than this one.

Brandon had thought long and hard about the lives they lived during that time. He felt certain that their time together had strengthened their relationship, but to be certain, he began this meeting with a question: "Do we all still want to be part of this team?"

"What kind of question is that?" Tony asked.

"It's a question that should be asked every once in a while." Brandon said. "We come into the world alone, and we leave it alone, but the time we spend in between is all ours. It might seem like our lives don't belong to us, especially living in the Centres, but they do. We began this when we were young, and we've seen more than most will come up against in an entire lifetime."

Easton stood and leaned against the door. "Everyone answer the question, please, and don't feel bad if you've decided to leave the group. I don't think anyone could blame you. Most people don't stay together for over forty years. We've done that. If you want a change, there's nothing wrong with that."

"I agree," Brandon said.

"I stay," Kay said quickly.

"Me too," Tony agreed.

"I'm not leaving," Alan said.

"A hand without a thumb is a sad thing," Easton smiled. "I'm staying."

Brandon nodded his head and a grin spread across his face. "I don't know what finger I represent, but my life truly began the day we all came together. I stay as well."

"So we've beaten the Sim and weathered the storm of time," Easton said. "What's next?"

"We play games with civilians," Brandon said.

"Civilians?" Tony asked. "So it's just getting easier, then?"

"I don't know," Kay said. "They might surprise us."

"Not for long, they won't," Brandon shook his head. "There is no one better at games than us. No one."

===

Thorn, Cooper, Wesley, and five of the other instructors sat at the large conference table, writing reports on the group of players they'd just debriefed. Thorn finished his report first, as usual, and looked up to wait for the rest.

When everyone stopped writing and looked up, Thorn nodded and began to speak.

"Give me the negatives."

Everyone remained silent.

"No one spotted anything negative from Brandon and his Hand?" Still no one answered. Thorn looked at Cooper and raised his eyebrows. Cooper could always find something negative.

Cooper shook his head. "They did better than I expected anyone would."

Thorn nodded his head. "I agree," he said. "This was the last group to interview. Thank you, everyone, for your participation. Send me your detailed reports before the end of the day tomorrow. Wesley and Cooper, please remain behind."

When everyone was gone, Thorn spoke again.

"Wesley," Thorn asked. "How many groups will we keep out of Beta testing?"

Wesley looked at his notes, then back to Thorn. "Only two."

Thorn nodded. "That's not too bad, considering the ordeal we put them through."

"When do they go in?" Cooper asked.

"Tomorrow."

"That doesn't give them much time to relax and wind down,"

"They've been living normal lives for the past thirty years," Thorn said. "Compared to normal days as players in the Sim, they've been on a thirty year vacation. We've held the start of Beta off as long as we can, and in three days ten thousand regular Beta testers are going to flood the system. There are already over a hundred thousand NPC's on Tygon; I want to give our kids some time to go in and scout around a bit."

"So they can have a day off and go in the following day?" Wesley asked.

Thorn sighed and nodded. "Okay, one day's rest and then they go in. All three of us will go in with them to see how they handle it."

"Is it different than the Sim?" Cooper asked.

"It's on the same digital platform so it won't seem any different. The major difference is that it is significantly less violent. The Sim was primarily training games and military style operations, even when the players didn't realize it. The civilian game reflects a normal life more closely." He looked at both men. "If that's all, then you can go."

Cooper and Wesley nodded their heads.

"Tomorrow morning, then, gentlemen," Thorn said. The two men stood and left the room.

Thorn stared at his computer monitor. He'd worked long and hard to get to this point. There were so many variables about to be put into play, and still too many wild cards. He shook his head and told himself to stop worrying. His skill and instinct had gotten him this far, playing a serious game that few even realized existed. Starting tomorrow he would play some of his best cards.

He would see how those cards fell, and move forward from there.

53

As instructed, the General placed the helmet on his head, flipped the switch, and closed his eyes. He then began to count backwards from ten. When he reached one, he opened his eyes and looked around.

He was no longer sitting in his office. Instead he stood in an empty, white room. The General spotted a door in one corner and strode over, turning the handle to open it.

It was locked.

No matter how hard he tried, the General couldn't open the door.

After trying for a few minutes he went back to the centre of the room and sat down. He closed his eyes and initiated the exit sequence like he'd been shown.

"Back so soon, sir?" the technician asked.

The General took off the helmet and put it down on his desk. "It didn't work," he said with disgust.

"It didn't transport you to the Sim?"

"It took me somewhere," he said. "A stupid, empty room."

"There should have been a door."

"Oh, yes, there was a door; a locked door."

The technician looked uncomfortable. "That's not possible. The doors to the entrance rooms are never locked."

The General glared.

"Right. Okay, sir. I'll get to work on it."

"I'm losing my patience," the General growled.

"I understand," the technician hurried out of the office, leaving the General to sit and stare at the headset in frustration.

It looked like he wouldn't be touring the Sim today.

The General lashed out and swiped the computer monitor from his desk. With a casual display of strength, he hurled it against the wall, staring with anger as it exploded from the impact. The General sat back down slowly; the act had given him no satisfaction.

54

"**If everyone can** give me your attention, we'll go through the login procedure for 'Tygon 3.0'," Wesley said.

It's a pretty looking game," Brandon said.

The load screen showed a large blue planet with a single land mass in the centre. Next a screen appeared with an avatar standing comfortably with a minimum amount of clothes on. Wesley had already taken them through the stages of selecting the attributes for their avatar; hair colour, eyes, height... there were an incredible amount of variables. On the main screen stood an exact digital replica of Wesley, dressed only in a pair of blue shorts.

"Next you spend points on a set of base skills," Wesley said. "Strength, endurance, appearance and charisma, to name just a few. Let's go through each attribute now."

"Oh, this is boring!" Tony whispered. "Why can't they just do it for us like they did when we played in the Sim?"

"Shh," Easton said. "They aren't going to do it for us, so pay attention. Keep your eyes open for tweaks and loopholes that might exist. You can bet that regular players will be talking with each other to find any exploit that will give them an advantage."

"We'll get it right, don't worry," Brandon whispered. "Plus we'll get some perks regular players won't."

"Really? Like what?"

"Like twelve years of full-time experience playing these types of games," Kay said.

"Shh," Alan flashed them a serious look and they all quieted down.

After they'd learned about the attributes section, Wesley moved on to server selection.

"Eventually there will be millions of players in Tygon. Each server will only accommodate a select number of players and NPC's. I expect the capacities will grow as our computing power increases, but for Beta testing everyone will play on the same server. Once the game goes live, we'll start with forty servers online to accommodate one million players per server."

"Is he serious?" Easton asked. "What's the world population? A billion? Will that many people want to play?"

Brandon shrugged. "Where would you rather be, playing or struggling through life in the Dream?"

"Yeah, he's got a point," Tony said. "Tygon 3.0 is gonna be popular, I think."

"It's going to be a whole new world," Brandon smiled, "and we'll be the kings and queens of the playground."

===

A day later, Brandon and his Hand went in.

The first few entries were less than perfect. The group erupted in laughter when Tony's avatar appeared with bunny ears and a long tiger's tail. A short time later, Alan suddenly sprouted a scarecrow mask, complete with leaking straw and buttons for eyes. After a round of jokes and jibes, the group had exited the simulation and fine tuned their avatar designs with Wesley's assistance.

The Beta testers hadn't arrived on Tygon yet, but the world was fully populated by non-player characters. Brandon's team travelled through the main city, riding on the transportation systems, eating in the restaurants, and doing everything they could think of to test the system. Each time they found a glitch or bug they called technicians on their cell phones to report the issues.

"Let's split up and get into some trouble," Alan said.

"Don't hurt anyone," Brandon said.

"There's no one to hurt," Kay grinned innocently.

"There are NPC's."

"They don't count. It's not like we're hurting anything if we knock a few of them down."

"In the Sim, every time we went in to play it involved elimination games," Brandon said. He held out his hands for the others to see. "There's blood on all of our hands. Virtual blood, but it feels real."

"We only killed avatars," Easton said.

"You're just an avatar at this moment in time," Brandon countered.

Alan started to say something, but he paused thoughtfully.

"This isn't the Sim. It will be more like our thirty year play, at least to begin with," Brandon said. "I'm not one hundred percent positive, but my guess is that playing in Tygon will be about more than killing."

"Okay, fine," Kay said. "We won't hurt anyone." She grabbed Tony by the arm and led him down the street.

Brandon and the others split up and started to walk in different directions.

"Brandon!" Kay called from across the street.

Brandon looked in her direction.

"If we can't kill anyone, then what are we supposed to do?"

Brandon looked at her for a moment, then laughed and shrugged his shoulders. Cupping his hands he yelled back, "Use your imagination!"

55

"**How can I** help you today, General?" Thorn smiled pleasantly as his boss entered the room. It was obvious that the General was angry.

"You can let me into the Sim, for starters!" the General snapped.

"What do you mean?" Thorn looked confused.

"I tried out my new VR helmet and found myself in a white room with a door."

"Yes," Thorn nodded, "that's the standard entrance area to the Sim. Then you open the door and take the hallway to your programmed destination."

"I'm not in the mood to be mocked, Thorn. I couldn't leave the room. If you're trying to stop me from entering the Sim, you're about to see a very different side of me."

"I'm not mocking you. Are you telling me that isn't how it went for you?"

"You know exactly how it went! I went into the Sim, stood in the white room, and couldn't exit."

"There was no door?" Thorn looked confused.

"The door was locked!" the General snapped.

Thorn frowned and looked at his computer screen. "When did you enter the Sim?"

"Yesterday."

"What time?"

"It was about a quarter past six."

Thorn nodded and continued to look at the screen and type in commands. Finally he nodded and sat back in his chair, looking up at the General.

"You locked yourself out," Thorn said.

"What?" the General stammered. "What do you mean, I locked myself out?"

"The Sim is designed to keep unknown programs out. I'm proud to say that no one has ever successfully hacked into the Sim. It was one of your primary directives: to keep security as tight as possible and to keep the Sim safe from enemy eyes."

"Well, yes, that's true," the General said, "but I'm not a threat; the Sim is my property!"

Thorn laughed to himself, but on the surface he nodded in agreement. "Of course that's true, sir, but the computer didn't know that it was you attempting access. The fact that you were able to enter the Sim at all is remarkable. I find it disturbing that for all these years you have refused my offers of assistance with entering the Sim on the grounds of maintaining safety, but yesterday you came closer to dying than I think you have in a long time."

"What do you mean?" the General's anger disappeared, replaced with concern.

"The helmet you used wasn't authorized technology," Thorn said. "One person managed to hack into the primary stage of the Sim a few years ago. He transferred his mind into the Sim, hoping to gain information for an outside source." Thorn turned his monitor around for the General to see. "The security measures of the Sim dealt with him. We found a man lying on the ground that same day just outside our facility, and we were able to piece information together to confirm that he was the one who'd hacked us. He currently resides in our medical facility. The Sim destroyed his mind, General. The same thing could have happened to you yesterday."

The scene on the monitor was horrible. A man hooked up to tubes and monitors lay in a hospital bed. His eyes were half open; his mouth drooped on one side. The General could see by the man's vacant stare that his essence was no longer there.

"He's a vegetable," the General murmured.

"Yes," Thorn agreed. "That's what happens to people who try to access the Sim without proper clearance."

"But I should have proper clearance!" the General shouted angrily. He realized how close he'd come to death, or perhaps worse, and he was infuriated.

"You do, sir," Thorn said. "When we know what you're doing. No one can decide what they want to do and proceed without going through the proper channels — not even you."

The General nodded his head. "I understand, Mr. Thorn. Computers have never been my strong suit. I suppose I should have consulted you before I made the attempt."

Thorn shook his head with concern. This was the moment he'd been moving towards during the entire conversation, and he struck hard. "Whoever built and designed that helmet for you would have known this, sir."

"What do you mean?" the General asked.

"Your helmet designer understood computers enough to know how secure the Sim would be. Whoever constructed your helmet expected you to die when you tried to access the Sim."

The General's face turned pale.

Thorn repositioned his monitor, allowing the General a moment to ponder that thought. It was possible, of course, that whoever had helped the General had no desire to kill him, and simply wasn't savvy enough to consider all the possibilities. What mattered to Thorn was that someone other than him existed who was clever enough to build a functioning virtual reality helmet, an unknown competitor who would be eliminated very soon because of what he'd just led the General to believe.

"Thank you, Mr. Thorn," the General stood up. There was death in his eyes. "I appreciate your help."

"General?"

The General paused with his hand on Thorn's door. "Yes?"

"When you are ready to safely enter the Sim I'm always ready, willing, and able to assist you. There is no one else on this planet that depends on your safety and continued well-being as much as I do."

"That's true," the General said. "Without me, this would all go away. Thank you, Thorn. I'll schedule a session for you to help me enter the Sim soon. There are a few security issues I must correct, first."

"Of course, sir," Thorn nodded solemnly. He waited until the General left before he allowed himself the luxury of.

Chapter 56

"There is big news in the world of video games and business today.

Computing giant 'Thorn Inc.' is opening up Beta testing for the first ever totally immersive virtual reality game.

Later this week ten thousand lucky video gamers will log in to explore the imaginary world of Tygon.

With over a million advance copies of the game 'Tygon 3.0' sold already, the business world is watching the event that could transform Samson Thorn into the richest man in the world.

If everything goes as planned, in just a few short weeks millions of citizens will disappear into virtual reality for short periods of rest and relaxation…"

56

"**READY FOR THE** REAL SHOW!?"

Brandon and the group raised their heads and looked towards the entrance of the bookstore. They were sitting at a reading area in the very back corner, but they could hear Cooper clearly shout his greeting from the front door as he walked in. People paused to watch as he moved past, but he was oblivious of their attention. A parent rushed forward to pull her child out of his way, staring at him as if he were crazy. Cooper ignored them all, grinning as he continued towards Brandon's group. He walked into the sitting area and flopped down on a beanbag chair.

"That was a bit rude," Kay said.

"Yeah," Cooper shrugged and grabbed a book out of Alan's hands. "It's just hard for me to care about NPCs." He pointed to a man standing nearby browsing a bookshelf. "They're... empty. They put so little thought into most of what they do." He looked back at Kay and shook his head. "They aren't... real."

"Well, they act real enough," Easton said. "We've lived our entire lives in the Facilities, but they seem identical to real people, from our limited experience."

"That's the biggest problem!" Cooper leapt to his feet and pretended to pull out a gun, pointing his finger at an NPC browsing a bookshelf close by. Squinting, he looked down the sight of the imaginary weapon. "They're more like real people than they should be," He pulled the trigger and his hand "recoiled." Blowing on the tip of his finger, he holstered his hand. "Which is the most depressing truth of all."

Cooper shook his head and gazed at the NPC with disappointment, flopping back into his seat and opening the book he still held in his other hand. He removed an energy bar from his pocket and took a bite, not even bothering to remove the wrapping. The others laughed at him; Cooper was acting a lot like a slightly older version of Brandon, "slightly" being the key word.

"So tell me," he said, still idly leafing through the book. "Are all of you ready for the civilian players who'll be coming in tomorrow?"

"I think so," Brandon said. He looked at the others who nodded in agreement. "There are still some issues to resolve, but that's what all the Beta testers are for. Small groups can only find so many problems, right?"

"Absolutely," Cooper agreed. "Have you run into any other Elites?" He was referring to other Sim veterans.

"A few," Tony said. "We've grouped up with some of them to test larger areas and general systems. We've caused damage, wreaked havoc and committed crimes around the world to make sure the automated peacekeeping forces reacted as they were designed to do."

"And?"

"Oh, yeah," Kay smiled, "they caught us."

"Because we had to let them," Alan said. "If we'd wanted to get away, we could have."

Cooper chuckled and looked at his watch. He stood up and tossed the book back to Alan. "We have a few hours left before they begin flooding into the world. Who wants to go grab one last free meal before the server goes fully live and we have to start paying for everything we consume?"

The group stood up. "Sounds good to me," Easton said.

"Great," Cooper said. "When we're done, we can go to one of the busier spawn points and watch civilian Baggers logging in for their first plays."

"I wonder how regular players will be different from us professionals," Alan said.

"For normal games, they'd clean our clocks," Cooper admitted, "but they're going to find this much different from the traditional computer games they're used to. Up until now, gamers sat in front of their monitors and mashed their keyboards. Now they're gonna have to feed their bodies, suffer from exhaustion, need rest, and feel pain when they're hurt. They're coming in here thinking virtual reality is a game."

"But it is a game," Tony said.

"No, it's more like life," Cooper said.

"The game is life," Brandon said.

"Hey, now," Cooper smiled, "that's catchy."

57

The General locked his office door, went to his desk and picked up the phone. This wasn't a call he'd been looking forward to.

"Hello, Madame President."

"General." The President's voice sounded cold and formal.

"What can I do for you, Ma'am?"

"Your... pet has become troublesome, Donovan. Thorn's little game has swept the world in a wave that could very well drown us."

"Yes, Madame President."

"You understand games better than most, General. They are useful when they help us train soldiers for battle, or workers to perform simple repetitive tasks. They assist with learning new ways to improve society. Games allow us to harvest knowledge and productivity from the masses. Mindless games are even useful for entertainment purposes, helping normal citizens escape for a brief time from the drudgery and dismal nature of their existence, giving the population harmless activities to look forward to performing during their off time."

The General knew all of this; he'd educated the President many years ago, teaching her about these exact types of benefits. She was angry, though, and he dared not interrupt her. "Yes."

"Games deliver control, General. That was your last sales pitch to me, wasn't it? The Sim and your successful Blurring project delivered control, turning regular children and adults into unsuspecting weapons who would gladly die for whatever cause we desired?"

"It was," he agreed.

"Six months ago, Thorn Inc.'s virtual reality game, 'Tygon 3.0' went live. Six short months ago, General. Do you know what has happened in that space of time?"

The General sat down in his chair. "Yes, Madame President."

"Tell me," she said.

"Tygon 3.0 has become the best-selling, most played game ever," the General said. "Samson Thorn is now the richest man who has ever lived."

"I wish it was only that, General. Tell me the worst of it."

The General closed his eyes and rubbed them wearily. "People are so immersed in Tygon 3.0 that they are ignoring their real lives. Adults aren't showing up to work, kids are no longer attending school, and essential businesses and services are having to shut down due to lack of manpower."

"This wasn't supposed to happen here, General," the President said. "You leaked it to our enemies and assured me this would occur there... but not here. You told me there would be fail-safes built into Thorn's game here. Limits to the amount of time a person could play, dampening programs to make the virtual reality not feel so real inside the simulation, that sort of thing. Do I remember incorrectly, General, or did you give me those assurances?"

"Yes, I did."

"Then tell me what's happening, General. Everything I've built for over eighteen years as President is slipping away in the span of mere months. Is this part of your plan? Because if so, it is treasonous. You assured me there were measures in place to stop Thorn if this type of thing began to happen!"

"There were. There are, Madame President."

"Do you know what happens if we try to unhook a VR helmet while a person is playing, General? They drop dead on the spot. We've tried to slow this down, but it's become an infection. It's worse than an infection! We are witnessing a digital plague that will destroy civilization as surely as any disease I have ever seen!"

"I can bring things under control, Madame President. Just say the word."

Laughter erupted on the other end of the line. Strained, stressed, fearful laughter poured from the President's lips. The General winced at the sound.

Finally the laughter subsided and he could hear her laboured breathing.

"Consider the word given, Donovan. Fix this. Now!"

There was a click on the other end of the line. A small wisp of a smile touched the General's lips. "Yes, Madame President," he said to the dial tone as he hung up the phone.

58

She stood backstage, smiling as the fans chanted her name.

Her manager had advised her to make them wait an extra ten minutes, and it turned out to be a great idea. The chanting and cheering grew in volume as the minutes passed.

She closed her eyes and remembered the long journey she'd taken to get here. All those nights playing in tiny bars with only drunks to listen, begging for small gigs just to earn a meal and a couple sales of her self-made albums. She'd travelled thousands of miles in a beat up old car just to follow her dream.

Her perseverance had paid off, though. While she was onstage in one of those small bars, a young music executive had walked in. He'd been searching venues in remote locations in hopes of finding the next big star. Fate had connected the two of them. She'd poured her heart and soul into her songs that night, and he recognized her talent when he'd heard her sing.

After that it had been a whirlwind. First the venue sizes increased. Then her music began to get picked up by the major radio stations. The appearances and live performances began to bring out increasingly large crowds. It had been worth it all; the sacrifice, the heartache, the miles covered.

Her manager walked up and grabbed her in a warm embrace, swinging her around before kissing her passionately. They'd become so much more than partners in music; they'd fallen in love and, before long, they'd gotten married.

"Okay, baby, I think you've made them wait long enough," he said with a smile. "Get out there and give 'em what they're begging for!"

She giggled and playfully grabbed at him; he was so good for her. "Come and watch me sing, lover," she said.

She turned and walked to the curtain where a roadie was smiling, ready to open it for her as she approached. Through a narrow slit in the curtains, she could see the crowd; this was the largest event she'd held so far. It would be a night to remember forever.

She pushed the curtain aside and smiled as she took hold of the microphone....

"Mommy, mommy! Please talk to me, Mommy! I'm so hungry, and you said you would make us some food soon!"

The sounds of the crowd vanished as her six-year-old daughter pulled the VR helmet from her head. She found herself in her apartment, sitting on her sofa, in her drab living room. She grabbed the helmet from her daughter's hands and pushed her off her lap as gently as possible, closely inspecting the helmet to make certain it hadn't been damaged. "Give me a second, honey. I told you I'd make dinner when I was done playing my game."

Katie would never have been able to take the helm off if she'd been fully within the game; it must have shorted out again. She shouldn't have come out of Tygon until the concert was finished and the celebrations had ended. A quick glance showed her that her helmet had overheated. With a flash of annoyance, she checked the timer and saw that she'd been inside the game for over thirteen hours. The helmet was one of the original models and tended to overheat after twelve hours or so. She would need to let it cool down for a bit before she could get back in and finish her concert.

Sighing with disappointment, she shuffled to the filthy kitchen to look for something to make for dinner. Piles of dirty dishes and food wrappers lay all around. She rummaged through the cupboard. It was mostly empty, save for a few bags of dried goods.

"How 'bout noodles, hun?" she said, looking down at her daughter.

"I'm still hungry after noodles, Mommy," she said. Her hair was dirty and she was still wearing pajamas even though it was late afternoon.

The mother looked at her daughter and felt a momentary twinge of guilt.

She smiled, though, because soon she'd be able to afford another headset. Then she could let her daughter play as well. There were new jobs inside the game where you could earn credits and even headsets to give to family members. Things would be better for both of them then.

"Soon Mommy will get you your very own headset and let you play in Tygon too, baby," she said. "There's much better food in there, but today noodles is all we got."

The little girl looked confused, but she believed and trusted her mother, so she nodded. "Okay, Mommy," she said.

The mother stood at the stove, waiting for the pot to boil and the noodles to cook. The entire time, she was daydreaming about her life inside the game. On Tygon she was a somebody. Here she was just a poor uneducated woman with a husband who had left her and a crappy little apartment. Here she had no job, no food, no real hope of anything good from life. There was nothing for her here.

She put the noodles in a bowl and put them on the table. "There you go, sweetheart, you eat those noodles up."

"Thanks, Mommy," her daughter said. "You gonna eat some too?"

Her mother smiled and shook her head. "No, Honey, I'll eat on Tygon. You go ahead."

She patted her daughter on the head and walked to the living room, grabbing her VR helmet from the table on the way. She looked at the timer and smiled. It had cooled down enough to let her log back in.

Adjusting a couple of dials, she placed the helmet on her head.

She thought she heard her daughter's voice from the kitchen, saying, "I love you, Mommy," but she was already back in Tygon, standing on the stage as the crowd cheered and applauded and chanted her name.

59

Brandon's plane was a small single propeller model, the kind with pontoons that could land on water. He exited the aircraft, collected his bag, and walked up the pier towards an elegant hotel.

Thorn was there to meet him at the entrance; Cooper stood beside him. Both men smiled and took turns hugging Brandon.

"How was the flight?" Thorn asked. "Not too long or bumpy, I hope?"

"It was fine, thanks," Brandon replied. "I had no problems at all."

In Tygon 3.0, Brandon was now a grown man, six feet tall with dark blonde hair and blue eyes. He was muscular, with an athletic build. A few weeks after the game had gone live, almost all of the Elite groups had decided to change their avatars from children to adults. Average players didn't choose child avatars, and being an adult was much more practical.

"Do you want to go to your room first and drop your bags off, or would you prefer to get right to it?"

"If everyone else is here, I'm ready to get started," Brandon said.

"Okay, then, right this way."

The three men talked and got caught up on the way to the main lobby of the hotel. Brandon had been here once before; it was a private island on Tygon, owned and controlled by Thorn. The only way to get here was by invitation, and in Brandon's experience this wasn't a place one would want to visit for pleasure.

They entered the main hall and walked to a private meeting room filled with team leaders from the Elite groups. Brandon smiled and nodded to some of them; many had become friends and allies over the years in the Sim. Brandon spotted Lohkam who scowled at him and turned away to talk with his neighbour. The two had never grown close. In fact, Lohkam tried to kill Brandon almost every time they ran into each other, although most of their encounters ended with Brandon getting the upper hand.

Thorn walked to the head table and sat down, with Brandon on his right and Cooper on his left.

"Thank you all for coming on such short notice; I'm glad you could all make it. I've called you here today to deliver a message. Real life, or the Dream as we call it, is in a state of extreme crisis."

Thorn paused for a reaction, but no one looked surprised or concerned. Thorn said something to that effect and Lohkam spoke up on behalf of the group.

"It's never been our world, Mr. Thorn. We didn't really get to live in it. All of us have spent our entire lives in the Centres and inside virtual reality. Quite frankly, if the Dream ceased to exist tomorrow, I wouldn't care one bit."

Others nodded in agreement; Thorn could see their point, and although he didn't share their sentiment, he could understand it.

"I have one entire Tygon server dedicated to crunching numbers and figuring probabilities," Thorn said. "The data overwhelmingly points to an outcome which we must avoid at all costs; complete extinction of our species from the planet. Even if you live your entire life inside Tygon or some other simulation, electrical power is still required to keep these virtual worlds in existence. That power is generated in the real world, and without it you will die in here as well."

The group of Elites looked at each other around the table and nodded grudgingly.

"How much time is there?" Brandon asked.

Thorn shook his head. "The absolute worst case scenarios indicate that we have a little over a year."

"How can we help?" one of the leaders asked.

"To begin with, I need you and your teammates to complete another thirty year simulation," Thorn said. "Because of the drain on our computer and energy resources from Tygon 3.0, that simulation will last three months rather than three weeks."

Lohkam groaned, "That part doesn't matter to us," he said. "Three minutes or three years, it will still feel like we've been inside the simulation for thirty years! I can't do that again."

Thorn pursed his lips and looked out over the leaders. "I can't force you to do it, but the experience you'll gain from living another lifetime will be invaluable. I can tell you that this time around will be more focused. We need you to master one skill."

"What skill?" another leader asked.

"I need you to become to become experts in the field of quantum computing design and programming."

<u>60</u>

Thorn sat at a small table in a corner of the resort's restaurant. It had been a long, stressful day making sure all the Elite leaders arrived in time and were present for the message he had to deliver. The last of them were boarding their planes to depart the island now. There were a few special guests still enjoying private meals around the dining room. It was the perfect time to relax with a glass of wine and a peaceful meal.

Thorn cut into his rare steak and raised it to his mouth. As he looked up, he saw Lohkam striding purposefully towards him, a frown on his face. That boy always has a frown on his face, Thorn thought to himself.

Lohkam stopped in front of Thorn, glaring at him but saying nothing. Thorn looked him in the eye but continued to chew his food, taking the time to enjoy the first bite of steak he'd had in quite a while. He looked down to cut another bite. When he put the food into his mouth, his eyes conveyed boredom as they returned to rest on Lohkam's. Could be lucky enough to eat this whole steak before I have to listen to this?

Three bites later, Thorn groaned inwardly as Lohkam finally spoke up.

"I can't do another thirty year session."

Thorn finished chewing the food in his mouth. "What if I could have you complete it in three weeks instead of three months?" he asked.

Lohkam shook his head negatively without a hint of hesitation, which told Thorn all he needed to know about the situation. "It's not the time that passes here, Mr. Thorn," Lohkam explained. "It's having to live another thirty years in there. I just can't do it."

Thorn looked Lohkam up and down with a critical eye. "You don't plan to live thirty more years?" he asked.

"Of course I do. I don't want to live more than one lifetime, though. One lifetime is enough; to live more than that just seems like... punishment."

Thorn was surprised. He assumed everyone wanted to get more life. He shook his head in wonder at the thought of someone not wanting to live as long as possible and experience all there was to experience. He looked at Lohkam for a moment, then nodded and waved his fork before he cut another bite.

"Okay, fine, Lohkam. If you don't want more years of life, then so be it."

Lohkam relaxed visibly, almost as if someone had just pardoned him from a prison sentence. "Thank you, sir, I appreciate it. If there's anything else I can do for you, I'm happy to. Anything at all."

Thorn nodded while he finished another mouthful of food. He wished the boy would leave him alone while he was eating, but he wasn't going to let this prevent him from enjoying his meal. Lohkam could wait between bites, since this was the time he'd chosen to chat.

"I have something else for you to do while the other Elites are out for the next three months," he said. "It seems that Tygon 3.0 is too... pleasant. It's better and more enjoyable than most people's real lives, which causes them to want to spend all their time in there. We are thinking of changing Tygon 3.0 to become less 'fun' to live in, in the hopes that people will decide to quit the game and get back to reality."

"How will you do that?" Lohkam asked.

Thorn smiled, "We're going to take Facility players into Tygon, one server at a time, and start killing every civilian player we see. Over and over until they get frustrated and quit the game."

Lohkam frowned. "Rather than live a boring life for thirty years inside VR, you want me to spend my days slaughtering unskilled avatars inside a game that doesn't really promote violence?"

"Exactly," Thorn nodded.

Lohkam's frown spread into a wicked grin. "I'm ready to start immediately."

<u>61</u>

Carl was starting to wonder if the computer running the Sim was glitching.

He opened the door of the house and examined the decorations. Well, he thought to himself, if it's glitching, the furniture and appearance of the houses continue to be different.

Carl had questioned this particular game since the very first time he played it. He expected a challenge, but so far there'd been nothing. He was beginning to lose count of the number of times he'd played this scenario; He was sure it was at least thirty-three.

The house was silent. As he moved from the hallway and into the middle of the house he heard a sound coming from a room in the back. Carl approached the room, gently pushing the door open to reveal a small bedroom with walls decorated in pink.

There was a video player on the dresser and a small girl, perhaps five or six years of age, sitting on the bed with her back to the door watching a children's program. Carl slowly closed the door, making certain that the girl didn't notice him.

He checked the other rooms and found his target in a room on the right. Entering the room, he immediately noticed the smell; it was musty, like stale body odour mixed with faded laundry detergent. The blinds were pulled down, although slight cracks in the blinds let in streams of sunlight. Motes of dust flashed in the narrow shafts of light. Clothes littered the floor as if someone had been looking for something specific. The bed didn't match the rest of the scene; it was made precisely, the covers clean and colourful compared to the drab dirtiness that surrounded it.

He approached carefully and slowly, although experience had taught him he didn't need to use any stealth; his targets never seemed to sense him.

This one was a woman. Sometimes they were women, and other times men. Their ages were all different too. She appeared to be around twenty-five and was sitting cross-legged on the bed, arms hanging loosely by her sides. On her head was a gold coloured helmet; smooth except for one small dial and knob near the right top portion. A black pair of goggles covered her eyes. Carl guessed they were too dark to see through, but he wasn't certain about that. Her mouth was turned up in a grin; they were always grinning, often with a bit of clear drool dribbling down from one corner of their mouths. There was no drool this time, but the grin was certainly there.

Carl stood and watched her for a moment, making sudden small movements to see if he could get her attention. Nothing. There was no reaction at all. Leaning in close, he read the logo on the front of the helmet. He already knew what it would say, but it had become part of his ritual and it felt odd not to do it. Plus it delayed what had become the worst part of the mission.

'Tygon 3.0, Thorn Inc.' He wondered what Tygon was, and if Thorn Inc. had something to do with Mr. Thorn. Often simulations included familiar names and situations because the Sim used details from existing data in the system to fill in unimportant blanks.

Carl shook his head and dismissed the idea that it was of any importance; he'd wasted enough time. Reaching behind his back, he unsheathed a long, sharp blade. With a quick slash he performed his task, watching grimly as the avatar crumpled silently back onto the bed. The blood pooled around her throat onto the clean sheets beneath her as Carl turned and left the bedroom.

He saw a towel lying on the floor in the hallway and he bent down to wipe his blade. He continued his search, checking the remaining two rooms in the house.

In one of them he found a teenage boy frozen in place, also wearing a helmet and a grin. Carl quickly dispatched him and exited the house through the back patio doors.

Hopping the fence, he made his way to the next house, looking for a back entrance. He looked at his watch and realized he'd have to pick up the pace. He had two hundred and ninety-two more targets to find and eliminate before his time in this game ran down to zero.

62

"**I heard you** want to add another member to your team," Cooper said. "I don't recommend a hand with six digits, Brandon. It isn't as useful as it might sound."

"I'm not adding another member to my team," Brandon said. "You showed me how to build a network, Cooper. Carl's a key member of mine, and I want him to join us in the thirty year Sim."

Cooper smiled. Early on he'd taught Brandon that his Hand was the General's best, not only for their skill and prowess in the field, but also because of the vast network that Cooper and his team had built over the years. Brandon had learned this lesson well, and built his own network among the Facility's Gamers that included almost every team and notable player who had played inside the Sim in the thirteen years that it had been live. The list of people that Brandon could rely on for help was impressive.

"A team is guided and controlled by its members," Cooper said. "A network is accepted for what it is, and tapped into when the situation allows."

"Exactly," Brandon nodded.

"Asking to bring Carl with you is controlling him, when you should monitor the situations and use Carl when the time and opportunity present themselves."

"I get it, Cooper — honestly, I do," Brandon said. "I'm not telling Carl to come join us. I simply see an opportunity, and if the situation presents itself, then I would like to get him an invite into the Sim."

"What is it you want to have him do for you?" Cooper asked.

Brandon explained his plan, and Cooper nodded in agreement. "Okay, I see what you're getting at. Carl will be perfect, but there's a slight problem."

"What?" Brandon asked.

"He's Blurred, and he's on assignment for the General."

A cold sensation gripped Brandon's stomach, and he felt ill. They'd heard rumours of what was happening with Blurred players but had tried not to listen too closely. To prevent it from happening to them, they'd increased their meditation sessions. The entire team had been relieved when they were removed from the Sim and put into Thorn's public virtual reality, where the dangers of Blurring seemed significantly diminished.

"What does that mean?" Brandon asked.

"It means," Cooper said with a grim look, "that he thinks he's inside the Sim killing computer generated NPCs for points, when in fact, he's in the real world killing people the General wants dead."

"This whole Sim project was intended to turn us into better killing machines for the General," Brandon said.

"Absolutely," Cooper said. "His plan was to create even better soldiers to help him solidify control over the real world."

"And Thorn helped him."

"Yes, Thorn helped him. Then Thorn took it to the next level, making things go from bad to worse."

"The General wanted to rule the people of the world, but Thorn might end up destroying them all," Brandon guessed.

Cooper nodded. "There are stories of people staying inside Tygon for so long that they're starving to death, sitting in their homes with their VR helmets on."

"That's horrible," Brandon said.

"Yes, and that's one of the less horrific stories. There have been reports of people stealing and killing each other to get enough money to subscribe to Tygon 3.0 for just a few more days. People are becoming hooked on the game almost immediately. Their lives are so much better inside Tygon that they abandon reality until they die."

Brandon shook his head in bewilderment. "So who do we help? The General or Thorn?"

Cooper answered immediately, "Thorn. The popularity of Tygon 3.0 wasn't anticipated. There have been interactive online games around for decades and none of those have ever resulted in this type of problem."

"It's the immersion aspect of it," Brandon said. "There should have been some type of control over who went in, a limit to how long each session could last... perhaps adults shouldn't have been allowed to play it."

"All good ideas, but it's a little late to implement them now. We need to help Thorn get this situation under control. I've told you what the General has Carl doing. We can't help the General or we'll all end up being his slaves."

"I have an idea, Cooper, about how to fix this."

"Which part?" Cooper asked.

"All of it." Brandon seemed possessed; Cooper wasn't sure what to make of it, but he nodded.

"How can I help?" Cooper asked.

Brandon scribbled a list of names and handed it to Cooper. "Get me Carl and the other players on this list. I don't care how you do it, or what favours you have to call in, Cooper, but I need these people to go into the thirty year Sim with me."

Cooper couldn't put his finger on it, but his gut told him that he had to help Brandon get what he was asking for. "Give me the names," he said. "I'll do my best."

63

Lohkam opened his eyes and quickly closed them. He made his right hand into a tight fist and put it to his forehead. Tapping the middle part of his head, he took a deep breath and opened his eyes.

"No!" he yelled. "I told you I couldn't do this again, dammit!"

The entry room for both the Sim and Tygon was plain, undecorated, and white, but this room was a clearly a bedroom that belonged to a teenager.

Posters covered the dark blue walls, clothes were thrown on the floor, and the far wall had a shelf with books and trophies on it. Thorn sat on a chair beside the bed, staring pleasantly at Lohkam. "I'm afraid you don't have a choice in this," he said.

Lohkam's eyes flashed angrily. He jumped up from the bed and grabbed a letter opener off the desk, holding it to his throat. "I have a choice," he said. "I can rip my throat out now, and ride on out."

Thorn shook his head, "You know better than that, Lohkam," he said. "The consequences of suicide have been explained since your first orientation day."

Lohkam growled and threw the blade. It sunk into the wall with a solid thunk. "Fine, then," he said. "I'll sit here and waste my entire life." He glanced at the computer in the corner of his room. "I'll play video games and eat pizza for the next twenty years until my bloated, sick body gives up and dies. I'll exit the

Sim that way; it's one of the acceptable ways to kill myself, right?"

"If you want," Thorn shrugged. "It's stupid, but entirely within your rights to waste a play."

"Then that's how I'll play it," Lohkam nodded.

"I didn't think you'd let Brandon win so easily, but I guess it must get tiring losing to someone better than you for so many years."

Lohkam stiffened at the mention of Brandon's name. "Why'd you have to bring up the Runt?" he asked.

Thorn smiled, "Because he's doing a thirty year Sim, too."

"I'm guessing all the leaders are doing one," Lohkam said. "Since I specifically asked not to and I'm still here, anyone else who did the same likely got the same treatment."

"You're correct, Lohkam. The real world is a colossal mess and I need everyone to do their part."

"Our part?" Lohkam yelled. "What do you expect us to do? You're an adult and you've managed to mess things up. What do you expect kids like us to do?"

"You're not regular kids. After you complete this second Sim you'll have the experiences and knowledge from having lived over seventy years. Plus you'll still be in a young body. All of you are more than regular children. You're much more than the General anticipated, and one of you could very well help save the world."

"The world's not gonna end, and none of us are gonna help to save it."

Thorn shook his head. "You have no clue what's happening in the Dream right now. Pay attention this time, Lohkam, and over the next thirty years you'll see why the Tygon 3.0 game became so addictive and destructive."

"Is this Tygon 3.0?" Lohkam asked.

"No, this is Tygon 1.0. It's a secure, standalone server with a billion NPCs living lives that mirror how our world was until a short time ago. The NPCs believe that they are as real as you and I. They are born, they grow up, work, love and struggle.

Then they die. For them, this is real life. Most of them don't believe they get another one when this ends."

Lohkam stood and glared at Thorn for a moment. Finally he sat back down on the bed. "Okay. What do you want me to do?"

Thorn stood in front of Lohkam. "Life in the Facilities and then the Sim didn't allow you to feel like you were a member of your own race," he said. "The General spent all his effort to make you into soldiers, but I need you to be citizens."

"Why?" Lohkam looked confused.

Thorn didn't expect him to understand, but he answered anyway. "Because if you feel like you are truly a part of this world, then perhaps you'll want to use your considerable gifts to help save the real world when you return to us. Gain some knowledge and empathy for your race, then be ready to work hard to save it when you come back."

64

"**Are you going** to kill me?" Thorn asked. He sat across from the General looking like a veteran lion tamer who'd just realized he'd made a terrible miscalculation.

"I haven't decided yet," the General said. "I likely should have killed you a year ago, but it looks as if I missed my opportunity. If I eliminate you now, then I'm forced to try and fix this entire mess on my own."

Thorn nodded. "I know for a fact," the General continued, "that there have been moments when you thought of eliminating me as well."

"Certainly," Thorn confirmed. "There always seemed to be something that made it not quite the perfect opportunity, which held me back. I assume those little 'somethings' were orchestrated by you to help keep me from making the attempt?"

"Of course," the General smiled. "You did the same, and I assume for similar reasons?"

"Yes," Thorn said. "Now here we sit, the world crumbling to ruin around us, and I think for the first time since we first met, each of us is absolutely safe from the other."

"Weird how the world works, isn't it?" the General said.

"Most of the time."

The two men sat and considered the situation. Finally, the General spoke up.

"I can't rule a nation that no longer functions," he said.

"I can't get subscription fees from people who don't bother to go to work to make money," Thorn responded. "I have some ideas that require your cooperation. I think we can slow this degeneration down, and if we're lucky, reverse it."

The General thought for a moment. "I'll do whatever I can to help."

"How many regular citizens belong to you, General?"

"What do you mean?" he asked.

"Don't pretend with me, sir," Thorn said. "Your endgame might be too bold for many to envision, but I've seen more than most. How many Centre graduates — how many people who wear your Infinity symbol, and are loyal to their loving 'Father' — exist in our society today as a result of your decades of quiet scheming?"

"A significant number," the General admitted. "Approximately one quarter of our society belongs to me. Most of them hold positions of power and influence within their communities."

"Or they are in the military," Thorn stated.

"Of course. The military belongs entirely to me."

"How many years have you spent building this force, sir?"

"This will be the thirtieth year of my plan. Why do you ask?"

"No reason," Thorn said, but his mind was curious. The Elite leaders had completed and were now in the midst of another thirty year simulation... An odd coincidence, he thought. When Thorn had come up with the number it had been random — or so he'd thought.

"Are your people playing Tygon 3.0?" Thorn asked.

"I would assume so. Video games were never a problem, and therefore not forbidden, until this one came along."

"All right. I know you've never gone into the Sim, General, but I have a few strategies that I want to show you for halting and reversing the situation. The most effective way for me to do that is to take you inside the Sim and show them to you." Thorn opened a cabinet and brought out two golden VR helmets. "I think it's time that you came in and took a look around, don't you?"

The General paused for a moment, and then nodded in agreement. "Yes, I think a visit to the Sim is long overdue, Mr. Thorn."

Thorn nodded and moved to place one of the helmets on the General's head. "It works the same as the copy that you tried to use before from your designers. Count backwards from ten to one and wait in the room when you open your eyes. I'll come and get you, and from there we can go to the main centre. Once we get there, I can present the ideas that I think will work best to get us back on track with minimal loss of life."

The General nodded and Thorn flipped the switch to activate the helmet.

The General started to count backwards slowly from ten and Thorn quickly sat down and put his helmet on. He wanted to get into the Sim immediately so that he could meet the General right away. He was about to hit his helmet's power switch when he heard something strange coming from the General's helmet. Thorn lifted his visor and looked in the General's direction.

As the General reached the count of four, his helmet made another sound, a loud, hollow sounding metallic click.

Throughout the room a woman's voice announced; "Recognized; General Donovan. Begin process Zeta. Mark."

Thorn tore his helmet off and rushed to the General's side. During the thousands of activations he'd witnessed, he'd never heard anything like this before.

The General stood up from his seat and lay down gently on the floor. He continued to count backwards, but as he reached zero his breathing became shallow, and Thorn noticed that he wasn't grinning.

Now Thorn immediately knew that something was seriously wrong. During the early days of prototype development, it was counterproductive to stop the helmet and ask if it was working, so they had built in the grin function. If a subject was properly immersed in the Sim, the corners of their mouth would turn up slightly and form a grin. The General appeared to be inside the Sim, but he wasn't grinning. Not at all.

Thorn grabbed his helmet and quickly put it on. He counted down to ten and opened his eyes inside the Sim, a process he was very familiar with by now. He threw open the white door and raced to the room where the General would be waiting...

Thorn swore loudly and ran towards the main control room.

The General wasn't there.

65

"**Is something wrong?**" Cooper asked. Thorn looked shaken as he entered the room to talk with Brandon and his group.

"It can wait," Thorn said. He sat down, put his hands flat on the table and stretched them as far out as they could go, then he took a deep breath with his head facing downwards, and exhaled as he looked up. His frown became a smile, and he nodded to the people surrounding him.

"Is everyone here?" he asked.

"Everyone is here, sir," Brandon said. "I appreciate you doing this; bringing them all together."

"All of you know what you're about to enter into, and you all agree to join Brandon in this simulation?"

There were twelve individuals sitting around the table. Thorn made eye contact and waited for them to nod before moving to the next person. He wanted to make certain that everyone realized that they would be spending three months on a table in a controlled coma, and thirty years living a full life inside Tygon 1.0. Of the twelve, five were Brandon and his Hand. The others whom Brandon had requested were no real surprise; they were influential players with serious skills who joined Brandon whenever they could.

Carl was present; he looked refreshed and much more alert Cooper had gone to great lengths to bring him out of the field, and help him become unBlurred. Carl still didn't know that the thousands of innocents he'd killed in cold blood were real people. The killings had been the General's attempt to cause fear among players, but the threat of psychotic killers coming in and killing players while they were playing Tygon 3.0 hadn't slowed anyone down from subscribing or playing as the General had hoped.

Thorn frowned slightly as his eyes came to rest on the final member of Brandon's chosen group. "Wesley? What are you doing here?"

"I want him with me," Brandon said, "and he agreed to come."

Thorn raised his eyebrows questioningly at Wesley, and the man nodded. "With your permission, sir, I would like to join them. I'm of no use here at the moment, and if they can find something for me to do to help, then I'm happy to try."

Thorn looked at Cooper, who nodded slightly. "Okay, that's fine," Thorn said. "Now, before we send you in, would you please tell me what you're planning on doing with all of these extra accomplices?"

"You said that you had plans to implement out here, but first you wanted the Elites to live one more lifetime to become adept at quantum computing and designing," Brandon said.

"That's right," Thorn said. "After you all come out with the experience we want you to get, that will leave us six to nine months to implement actions on a global scale with the goal of safely ending this crisis."

"What if it doesn't work?" Brandon asked.

"Then we've done our best and we move forward ," Thorn said.

"How would you like to double your chances for a solution?"

Thorn leaned forward. "I'm listening," he said.

===

They sat at their regular table in the mess hall. The other tables were empty, but the cooks had come in to prepare a meal for them before they entered Tygon 1.0 for their long simulation.

Everyone joked and talked; it was like being a kid again on a good day in the Facility, even though good days had been far and few between.

After the meal, Brandon stood up to address the group. "This simulation is a bit different from others. Some of us have done it before, but some haven't. I'm going to tell you how it should go and then cover our basic plan. Interrupt me with questions any time."

The others nodded and Brandon began the briefing. "We'll be placed in avatars that match our current appearance and age. With one billion NPCs in the simulation, there will be more than a few avatars that match us, but most of us will likely end up being placed far from each other when we start off."

Brandon paused to see if this raised any questions, but the group seemed to understand. "When we enter our avatars, the consciousness from that avatar is deleted."

"That's a bit harsh," one of the kids said.

"How do you mean?" Brandon asked.

"We're killing a person to take their place."

"No, we're not," another shook his head and laughed. "They're computer programs, with pre-programmed everything. They aren't real, or important."

"Good," Brandon smiled. "I'm glad this came up. Let's deal with it now and all come to an agreement."

"About what?" Tony said.

"How to treat the population of the world we're about to join," Easton said.

"I think we treat them like we would each other," Kay said. "They will be just like us, in shape, thought, and form. Our avatars will interact with their avatars. Our brain patterns will match theirs. We treat them like we treat each other, simple as that."

"Does anyone disagree?" Brandon asked.

"They aren't real," Carl said. Others nodded in agreement.

"They will be very real to us for the next thirty years," Brandon said. "We will be just as unreal, if you want to look at it that way."

"But we come back here," Carl said.

"As long as nothing goes wrong with the transfer," Alan said. "There have been some kids lost in the trip out. Does that mean they weren't real? And who's to say the NPCs don't go somewhere as well? Maybe it's the mainframe to be debriefed and recycled, but that's still a place for them to go."

"I can tell you all from experience," Brandon said, "that this can become a confusing topic. The easiest thing to do is agree that everything in the simulation is real, because it is. We feel it, we affect it, we live with the repercussions of each choice we make. I say we choose to value the citizens of Tygon as real entities."

"What if a million of them die, or suffer?" Wesley asked.

"Then we react the same way we normally would," Brandon said. "A million people could die from starvation playing Tygon 3.0, followed by millions more. I hear that number and although it's a shame, it doesn't change the way I live my life, for the most part."

"I agree," Easton said. "It's not a war game that we're entering. Let's play it correctly. We value and respect NPCs because they are real beings."

No one else disagreed. Brandon looked around and everyone nodded, although some shrugged their shoulders indifferently. "Okay, then, back to the plan. When we are solidly in place, the mainframe will reset the names to match ours, so when we go to bed and wake up everyone will call us by our names. Then we begin our lives at our current age. Some of us will have to finish school, some will have jobs they need to go to. We continue on the path we inherit until we are eighteen years old inside the Sim. Sound good to everyone?"

Everyone nodded.

"We need to find each other sooner than that, though. Tygon 1.0 uses social media the same as ours, so we will use the catch phrase 'Thorn Protects The Sim.' Start a blog, make a website, do something, so we can track each other by looking for that phrase."

Brandon grabbed another plate of food and sat down. He took a bite and waved his hand. "That's it for now; we get into the simulation, gain our bearings, and we contact each other. We can talk about the rest inside when the time is right. Any questions?"

No one said a word.

"Good," Brandon said. "Let's have some fun and get old."

66

The General opened his eyes. The room looked exactly like the last time he'd attempted to enter into the Sim; the door was even in the same place in the wall.

He knew his instructions were to remain in the room, but curiosity got the better of him and he went to the door and attempted to open it. This time it opened with a soft click. He stuck his head into the hallway, peering left and right. A plain white hallway extended both directions with a closed door at one end, exactly how Thorn had said that it would appear.

The General nodded and closed the door. His instructions were to wait for Thorn, and he would wait, even though he was excited about finally getting to tour what he had hired Thorn to create.

The General had always been cautious, especially as his career grew. Kill a few people, then a few more, then take children who showed genetic potential away from their families to raise according to his plan... that kind of thing could eventually come back to bite a person if they weren't careful. The past thirty years had been full of challenges, but the plan was sound. Taking each step had enabled him to make the next, more difficult one.

He had convinced himself early on that he wasn't doing this for himself, he was doing it to save his people.

As a young soldier, Donovan had been different. He'd moved up the ranks through skill and by creating networks and allies in all aspects of both military and private life. His family had helped, of course. Donovan came from generations of wealthy leaders and public figures; his family connections ran far and deep. Before Donovan had drawn his first breath, his father had already made plans and set goals for his son's entire life.

His upbringing, instilled values, and family connections had paved the way, but it was Donovan's ingenuity and ideas that had set the stage for his long term goals and plans after he became a General. His father wanted Donovan to become President, but after living in the system and seeing the limited potential which could come from that, he'd decided to change the entire political system instead. A normal person would never consider such a thing, but the General saw it all very clearly. He understood from his extensive study of history that special men during critical moments could affect monumental changes to the world, and he'd decided that his father's goal wasn't nearly ambitious enough for him to pursue.

Donovan had developed an intricate and long term plan to reach his goal. Thirty years... a period too long for most people to comprehend, much less execute, but after he'd spent years developing it, he knew it was his life's calling. To lead a world inhabited by a population of devout followers.

As the final year approached completion, Donovan knew he was close to getting exactly what he'd been striving for.

Tygon 3.0 appeared to be a catastrophe in progress, but Donovan had seen many threats to his plans before. He'd managed to deal with them all, and he was confident that with Thorn's help they would bring this latest situation under control. With cleverness and hard work, and the bit of luck that always accompanied anyone truly successful, the General was certain that he was only months away from removing the President and installing himself as the nation's new leader.

The door opened, interrupting the General's thoughts. He stood and brought his full thoughts to the crisis at hand. He was interested to see what ideas Thorn had to fix this problem.

It wasn't Thorn who entered the room, however. The General took a slight step backward, and his practiced façade of control faltered as he stared at the man facing him.

The man's face lit up at the General's reaction. He entered the room and closed the door behind him, deliberately taking his time to savour the moment as he turned to face the General.

"What's the matter, Donovan?" there was danger in his tone, and the promise of much pain, "You look like you've seen a ghost."

The General quickly regained his bearing. In a confident, commanding tone he answered, "It's not often I'm surprised, but I certainly am right now."

Brad laughed, his eyes filled with hatred and madness. "The surprises are only beginning, General. I promise you that."

67

Brandon opened his eyes and looked slowly around his room, making a complete circuit before stopping to look at Thorn, who was sitting in a chair beside his bed.

"Is this real?"

Thorn's mouth twitched into a sly grin, "Well... no, it's a simulation."

Brandon laughed, "I know that! Am I in a bedroom or a house? This room is huge! It looks like my avatar is a rich kid."

"He is indeed, a very rich kid, Brandon." Thorn smiled, enjoying the look of happiness on Brandon's face. He'd always felt bad for this poor boy. His parents killed, abandoned by his only remaining kin, then sent to live the life of a slave to a megalomaniac bent on world domination. Every parent wanted to give their children the best possible life, and this was Thorn's attempt to do that for Brandon. It also happened to fit in with what Brandon would need if he was to have a chance to pull off his plans, but that was a happy coincidence.

"Which makes me a very rich kid," Brandon laughed and threw himself back into the huge soft bed. "What's my last name here?" he asked.

"Your last name is Strayne," Thorn had built this avatar custom perfect , even down to the last name. Brandon would never know that his new surname was his true one, but Thorn would know, and that was something.

"Brandon Strayne," Brandon said it out loud and nodded his head. "That's a very good name."

"It sure is."

"So what about the parents?"

"Sorry on that end of things," Thorn said. "Your mom isn't around, and your dad is a super successful computer genius who's always travelling."

"That's handy, considering that you want me to learn quantum computing and design,"

"It's your reward for learning it already," Thorn said. Brandon had spent his first thirty year Sim becoming a computing expert. Of all the teams, Brandon's had the greatest advantage. His exceptional talents, combined with thirty years of experience already in computing, would help his odds of finding a solution to the problem occurring in the Dream.

"Your father is never here. I'm sorry, Brandon, but you won't have much of a childhood during this Sim."

Brandon stood up and grabbed Thorn in a sincere hug. "That's okay," he said, "my first thirty year Sim was incredible. I had the best parents and family life a person could ever dream of having. Besides, I already have a Father who takes good care of me."

Thorn hugged the boy back, closing his eyes and losing himself in the warmth and emotion of being loved with such sincerity. Despite the way life had played out to this point, Brandon was a passionate boy who sincerely cared about the special people in his life.

They hugged for a long moment before Brandon let go. Thorn blinked his eyes rapidly to make the tears disappear as best as he could before he stepped back to face the boy.

"I'm very proud of you, Brandon," Thorn said. "If anyone can find a solution, it's you."

"Thank you, Father. I'll do my best to make you proud."

Thorn knew the next thirty years would be hard on their relationship. There would be times that Brandon would hate him, but that would be necessary if he was to get Brandon to work and develop to his fullest potential. "I know you will, Son," he said.

"Can you tell me where the others ended up?" Brandon asked. He walked over to his desk and turned on the desktop computer, expertly pulling up a program to make notes for reference.

"I was able to put your Hand members close to you," Thorn said. "Tony and Kay are in your high school, and Alan and Easton are just a few blocks outside your school zone. You'll be able to spend a lot of time with all of them."

"That's great news," Brandon said. "What about the others?"

"Some of them are close, others you might not meet in person for a few years since they are on other continents." Thorn shook his head. "I did the best we could, but you sprang some of them on me last minute."

"I did," Brandon nodded. "It's no problem. Are Carl and Wesley close?"

Thorn shook his head, "Wesley is an adult, so he'll likely quit his job and start making his way towards you. As for Carl," Thorn didn't look pleased. "The absolute best avatar I could find for him to inhabit has put him in some... unpleasant conditions."

"That's fine," Brandon said. "I'm not worried about Carl, he's very resilient. He will leave his placement early, likely, and find his way here."

Thorn nodded. "The rules for this game are on your computer. Learn them well. There are stages you can unlock, outside help you can bring in under certain circumstances, and a large assortment of other perks and rewards. Rules and prices for cheating death or, if someone gets killed, we might be able to put them back in. All of it is costly, though, so learn the game well. I will continue to do what I can, although it won't be very much, Son. This has to be your solution. My involvement could prevent you from going down a path that would lead to our salvation."

"I understand, Father," Brandon said. "Will I see you again soon?"

"You will only be allowed so many visits, including myself and others," Thorn said, "but yes, we will see each other again soon."

The white door appeared, signalling Thorn's time to depart had arrived. Brandon ran over and gave him another fierce hug, which Thorn returned with as much fervour.

"Good luck, Son."

Brandon smiled as Thorn walked towards the doorway. "Thanks, Dad."

After Thorn disappeared, Brandon looked around for a moment. Then, remembering the hard bunk that he'd spent most of his thirteen years sleeping on, he ran back to jump into his huge comfortable bed. Saving the world could wait for another hour or two.

===

Thorn and Cooper sat together, eating a meal. The two men were so busy that the only way to fit it all in was to do more than one activity at the same time.

"Did Brandon's group go in?" Cooper asked.

"Yes," Thorn said. "Each of the Elite teams are now inside their own private worlds."

"Some of them have interesting plans," Cooper said.

"That's what they were selected and trained to do," Thorn said, "come up with plans and execute them. The General believed that games could produce extraordinary results, and he was right. We've seen things over the years that most would never believe. I always loved the idea, even when I didn't agree with the specific tasks he was trying to accomplish."

"Do you think any of them can do it?"

"I don't know," Thorn said, "but I've pointed them all in the right direction. Brandon was right; doubling our odds of success is much better than a single chance."

Cooper chuckled. "Yes, and if each team makes a solid attempt, then we have thirty chances to find a solution within the next three months."

Thorn looked up from his food. "How many?" he asked.

"Thirty," Cooper said. "That's how many teams we just put into simulations. You knew that."

"I didn't really pay attention to the number before," Thorn said. "How many years does the simulation last?" he asked.

"Thirty years."

"Do you know how long the General's plan was?" Thorn asked. "His life plan for world domination that's in its final year?"

Cooper shook his head, then he saw Thorn's look and took a guess. "Thirty?"

"That's right."

"Does it mean anything, or is it just coincidence?"

"I've lived in computer simulations myself," Thorn admitted. "You've done three tours, I've done six."

Cooper whistled, "180 years, Doc, that's a lot of living."

"It is," Thorn nodded. "When you get to live a certain amount of years, you stop calling it coincidence, and start calling it fate."

"So what's it mean?"

"I have no idea," Thorn admitted. "Perhaps we won't live long enough to know."

The two men ate quietly. During desert, Cooper asked another question.

"Any idea where the General is?"

"I don't have a clue," Thorn said, "but if he's in the Sim, we have to find him, and soon."

<u>68</u>

The General couldn't move his head. They'd somehow rendered him immobile, even though nothing was physically touching his body.

At one point, as they released him from their invisible grip and he'd tumbled towards the cold, hard floor, he'd thought to himself, I really should have used the Sim for torture. Then he'd felt his face smash hard into the floor and his mouth had erupted into blazes of pain as his teeth broke, followed soon after by the sweet embrace of unconsciousness.

The worst part of the torture was waking up feeling great, and looking down to see not a single scratch or mark on his body. The General had learned how easy it was to repair an avatar so that it could be destroyed yet again. The days when he felt the best had become the most terrifying, because it meant they were about to start from the beginning and hurt him all over again.

Decades of easy living as the top man in the system, with years of having neglected his physical training, protected from harm by bodyguards, had made the General an easy subject to torture. On most days, less than five minutes into a session he was begging to tell them anything they wanted to hear. The General wasn't proud of it, but it was the plain and simple truth.

Of course they hadn't asked him for any information. Brad came in every morning, made some polite small talk and drank a cup of coffee. Then he went to the sink, washed his hands, and approached the General to begin the daily session of pain.

It was impossible to know how long he'd been here, but it seemed like eternity.

"Good morning, Donovan," Brad said as he opened the door. He swung it shut with his foot. He had two cups of coffee in his hands this morning, and a bag that must have some food in it. This was new.

"I thought we could take a little break and enjoy a hot beverage and a sinful pastry treat together. Would you like that, sir?"

Brad was being polite and respectful, two things that he'd not bothered to be since the General came here, but the General was too tired and worn down to mention it. He nodded his head slightly, hoping Brad could see the gesture, which apparently he did.

"That's wonderful, sir," Brad smiled. "I think we'll just have a little talk today, and if everything goes well, we can see about giving you a rest from our daily sessions. How does that sound?"

The General bit his lip to keep from weeping in relief and nodding his head wildly. Instead he blinked back the traitorous tears forming in his eyes as best as he could, and nodded slightly twice.

"That's great," Brad said. He pulled up two chairs and set the coffee and bag down beside one. He walked over to the General and, with a simple wave of his hand, released the invisible bonds that held him suspended in place.

They always left him anchored there against the wall when they were done with him; standing upright with his arms stretched outwards. Lack of blood flow and movement for so long had robbed him of his basic strength. The General fell to the ground with a heavy thud, where he lay unmoving. Brad stood over him with a pleasant look on his face, but made no motion to help the General stand. "I'm afraid if you want your treat, you'll have to come get it yourself."

Brad walked back and sat comfortably in one chair, reaching down to grab a coffee. He took a sip and pointedly looked away from the General, gazing with intense interest at some imaginary point on the wall. The General began to flop his arms and slowly moved his way towards the chair. Inch by painful inch, after what seemed like an eternity the weakened old man finally made it to the chair. He half leaned against it and panted for breath, his lungs burning and all of his strength used. With a look of desperation he croaked out the word, 'help' and raised his hand slightly towards Brad.

Brad looked down at the General. His face softened and he nodded with mock sympathy. "Well done, sir, well done! Here, let me help you the rest of the way." He lifted a hand and the General floated into the air and came to rest on the chair. He slowly began to slide sideways, but a strong invisible force held him securely. This time he was glad for the support.

Brad handed the second coffee to the General, who accepted it with a shaky hand and took a sip. It should have been cold after sitting so long, but it was scalding hot. The General burned his lip and the roof of his mouth, but he didn't flinch or care. After the things that had been done to him he barely felt the pain. He blew on the coffee and took rushed, greedy sips, afraid that Brad would suddenly change his mind and take the delicious liquid from him.

Brad sat comfortably as if they were two old friends sitting on a park bench on a lovely summer's day. "You've probably been wondering how I managed to stay alive," Brad said. He looked sideways at the General, who nodded weakly as if he was nodding off to sleep. "I guess I should thank you for putting that RFID in my neck and not my head. When you activated it I was landing in your enemies' airport. I know you said they wouldn't be interested in helping me, but it turns out that they were. That nasty little explosive blew quite the hole in my throat. There was a lot of pain and blood. It's hard to describe but don't worry, eventually I'll let you experience that sensation a few times, then you'll have a better understanding of what I mean. Anyway, they had a medical team right there in the plane with me and as soon as I blew, they got to work on me. I almost died a few times, but medical professionals really are amazing. They eventually fixed me up and put me into hiding so your spies wouldn't know that I had survived."

Brad paused and took a drink of his coffee. The General's coffee was gone. Brad noticed and handed him a pastry from the bag. The General began to shove the treat into his mouth noisily.

"So after a few months, I was healed enough to talk with them. I knew you very well, sir, and they were impressed. Spies kept an eye on you and I scoured every report looking for things that we could use against you. I was very excited when I learned about this virtual reality program and your work with Samson Thorn."

Brad took a bite of his pastry and kept talking. "At first we didn't know what to do with it, but then we found out Thorn had a helmet, and that he was going to be making millions of them to sell to the public. Well, by that time we already had our version of virtual reality, stolen from you — too easily, I might add, we knew you wanted us to have it and had to spend months finding and eliminating all the spyware and viruses — but we weren't sure how to get access to you. It was very shrewd and clever of you to never enter the Sim. I had your DNA, hair I'd collected from a comb, so we decided to set a trap for you. We bought every company who could possibly make the helmets and waited for the contracts to come in. Once we had the contracts, we installed a small program into every single helmet. It was a program that would recognize your DNA and, once you put a helmet on, would send you to our simulation instead of Thorn's. We've waited for years for you to break down and put a helmet on, sir. There were times when I actually thought you might never do it."

Brad smiled and patted the General on the knee. "But you did, and let me say that it was well worth the wait."

Brad stood up and brushed the crumbs off his pants. "Thank you for joining me for the drink and the chat, General. It was good to talk with you. We've been very busy with the sessions, and haven't talked much at all."

The General felt better after the nourishment and the drink, but he was still too weak to stand or speak.

"I'm gonna call it a day, now, and some nice men will come take to you to a room with a nice, comfortable bed for you to sleep on. We'll get you some food and let you rest up fully. How does that sound?"

The General knew it was likely a bad idea, but he was so weak, tired, and sore that he didn't care. If he was going to be tortured again, he preferred to sleep in a nice bed once more. He nodded and tried to smile.

"That's great," Brad said. "You rest up, sir, and when we meet in a couple days, I'll finally be able to start your sessions with some real intensity."

He walked out the door whistling.

The General sat there and hung his head. He couldn't hold back the tears any longer, and he began to sob.

69

"**I asked you** a few weeks ago about changing your names, but we didn't discuss it. How do you all feel about it?" Brandon asked the group.

They were sitting in a local restaurant that had become their regular hangout in the three years that they'd been inside Tygon 1.0, or simply Tygon as everyone now referred to it. Brandon, his Hand, Wesley and Carl were present; Wesley had pulled into town just a couple weeks after they entered the simulation, and Carl had appeared only a couple of months ago. He looked and acted... different in some ways, although Brandon couldn't tell whether that might be a problem or not. When they asked him what took so long, Carl had just shrugged and said, "Had some housekeeping to do."

"I have no problem with changing my name," Alan said. "What are you thinking, Brandon?"

"I'm thinking of making a major move in the business world," Brandon said. "Not until I turn eighteen in a couple of years, but if this takes off like I think it will, then I'm going to need you all in place close to me. My past is cloudy, being the son of a rich and powerful man who has paid to keep his family out of the press, but you guys could all be easily researched. When everything starts to fall in place, I think it would be easiest if searches turn up nothing."

Tony nodded. "We can set the parameters on new names so that the net doesn't retain or pool information about them."

Brandon nodded, "That's right."

Brandon and his hand had all learned a lot about computers in their past thirty year Sim, and this time around they were all ahead of their field. The five had graduated early from high school and were almost finished earning their university degrees. Easton was nineteen, and the other three were eighteen. Brandon remained the youngest at sixteen; everyone was hanging around waiting for him to become a legal adult before they made major plans.

"What's the move you're thinking of making?" Kay asked.

Brandon smiled, "There's a company called VirtDyne attempting to create working virtual reality technology."

Wesley laughed. "The timing on VR appearing here seems less than coincidental."

"Yeah, I think Thorn programmed it to occur this way," Brandon said. "I haven't spoken to him, but it seems like we need to control this technology from the beginning or it could turn bad like it did in the Dream."

"Is it functioning technology yet?" Carl asked.

Brandon shook his head, "No, and it won't be until I'm eighteen."

"How can you be so sure?" Alan asked.

"Because I infected the technology," Brandon smiled. "It won't work properly, no matter what they try."

"They can always remove the infection," Easton said.

Brandon shook his head, "It's a quantum logarithm which rotates and changes a thousand times per second. They'll never be able to isolate it long enough to fix it. I don't think they'll even detect it, since it mimics legitimate code for much of its life cycle."

"So what's the plan?" Wesley asked.

"You all change your names and we live life normally for the next two years," Brandon said.

Everyone laughed. Being finished school early and having a friend with the richest Dad in the world made for anything but a normal life. They spent most of their time travelling the world and having fun. They all knew that would soon change, but until then everyone was enjoying themselves.

"Okay," Brandon said. "We live normal lives for the next couple of years. Then, when I turn eighteen, I make a move to take control of VirtDyne."

"I assume it will be an easy thing to do?" Alan asked.

Brandon nodded, "By then I'll be able to walk in like the hero and save the day. The only other thing we need to do until then is to make certain that no one else develops working VR technology."

"We can take care of that," Easton waved his hand and the rest nodded. They would simply scan the net for any companies working on the technology and destroy their work. For these kids it was a simple task.

"Then I take control of the company and bring you all in to help me run it."

"Okay, then," Kay said, "shall we pick our new names now?"

Brandon nodded. "Yes, please. We'll use the reset function so that when we wake up tomorrow, everyone will call you by your new names and you'll have new documents that reflect the change. Don't worry, I'll make certain it doesn't alter your past history like a normal name change. The old names will exist with history, and these will move forward from tomorrow."

"I don't want to do it," Carl said.

"Why not?" Brandon asked.

"The only thing I've ever had is my name. I was abandoned by my parents and the Centre turned me into a killing machine. I know what they did, Brandon; they Blurred me. They took away my grip on reality and almost drove me insane. Or maybe they did drive me insane, but you brought me back."

"We don't have to worry about that, Carl," Alan said.

"I know," Carl shrugged. "Even coming into this Sim, the rest of you had it good and I had to fight and claw my way out of a garbage heap to get here. It's fine — there's nothing I can't handle and get through, but there have been a lot of times when the only thing that got me through was having something to hold onto, and that was my name."

The table was quiet; Carl looked up and shrugged. "I'm not saying I won't do it, Brandon, if that's absolutely what it's gonna take. I'm just saying I don't want to."

Brandon nodded and thought about it for a moment. "Okay, Carl. You can keep your name, and so can anyone else who wants to. Raise your hand if you want to keep your name."

Carl's hand was the only one that went up, and Brandon nodded.

"Okay," he said. "It looks like Carl and I will both keep our names, and everyone else will change theirs. Each of you tell me what you've decided on."

Wesley spoke up, "I like the biblical names they have in this world. I pick the name Daniel."

"Change my name to Gabriel," Tony said. "Not sure why, but I like that one."

Kay laughed, "You can start calling me Angelica."

"Alan?" Brandon asked.

"A lot of names ending in 'el' here," Alan said. "I wonder if that's some sort of sign? If it is, then I guess I'll add to it. I choose the name Raphael."

Brandon nodded and wrote the name down. "That just leaves you, Easton. You want one that ends in 'el' also?"

Easton squinted his eyes and stroked his chin thoughtfully. "No, I think I'll be like Kay and pick a name that ends differently."

"Okay," Brandon said. "What's it gonna be, then?"

Easton smiled. "I think I like the sound of the name Shane."

70

Cooper travelled ten levels below the main floor of the Game Facility to meet Thorn in the medical zone. He was standing beside the General, who lay quietly in a bed hooked up to monitors. He still wore the VR helmet.

"How long has he been like this?" Cooper asked.

"A couple of days," Thorn replied. "The helmet should have lost power and ejected him back to this reality long ago, but the power indicator shows that it's almost fully charged."

"The same thing is happening everywhere," Cooper said. "At first the helmets powered down after twelve hours or so, but now they all seem to last until the person dies."

Thorn nodded. "We've brought subjects here to figure out what's going on. The helmet seems to be much more than it appeared at first."

"Any theories?" Cooper asked.

"Yes," Thorn said. "I think the computer programming inside it has evolved, learning how to recharge itself from the bioelectric energy of the wearer."

"The person wearing it actually recharges the unit?"

"Exactly."

Cooper looked at the General. "Why isn't he hooked up to life support?"

"We're letting him die," Thorn said. "The helmet is supposed to sense any stresses or health issues, and eject a player so they can receive medical attention. Where ever the

General is, as his body becomes stressed from deterioration, he will hopefully return to us."

"Or die," Cooper said.

"Or die," Thorn agreed.

"Any idea where he is?"

Thorn nodded. "We traced the manufacturers of the helmets to their true source. Our enemies own the companies that build the helmets."

"What? How was that allowed?"

"It wasn't *allowed*, but it happened the same way we infiltrate their society and businesses — through time, patience, and layers of deceit."

Cooper nodded.

"Have you secured control of the General's military forces?" Thorn asked.

"Yes," Cooper said. "The chain of command has always fallen to me in the absence of the General. It was an easy transfer of power."

"Has the President contacted you?"

"She's left messages."

Thorn chuckled, "I would enjoy hearing those, I'm sure."

Cooper smiled. "She doesn't seem too pleasant in most of them."

"I want you to bring the bulk of the military to this location. Have them bring rations, water, and as much weaponry and ordnance as they can carry."

"I'll begin the process immediately."

"How long will it take to get them here?" Thorn asked.

"Less than a week."

"Good," Thorn looked up as the door opened and two nurses and a doctor entered. Thorn sand Cooper stepped aside to give them room.

The medical team began to hook the General up to additional sensors and they inserted an intravenous tube into his arm.

"What are they doing?" Cooper asked. "I thought you were going to let him deteriorate?"

Thorn shook his head as he watched the doctors and nurses go to work. "I allowed that when I thought the helmet would lose charge. If someone has the General, that isn't good news. The longer they have him, the greater the chances of him spilling secrets."

"So what are you doing?" Cooper asked.

"Now we are putting his body into accelerated distress."

"Killing him?"

Thorn nodded grimly, "If we have to, but I'm hoping our good medical professionals can trick the artificial intelligence of the helmet into thinking he's dying so that it'll eject him."

"What if they can't do it?"

Thorn looked at Cooper and shrugged. "Then we remove the General from enemy hands and continue on without him."

===

The General's head hung downwards, weak and exhausted from the current session with Brad.

He wished that he could raise his head, but this time they'd locked it downwards so he could watch. Brad had slowly and painfully skinned the General's lower torso. As the fiery pain spread and lingered, he'd had screamed so loudly, and for so long, that his voice had eventually left him.

Then Brad told the General he could heighten his sense of pain, which he did before resuming his work with a knife to remove the tendons and select muscles from the Generals flayed lower torso.

The heightened senses had shown the General that he could still scream some more.

For a few moments the General had lost consciousness, but he awoke to feelings of fire and throbbing liquid white pain. Through the haze, he saw Brad shake his head and heard him say that passing out wouldn't be allowed. The torture resumed.

That was hours ago.

The General had endured more than he thought he could. He knew that if he'd been in the normal world, he would have died days ago.

The General now knew the meaning of true helplessness and despair. Yet he still retained his sanity.

Early on, the General remembered his military training enough to form a small compartment in his mind and allow his true self to be hidden away safely. Then he'd locked the door and hoped it would hold long enough to survive this ordeal.

Now, inside the inner recesses of his brain, he could see Brad had found that door, and he was beginning to hammer at it with all his considerable might. Cracks were forming, and soon the door would break.

When it did, the General would be lost forever.

Suddenly the General felt a jolt. Something rushed through him that didn't hurt, but felt very strange. He lifted his head and looked at Brad questioningly.

Brad's confident smile was replaced by a frown. He walked quickly to grab the General's face and peer into his eyes. Then Brad's eyes turned to steel.

"Damn it! I was supposed to have more time. A lot more time!"

The General didn't understand, but he was too weak to speak. He just looked at Brad with confusion.

Brad looked at the General with disgust and spat on him. He turned away, and then suddenly he swung around and punched the General forcefully in the chest.

The General's eyes bulged as Brads hand penetrated his chest and gripped something deep inside him. With a laugh, Brad pulled his hand quickly towards himself, and the General felt the most horrifying pain. It made all the other pain seem like gentle tickles. Tears streamed down his face and he began to scream, but this time it was a primal, shrill screech.

In his hand, Brad held the General's beating heart. Blood ran down over his fingers as the heart pulsed strongly. He let it go and it floated in the air in front of the General's eyes. Brad turned around and walked to the sink. He turned on the water and washed his hands calmly, taking his time to scrub under his nails with soap.

The entire time, the General screamed in agony and watched his heart pump forcefully, suspended in the air in front of him.

Brad turned around and smiled at the General as he toweled his hands dry. "They want you back, Donovan," Brad said. "I don't think they can get you in time, but I hope they do. It's been fun, and well worth the wait. If they're able to bring you back, then I'm certain we will see each other again."

Brad walked towards the General and patted his face with the flat of his hand. "In the Sim, I own you now. If you live and come back in here, I will find you."

The General was beginning to lose consciousness. His eyes faded shut but he heard Brad's voice as he drifted off.

"When we meet again, I won't be so kind to you, General. Remember that."

===

The General opened his eyes and sat straight up on his hospital bed. He blinked twice, looked around, and then let out a blood curdling scream.

Thorn looked at Cooper calmly and nodded. "Looks like we got him back," he said.

71

"**Once this world** has Virtual Reality technology, they're going to go crazy." Easton said.

Brandon took a bite of his hamburger and chewed thoughtfully. He swallowed, wiped his mouth with a napkin, and flashed a smile. "Duh," he said.

Easton laughed and shook his head. "Shouldn't we just squash it? We aren't here to work with VR technology, we're here to learn how to design and program computers."

Brandon looked at Easton and raised his eyebrows.

"Okay, I know what you're going to say. Virtual reality functions entirely on quantum computing. There's no better method for developing and learning the field than by working with VR."

Brandon laughed. "You know what I'm going to say before I say it. Do I even need to be here for this conversation? Why don't I go see a movie with the others while you argue with yourself about what we're planning? As long as I get to win the conversation in your head, that is."

Easton smiled. "We've been a team for so many years now that it's only natural we all know what the other is thinking."

"I bet you don't know what I'm thinking at this exact moment," Brandon said.

Easton's smile disappeared. He looked at Brandon blankly for a moment and then shook his head.

"I'm wondering how long I have to wait until you betray the group."

Easton frowned and squinted his eyes, then cocked his head slightly. "Why are you asking me something so ridiculous? Have I ever betrayed the team?"

"Never," Brandon said with absolute certainty, "but that's what moles do, Easton, they infiltrate and eventually betray the group. If it hasn't happened yet, then it has to happen sometime."

Easton stared at Brandon, his composure relaxed and calm. "How long have you known?" he finally asked.

"Before I invited you to join the Hand," Brandon said.

Easton shook his head in disbelief. "Yet you still invited me? How could you keep it hidden all these years?"

Brandon smiled "I'm the best of us, remember? If you could keep it hidden, then so could I."

Easton nodded thoughtfully, looking guilty and ashamed for the first time that Brandon could ever remember. "Why bring it up now, then?" he asked.

Brandon sat forward and fixed Easton with an intense stare. "Because now it finally matters, Easton. For our entire lives we've just been playing harmless children's games. We've been put in here to learn the most we can, but I have another plan for this lifetime, and it relies on all of us working together like never before. Over the next thirty years, from inside a computer simulation, I think we can do something pretty impressive."

"What's that?" Easton asked.

"I intend to save our race from total annihilation," Brandon said.

The two sat quietly for a time.

"The General approached me personally," Easton said. "He told me I would be doing him a great service to infiltrate your Hand and help you develop as a team."

Easton looked up at Brandon. Brandon nodded quietly for Easton to continue.

"He said that there would come a time when I'd need to share information with him about you. That he might need me to bring you down at a crucial moment during a game, or even after that, once we'd graduated and become a real Hand in his army."

"When he would come to you," Brandon said, "for information about us. What did you tell him?"

"I told him what was safe to tell him, and that's all. I swear to you that I never once told him anything secret that he couldn't have learned from other sources."

"And during crucial moments of games? Did you throw opportunities that caused us to lose?"

Easton shook his head vehemently, "Never! I'm sure you can recall many times over the years when I would recommend a change to your plans? When you wanted to use me for a specific role and I would encourage someone else to perform the task?"

Brandon nodded.

"That was how I helped us win and still kept the General's trust. I would tell the General that you made changes at the last moment and put me out of the situation he wanted ruined."

"You removed yourself from situations to avoid throwing games," Brandon said, "but that could have put us in danger of still losing. If you were the best person to do the task but persuaded us to use another team member, then you were still effectively helping the General."

Easton smiled proudly, "When no one else could do the job as well as me, and the General ordered me to fail, then I disobeyed the General and did my best for you and the Hand. Every time, without fail."

Brandon scrutinized Easton for a moment, then nodded. "You have always been on our side, Easton. When I brought you in I knew the game you played. I hoped that being part of something more would persuade you to be with us. It's impossible to have two lovers and be faithful to both, Easton."

"I know, Brandon," Easton said. "That's why I chose the Hand years ago. I can assure you that I will never betray you or the team. We're family, and I think my character and record have shown you that I can be trusted."

Brandon took a bite of his burger and smiled. "I believe you, brother. I'm glad we finally had this conversation. It's been hanging over us for years."

Easton smiled and nodded. "I agree, brother."

"Let's finish lunch and go to a movie," Brandon said. "I'll text the others to meet us."

72

Brandon Strayne's eighteenth birthday party was an extravagant event. His father, feeling guilty for never being around during the boy's upbringing, spared no expense when it came to celebrating this coming-of-age celebration.

During a brief and rare moment, he embraced Brandon and told him that they would spend much more time together now that Brandon was a man. Brandon smiled graciously and returned the hug, acknowledging in his mind that this father was just an empty computer NPC doing the best that it could, even though it wasn't enough to make a difference in the life of a son. Then, his father slapped him on the shoulder and apologized for having to leave immediately for a business meeting on another continent, and he had left.

Brandon laughed and went to join his true friends, the ones he'd spent his lives with, the ones who would help with his bold plan to save the Dream.

After enjoying a private and lavish dinner, Brandon stood in the small, private room, surrounded by his closest friends, and proposed a toast.

"Today we gather here not to celebrate another birthday, but to begin the operation that we've been planning for the past five years."

Brandon sat down before continuing to speak. The room was small, and there were only twelve people present. He didn't need to stand like some great leader addressing his troops before a historic battle, although that is exactly who he was, and what he was doing.

"This world perfectly mirrors our own before it was struck by the virtual reality plague. Thorn wants us to live a full and constructive life here so that when we get back to the Dream, we'll have the tools to help him fix the tremendous problem created by a game."

His friends nodded in agreement.

"If this world is like ours, then we can do more than learn here, we can create our own virtual reality simulations. We can work on fixing the problem out there, from inside this reality. Time is running out in our world, but here we have more than mere months, we have decades."

"Tomorrow I approach VirtDyne and begin the process to acquire the company and its technology. You all know your initial roles. We will constantly communicate and adapt to what needs attention, modifying each of your parts in this operation as required. We've spent our entire lives playing games for this moment. I will be the face everyone sees, but each of you helps to make up the team that will make this happen. The skills and experience we have in this room are extensive, and I know we can succeed."

Brandon raised his glass as did the others. "To the Game," he toasted.

"To the Game!" the others cheered.

73

"**They're developing virtual** reality technology, Lohkam."

Lohkam looked up from his computer screen and frowned. "Who is?" he asked.

"Some company called VirtDyne," his team mate said, turning his monitor to face Lohkam and tapping the screen to point at the news feed. "Says they're having a few issues, but they expect to get the bugs out very shortly and will soon be introducing the technology to the world. Experts predict that it'll change the way everyone does business and plays games."

Lohkam snorted and looked back towards his monitor. "There's an understatement for ya," he said.

"Should we do something about it?"

"Give me a second. I'm about to do something right now." Lohkam said. He pulled up a number from his computer directory and initiated contact with one of his other teammates off-site.

"Hey, Boss, what's the word?" The man on the view screen was a handsome man dressed in a business suit standing on the street in the busiest city of Tygon. He was tall and athletic, with dark hair and blue eyes.

"VirtDyne is the word," Lohkam said.

The man nodded. He took out a hand held device and typed the name into it. "Okay, what do I do with it?"

"Find out who runs the company, who the major stockholders are, and how close they are to making their technology operational."

"What are they working on?" the man asked.

Lohkam frowned. "VR technology," he said.

"Oh, crap," his team mate said. "This is top priority?"

"Absolutely," Lohkam nodded. "Word is that they're having trouble keeping people alive when they put them inside the Sim, but I want to confirm that."

The man on the street nodded. "Okay, Boss, I'll get right on it."

"Good," Lohkam said. "If you find out they have it working, or will soon have it working, go in and kill them. Then lock it down until we get there."

"Kill who? The programmers?"

"All of them," Lohkam said. "Right down to the janitor who cleans the building at night."

The man nodded comfortably. "Roger, Boss. Anything else?"

"They likely aren't up and running. Confirm where they are right away, Randy, I want to contain this and control it."

Lohkam concluded the call and brought up the screen he'd been working on before. "Let me know if you find anything else, boys." He said to the others in the office.

The two men nodded and kept working.

===

"There's a VirtDyne in two simulations?" Cooper asked Thorn as he looked up from reading update reports on the Elites' progress.

"There's a VirtDyne in every Elite simulation," Thorn said. "Each Elite group's simulation began identically the same way," Thorn nodded. "How they interact with their world will change it, but until a certain point we've replicated the same conditions for each of them. The natural progression of their reality will lead Tygon 1.0 down the same path as our world. Each team will alter the outcome, first by their direct involvement, and then by the ripples that their actions cause."

"Why only the Elites?" Cooper asked. "You could theoretically create simulations within simulations and, within just a few weeks, have millions of individuals working on the problem. The more chances you have the better, right?"

Thorn frowned and shook his head. "Thirty simulations is all we could manage. The drain that the population is causing on our energy and computing resources is greater than we anticipated, and it's increasing each day. Also, if they build a simulation within the simulation it draws even more power from our grid, exponentially more. So if they made a VR world, and then another inside that one, and then another inside that one... it would exceed the resources of our power grid very quickly and it would all shut down."

"How do you prevent it from happening?" Cooper asked.

"We put limitations on the physics of the simulation," Thorn answered. "If they try to go too deep it simply will not work, they won't be able to get around it, because the simulation won't allow it. It's a big enough struggle keeping thirty simulations going along with the worldwide Tygon 3.0 game. We're trying to eject players safely and permanently, but they're banding together and forming defensive compounds to enable each other to play."

Cooper nodded, "Game nodes," he said. "We've tried to raid some of them, but they're fortified and protected. It's not worth losing my soldiers to stop a few Baggers from playing a stupid Sim."

"Exactly," Thorn said. "The best I could do was send in the Elites and hope they can do something. Maybe one or two of them will be clever enough to build games within their own realities, but I couldn't suggest it."

"Why not?" Cooper asked.

"I don't want to get in their way," Thorn said. "These kids are brilliant. They've solved hundreds of impossible challenges over the years. Planting certain ideas in their heads might cause them to be stuck on a tangent, resulting in them spending their entire lives on the wrong track."

"I doubt your involvement would have hurt," Cooper said.

"It's not a chance we can afford to take," Thorn said. "Besides, we have other options to fix this. The Elites are one possible solution; our safest and best if they can come up with something, but there are other ideas to implement."

"What if they don't succeed?"

Thorn's face became grim. "Then we initiate the Beta option."

"When?"

"The Elites come out of their simulations all at the same time, three months after they entered. If none of them have shown us a solution by then, we hit the button immediately."

"Refresh me on what the Beta option is, because it sounds more like the Omega option."

Thorn shook his head. "The Beta option is to shut down the servers totally, killing everyone who is inside Tygon 3.0."

"How many people is that?"

"Current count is two billion people," Thorn said.

"It won't be more than that in a couple of months," Cooper assured him. "They stopped shipping helmets, right?"

Thorn shook his head. "There are techies springing up out there who can build their own versions of the helmets. If you're a 'builder,' as they call them, you quickly become a very popular — and wealthy — member of the VR community."

"This is insane," Cooper shook his head.

"This is a challenge, but there's still hope," Thorn said. "If we finally get to the Omega option... that will be when it's truly insane."

74

Brandon stood at the front of the conference room wearing a custom tailored black suit. His hair was professionally styled and he was clean shaven, although at eighteen facial hair wasn't much of an issue. An attractive platinum watch peeked out from his right cuff as he reached for a glass of water from the small table nearby. Taking a sip, he gazed out confidently at his audience. A small group composed of twenty men and women sat around a very elegant conference table. All of them regarded him with impassive faces and straight backs. They were the controlling board members and major stockholders of VirtDyne, a group of wealthy people backed against the wall by failure and misfortune.

Their company was failing, and they had gathered today at the request of Brandon Strayne to hear his proposal for saving it from certain death. It was obvious from the looks on their faces that they expected nothing but empty promises and unrealistic results from this young man, but they were sitting here because their only alternative was to accept failure and financial ruin.

Brandon smiled warmly as he began his address.

"I would like to thank you for agreeing to meet with me today. I have followed your company with intent interest during these past two years, and I'm as disappointed as you to hear of its difficulties."

Brandon scanned the crowd and noticed some of the attendees visibly squirming in their seats. They were most likely the ones who would be completely ruined when VirtDyne closed its doors. He mentally noted these individuals; they could be his strongest supporters.

"Most of you know my father by reputation; some have even worked with him in the past." A few people nodded in agreement. "But none of you likely know much about me." He flashed them a wide grin, "I have sufficient funds to buy into this company as a shareholder, and I'm certain the money would help keep you afloat for a few more months." Some people looked at each other hopefully, nodding as if this would be desirable.

Brandon shook his head and continued to speak. "That isn't going to happen. I might be young, but I'm certainly not foolish when it comes to money, business, or computer technology."

He began to slowly move back and forth on his small stage, making eye contact with people as he spoke. "To spend money on a business that can't produce a working product would be a waste of time, and so I won't offer you any."

Some members began to grumble and mutter to each other, while others scowled and looked at their watches with impatience.

"Instead, I'm here to offer the thing that everyone in this room needs most." Brandon stopped in the middle of the stage, paused, and then raised his right hand. "I'm here to offer you fully functioning virtual reality technology."

Brandon put his arms behind his back and waited quietly.

"Kid hasn't got a clue of what he's talking about," one man said.

"There's no way a child could fix something that the best programmers in the world can't solve," said another.

"His father is a computing genius," one shareholder mumbled.

"We have nothing to lose by letting him try,"

"It's not like he can do worse, people have already died,"

As the volume of conversation increased, Brandon listened closely and could hear two streams forming; one for him, and one against. Minutes passed, and as the noise grew to a loud crescendo, an older man dressed as impeccably as Brandon stood up and spoke.

"That's enough," his deep voice boomed loudly, sounding like a fog horn being blown inside a tunnel. "Let the young man finish his proposal."

The room quieted, and the man swept his arm towards Brandon and nodded. "Please go on."

"Thank you," Brandon said. "Instead of money, I propose to buy into VirtDyne with expertise and results." He looked pointedly at the people who could lose the most and continued. "I'll come to work at VirtDyne and take no wage. I'll deliver fully functioning virtual reality technology, providing the results that VirtDyne has promised to Tygon."

There was more talking and discussion, but the old man raised his hand for silence. "What do you want if you succeed?" he asked, getting straight to the point.

Brandon smiled, "I want a 51 percent controlling interest in VirtDyne."

People shot out of their seats and started shouting at Brandon, pointing at each other and raising their hands in outrage. Brandon smiled calmly and let them rage at the offer. After a few moments he straightened his tie, adjusted his cuffs, and began to walk towards the door. As he opened the door, he heard someone call for quiet again and he paused.

"That's a very large demand," the old man said.

Brandon turned around and looked at the man. Control of VirtDyne currently rested with this gentleman, who'd founded the company years ago with a bold vision and an aggressive plan. Brandon walked back towards the stage with a nod.

"It is a large demand," he said, "if it were for a company that had a product to sell." He looked at the shareholders and his smile faded to be replaced by a look of disgust. "I don't see that, though. I see a company with massive debt, stockholders who've spent all their money on failure, and a product whose only accomplishment so far has been to kill dozens of people."

He held his hands up before anyone could protest, the smile back on his face. "I assure you, folks, I can make this thing work. When I do, then you'll all be extremely wealthy. I think you might as well take one more chance. What's the worst that could happen? The company will die and you lose all your investment?"

People slowly nodded, they knew there was nothing to lose at this point, and everything to gain. Brandon had left this meeting until the last possible moment; he knew they were desperate for any chance, and he'd made certain that this was the only offer they would get.

The old man stood up and looked at the crowd. "We don't have time to debate this for weeks, you all know that. Let's put it to a vote now. Those of you who want to take one more roll of the dice and agree to Mr. Strayne's proposal, raise your hand. Those who want to lose everything invested so far, keep silent. Who's interested?"

The vote was unanimous as everyone's hand shot into the air. The look of hope was visible on many faces. Brandon smiled and nodded positively; he knew it wouldn't take long to get the VR technology up and working. Standing at the front of the room, Brandon raised his hands and smiled.

He'd just become a very powerful man.

75

Many of you may recall VirtDyne, the company that unsuccessfully attempted to invent and implement virtual reality technology over the past few years. Less than one month ago, founder and CEO Bertrand Crain indicated that the company would be shutting its doors due to repeated failures and lack of direction. Yesterday, Mr. Crain shocked the world by announcing that the company had completely turned things around and achieved success in creating a safe, reliable virtual reality experience.

Now the world is buzzing at the limitless possibilities that this new medium will bring. The business community is lining up at VirtDyne's door to tap into the marketing and sales potential, the entertainment industry is clamouring to get an audience with VirtDyne's top brass, and every other significant power on Tygon is posturing for an opportunity to discuss using the new technology.

This morning the world was shocked yet again, when Mr. Crain announced that he would be stepping down as CEO of VirtDyne. During what should be the greatest moment of his career, he's announced that his replacement is to be none other than Brandon Strayne. Everyone knows Russell Strayne, the world's most brilliant computer innovator and programmer, but his son Brandon turned eighteen only a few weeks ago.

It appears that Brandon Strayne's entrance onto the world stage has eclipsed even that of his father.

News report

"**This is outrageous!**" Bertrand Crain bellowed as he slammed his fist on the table in anger.

Brandon sat and looked at Bertrand curiously.

"You can't simply remove me from the equation, Brandon. I built this company from the ground up. For years I've invested and encouraged others to believe in this dream. VirtDyne would be nothing without my vision!"

Brandon smiled coldly. "Are we really having this conversation, Bertrand?" he asked. "Do you seriously believe the words dribbling out of your mouth?"

Bertrand looked at Brandon for a moment, his mouth moving but making no sound. The man was angry, which Brandon could understand, but he had no patience to listen to him whine because a deal made in desperation suddenly came to pass. He started to say something, but Brandon held up his hand to silence him.

"The deal has been struck, Bertrand. 51 percent of the company already belongs to me. The offer I'm making you right now is for an additional 30 percent of the remaining stock. A portion of that 30 percent is yours; I've already spoken with other shareholders and they've accepted. Now listen carefully to my offer, and either nod your head to indicate yes or no when I'm done making it."

Bertrand's face turned red but he said nothing.

Brandon nodded. "Stock price prior to our announcement was five credits per share. After we made the announcement, it jumped to more than 300 credits per share."

Bertrand couldn't help but smile at that. No company had ever made such a leap in value in the history of Tygon.

"I estimate," Brandon continued, "that the shares will drop in value significantly after my next announcement, but you shouldn't be penalized for that, so here's my offer to you. I will pay you 600 credits per share."

Bertrand's eyes widened in surprise. From the 300 credit jump he was already an incredibly wealthy man. This additional offer made him instantly one of the wealthiest men in the entire world. Still wanting to maintain some semblance of control, Bertrand nodded thoughtfully and tried to prevent his grin from surfacing. "I would like some time to think about the offer, if you don't mind?" he said.

Brandon smiled amiably and nodded. "Of course, Bertrand." Then his eyes turned to ice and his smile disappeared. He pushed a piece of paper towards the old man and placed a pen on top of it. "You have thirty seconds."

Bertrand quickly grabbed for the pen and scribbled his signature on the bottom of the agreement. He stood up and shook hands with Brandon. "It's been a great pleasure doing business with you, Brandon. I wish you good luck."

Brandon grinned. "Thanks, Bertrand. Luck is always welcome in my games."

76

Three months ago, Brandon Strayne entered the world stage and turned finance and technology on its head. When his company, VirtDyne, announced that they'd successfully invented virtual reality technology, investors couldn't buy stock fast enough. Share prices soared overnight from five credits to 300, and the world lined up at Brandon's door to discuss integrating the new technology into their business models.

Not one single deal has been struck during the past three months and stock prices have dropped at an alarming rate considering Mr. Strayne's recent press conference.

Mr. Strayne announced this week that VirtDyne will not be making their technology available to any business or commercial venture. Instead he stated that his company will commit their resources entirely to developing a new and more effective type of educational system. Children will be submersed in a virtual reality world where they will learn at an accelerated pace. Initially met with skepticism and doubt, VirtDyne convinced a few small countries to try this new schooling method for a period of two months.

Early results are showing that students of this virtual reality school are scoring significantly better than children who attend traditional facilities, which is causing most countries to take notice and consider the new option as well.

Society has been in a state of decline for some years now, with the gap between classes widening drastically. Experts around the world are praising Brandon Strayne's new virtual school and labelling it, 'The best hope for the future of our planet.'

Mr. Strayne adamantly maintains that he will not allow his technology to be used for anything other than this educational program, which he has named, 'the Game.'

The world continues to watch developments unfold...

Carl sat at the bar and nursed his drink. Occasionally his gaze went to the mirror behind the bar, resting on a wealthy man sitting at a booth.

The man was laughing and pouring drinks for three women and one man. The women were obviously hired; they were too beautiful and laughed just a bit too much to be girlfriends or wives. The group had been here for the past three hours, partying and making noise, drinks and food moving back and forth in a constant train of servers from the bar to the table. This was a popular hangout for the rich clientele of the business district, and Carl knew the man came here at least two or three times a week to relax and unwind. This man was a very powerful individual in the business world, so powerful that he'd aggressively pursued VirtDyne, trying to force them to work with his company to incorporate VR technology into his business. Two days ago, during a personal meeting with Brandon Strayne, this man had threatened to make Brandon sorry if he continued to refuse a working relationship. Brandon had nodded and agreed to consider the proposal more seriously.

Tonight, the man would die for threatening Brandon and his plan.

Carl sat patiently at the bar, sipping his drink and waiting for the man to leave. Two hours later, the man pulled out a wad of bills from his pants and dropped it clumsily onto the table top. He stood up, grabbed one blonde woman around the waist, and began to weave his way towards the exit. Carl finished his drink and left money on the bar, then stood up and left through the same door.

The man was standing at the curb, holding onto the blonde girl tightly he wobbled uncertainly from the effects of accumulated alcohol. " Wheresh the limo?" his voice slurred turning his head raggedly from side to side.

Carl approached him and grabbed his arm lightly. "It's right this way, sir," he said. "I moved it out of the view of the press and photographers. If you'll just follow me, we'll get you home right away."

The man peered intently at Carl, his eyes trying to focus on the man offering help. "Are you my normal driver?" he asked. "You don' look like my normal driver."

Carl smiled pleasantly, "He's sick tonight, sir. I've driven for you before; my name is Dan."

The man tilted his head and then nodded confidently. "Oh, thash right. Heya, Dan, wheresh the car parked?"

"It's right this way, sir," Carl began to walk towards the alley, still holding the man's arm. The girl started to follow them, but Carl looked at her and shook his head slowly. She sensed danger, and quickly walked away in the opposite direction.

Carl put the man into the back seat of the car, got into the driver's seat, and pulled out of the parking lot.

"Where are we goin', Dan?" the man slurred from the back. "I don' think this ish the way home." Carl ignored him and continued to drive.

Ten minutes later, Carl pulled into a quiet area under a bridge. There were no cameras and the area was poorly lit. He turned the motor off, got out of the vehicle and walked around to the back passenger side door. Reaching in, he grabbed the man and roughly dragged him out.

"Hey! What're you doin', Dan?"

"Quiet," Carl growled. He placed the palm of his hand against the man's head and felt the energy transfer begin. A few moments later the man's eyes became clear, his drunkenness completely gone.

"Wow, I feel totally sober," the man said. Then he looked up at Carl as if seeing him for the first time. "Wait a minute, you're not Dan. Who are you?"

Carl's mouth pulled back to reveal his teeth in more of a snarl than smile. "I'm the man you meet when you threaten Brandon Strayne," he said, pulling the man up effortlessly so that he was now standing.

The man looked around, seeing that he was alone and completely unprotected. He began to stammer. "Please, I meant nothing by it. It's just business. I wanted to do a deal with Strayne and he was playing hardball. I had to say something to try and get his attention."

Carl pulled out a knife and held it in front of him. "I think you got his attention, sheep," he said. "I also believe Mr. Strayne agreed to join you for a game of hardball."

Before the man could say anything else, Carl slid the knife between his ribs and into his heart. He watched the man curiously as life slowly drained from his body, then he let him drop to the ground.

Carl cleaned his blade, got back into the vehicle, and drove away.

77

"I don't know exactly why Mr. Strayne has declined to sell his virtual reality technology to private businesses, but I can tell you that it's a great relief that he has. Many jobs would be lost if companies began to use computer generated resources instead of the physical components currently used. I for one am a supporter of Brandon Strayne, and I hope that his new education system brings about effective and lasting change to Tygon."

Businesswoman Lilith Avernare

"**Mr. Thorn is** here to see you, Sir,"

"Send him in right away." Brandon stood up and walked towards the door.

A moment later the door opened and a pretty secretary held it open for Thorn. He smiled and nodded at her as he entered the room.

"Thank you, Jenn," Brandon said. "That will be all for now,"

"Of course, Brandon," the young woman smiled and closed the door.

Thorn shook his head as the door closed. "They could very well be my greatest creation," he said.

"Who could?" Brandon asked.

"NPCs," Thorn said. "When I first created them, they were mindless automatons, placed in situations to carry out simple tasks. Then we installed better programming to make them witty opponents against players in the Sim. Next, I took what

I'd learned and increased the programming parameters to allow them to learn, feel, teach, and replicate. They then began to evolve by passing on their information from one generation to the next. I've developed simulations where NPCs have lived normal existences and reproduced for millions of generations."

"Really?" Brandon asked. "I had no idea."

"Oh, yes," Thorn said. "Now look at how they act. Extremely realistic."

Brandon nodded, "When I entered my first thirty year Sim, I was concerned that I'd go insane from being all alone in a world with only NPCs for company, but I was surprised to learn that they are just like you and me."

Thorn chuckled, "There's nothing that is as similar to us as they now are, but there are still some differences."

"But that might not always be the case," Brandon said. "If they continue to evolve... you may have created an entirely new sentient, self-aware species."

Thorn nodded thoughtfully, and then he shook his head. "Enough talk about NPCs, I'm here to discuss the developments going on in your reality at the moment."

Thorn walked over to the window to admire the view. Brandon got them both a drink and came to stand beside him.

"When people knew that I had working VR technology," Thorn said, "I needed to quickly choose a partner powerful enough to protect me and rich enough to fund my development. You've managed to do both and stay totally independent; an impressive accomplishment in such a dangerous environment."

"I had help," Brandon said. "I'm sure if you'd had a team like mine, you would have fared better than I have, Father."

"Maybe," Thorn said, continuing to look out over the skyline. "How are things progressing?" he asked.

Brandon sighed. "On track. I wish I had more time, though. I'm twenty now, which means I've spent seven years here already. Twenty-three years is aggressive for what I'm planning."

Thorn nodded.

"I guess we'll just do the best that we can," Brandon said. "If we fail, then there's still time to try your other alternatives."

"About that," Thorn said. Something in his tone made Brandon glance at him with concern.

"What's wrong, Father?" Brandon asked.

"The situation has escalated in the Dream," Thorn said.

"Escalated, how?" Brandon asked.

"Time is running out," Thorn said. "Everything is deteriorating much more quickly than I'd anticipated. I'm afraid there won't be enough time to try anything else. This experiment... you are our last hope."

"What's happening?"

"We can no longer stop people from entering the simulation."

"Of course you can," Brandon said. "You told me you stopped producing VR helmets. If a person doesn't possess a helmet, then there's no way to enter the game, right?"

"There is another way into the simulation," Thorn nodded. "The purpose of the helmets was to focus the subject's brain waves to a specific wavelength. We selected a familiar wavelength for the brain so that people could stay inside the simulation longer. I didn't think it would become a problem, but it has."

"What wavelength is it?" Brandon asked.

"The same one that we generate during sleep," Thorn said.

"Oh."

"Yes. Oh." Thorn said. "People are beginning to enter Tygon 3.0 without the aid of any electronic focusing devices, when they fall asleep."

"Do they exit the simulation when they wake up?"

Thorn shook his head. "They don't wake up."

"Is there any way to prevent it from happening?"

Thorn nodded, "If we can get them to shielded underground locations, then we can prevent them from being pulled into Tygon 3.0. We don't have the resources to gather large numbers of people, nor do we have large shielded facilities. In a very short time, the entire population is going to be pulled into Tygon 3.0 against their will when they fall asleep, and once inside the simulation they will have no way to get out."

Brandon considered this new information, taking a drink and looking out the window.

"So you have to wake them up, somehow." He finally announced.

"Yes," Thorn nodded.

"Shutting the simulation off won't work," Brandon said. "That's like closing the only gateway back to reality."

"Correct."

"Why don't they try to get back?"

"Because," Thorn said, "they forget there is anywhere else to get back to."

"What do you mean?" Brandon asked.

"We can observe players inside Tygon 3.0, and it appears that they believe the VR Sim is their only reality. There are billions of souls trapped inside a virtual prison who have no idea that they aren't where they're supposed to be."

Brandon nodded thoughtfully, "Okay," he said, "I can simulate that."

"Where?" Thorn asked.

"Inside my Game here," Brandon said. "Do you have any idea how long it will take for everyone in the Dream to transfer into Tygon 3.0 from going to sleep?"

"I estimate that by the end of this month, everyone except myself and a few thousand key people will be immersed in Tygon 3.0."

"How can you protect yourself?"

"We are underground, and protected by layers of concrete and minerals."

"Will the servers lose power and go dead?" Brandon asked.

"Not for six months, at least," Thorn said. "I have a generator and enough power underground to keep Tygon 3.0 online for that long."

"How long can the bodies live while their minds are inside the simulation?"

"Less than six months," Thorn confirmed.

"How much less than six months?"

"I'm not sure," Thorn admitted. "The body seems to slow its function down considerably when the mind enters the simulation. I've seen some live for three to five months."

"That's incredible," Brandon said.

"Yes," Thorn agreed.

Brandon considered this information, writing key points down and making notes furiously in a black notebook.

"Since you are now our best hope of finding a solution," Thorn said, "I've managed to increase your stay in this simulation."

"By how long?" Brandon asked.

"It's uncertain. The mainframe that runs this simulation has been set to monitor the situation in reality. There will come a point when most of the bodies on our planet will begin to die in mass numbers. Just before that occurs, the mainframe running this simulation will give you a sign and begin a countdown. "'I'm not sure how clear it will be, but there will be indicators." Thorn made a wry face, "If I had to guess, you likely have thirty more years from a set date in your reality here."

"Why thirty?"

Thorn raised an eyebrow. "It's a number that keeps coming up."

Brandon sighed and looked at his notes. "Let me recap what you're saying, then."

"Go ahead."

"I have maybe thirty years to figure out how to wake the entire world out of a virtual reality simulation before their real bodies die?"

"You make it sound simple," Thorn said.

Brandon nodded confidently, "One of us will find a way. It's a good thing you have thirty of your best minds all working on it for thirty years."

Thorn nodded. "You're our best hope, Brandon. You truly are the best Gamer I've ever seen."

Thorn stood up to leave, pausing as he reached the door. "One more thing," he said. "Tygon 3.0 is a mouthful, so I've changed the name of that simulation."

"To what?" Brandon asked.

"Earth," Thorn said.

===

Thorn took his helmet off and placed it carefully on the desk. He stood up and walked down the hallway to a large room. Thirty tables were spread evenly around the room, each holding an elite leader. Their teammates were in adjacent rooms.

Cooper leaned against the wall, looking out over the tables. Thorn came to stand beside him.

"How's the General doing?" Thorn asked.

"He's responding to my voice now," Cooper said. "He still isn't talking, and his eyes look a bit... unstable, but I think he's coming around."

"Good," Thorn said. "We'll need his help."

Cooper nodded at Brandon's still form on his table."You told him more than I thought you would," he said, referring to Thorn's conversation with Brandon just a few moments ago.

"I had to make it clear to him that he's our best chance for surviving this."

Cooper nodded his head at the tables in front of him. "He's our only chance for survival now."

Thorn looked at the bodies lying on the tables, sheets fully draped over twenty-nine of them, the monitors turned off and unhooked. Twenty-nine of the best teams the game facility had produced, 172 children, were now dead because their simulations had been powered down while they were inside. Brandon and his team were the only ones still connected to their simulation, and therefore the only ones who could be brought back. Keeping the other teams alive after turning off their simulations would have meant spending wasted energy on maintaining empty biological husks, so Thorn had ordered them disconnected from life support.

"The power drain was too great," Thorn shook his head. "We could only keep one running and be sure it would last the full length of the program. I had to make a choice."

"Do you think it was the right one, Doc?" Cooper asked.

"Yes," Thorn said. "Do you?"

Cooper looked at Brandon for a few moments, "Yeah," he said, "I think so."

<u>78</u>

"Something's different, Lock,"

Lohkam frowned, he could feel it too. "I agree, but what? Can anyone put their finger on it?" he asked. The other members of his Hand surrounded him as they walked down the street. Lohkam wasn't sure where they were going; he could distinctly remember being away from his teammates a moment ago and on his way to dinner with a cute girl he'd met the other night at a club.

"I was in a different city, heading to meet with that jewel dealer," one of his teammates said.

"Whoah, wait just a minute!"

"What?" Lohkam stopped and the entire group stopped with him.

Aaron, the team member who'd stopped them, pointed up at a large building. "Either we glitched, or we aren't in our Sim anymore."

Lohkam followed Aaron's gaze to a large sign that read "VirtDyne."

"You're right," he said. "We took that sign down when we dissolved the company. We're not in our Sim."

"What kind of game are they playing with us?" one of the others asked. "They told us they wouldn't Blurr us or switch things up without our knowledge."

"I have no idea," Lohkam said. "Let's go see who owns that business. Then we'll try to figure out where we are and how to proceed."

79

Joe never dreamed.

That likely wasn't true. Everyone dreams when they sleep, it's just that Joe didn't remember ever having one. Whenever he'd heard others talk about dreams, he would shake his head and tell them that he'd never dreamt once during his entire 42 years on the planet.

Tonight was different, though. When Joe closed his eyes, he opened them almost immediately and looked around with a mixture of wonder and surprise.

There was no doubt in his mind that he was dreaming...

He'd been watching the news reports about the new virtual reality game called 'Tygon 3.0' that everyone was playing. Joe had always been a gamer; getting older hadn't stopped him from keeping up with the new computer games and being able to compete with the kids. Reviews of Tygon 3.0 started to spread around the globe, and everyone talked about how real it was, but something made Joe decide to pass on playing it. Friends and family were surprised that he wasn't in line to buy the first special editions. Joe was known for getting the special perks that came to early adopters, but this time he wasn't interested. When people asked him why, his answer was simple.

"It looks too much like real life," he'd said with a shake of his head.

All the reviews agreed with Joe, but everyone else seemed to view that as a positive fact. Joe had continued to stay away, even when some of his close friends and family members who'd never played games before told him that they were playing and that he would love it.

"If I want to spend time working in a restaurant, or building a successful business, or learning how to fly an airplane, then I'll go ahead and do that in real life," he'd said with a smile.

Weeks later, Joe watched with interest as increasingly more people began to play Tygon 3.0. Weeks after that, he'd watched in alarm as millions of people from every facet of society began to ignore the real world in favour of playing inside a virtual one.

Then it had gotten even worse as local municipalities began to decline. Most towns and cities were no longer picking up garbage or delivering fresh water to households; the world was in grave danger. News reported that people simply stopped showing up for work because they were too busy living inside the virtual game. Power companies began to struggle with keeping neighbourhoods lit and heated during the nights, and society slowly toppled from being inconvenienced into full blown crisis.

Eventually, people began to die.

Not violent deaths; lazy deaths caused by a lack of desire to exit virtual reality to take care of necessary things, like eating. Violence came later when Thorn Inc., the company who had invented the game, stopped making VR helmets in an attempt to prevent people from playing.

It was at that point that Joe had packed up his family and grabbed as many supplies as possible, then headed for the woods to escape the looting, and stealing, and violence that was spreading like a rampant disease.

Most people left Joe alone once they saw his size and the serious set of his eyes. They walked towards the wilderness on the horizon for three days, searching for safe places to hole up on their journey.

On the third night, they approached a house which looked deserted. After a quick search he'd waved for his family to enter. "There are two gamers upstairs," he said, "but they're stuck in the game and don't look like they want to come out of it anytime soon."

Joe and his family searched through the kitchen and found food to eat. They made up beds on the ground floor to sleep on for the night. Before the stations went offline they'd heard that people were becoming locked inside the simulations. Because of this, they felt safe sleeping with two gamers upstairs.

Joe and his family didn't know that it was now dangerous to sleep near active headsets. They hadn't heard that you could get pulled into Tygon 3.0 against your will simply by sleeping near someone already inside.

They certainly didn't know that once you entered Tygon you no longer came out...

"I'll remember this dream, that's for certain," Joe said as he walked towards the wall sized computer screen. An avatar of plain appearance rotated slowly in a circular motion on the screen, while a large banner above its head read, 'Tygon 3.0". Joe put his hands on the keyboard and scanned the attributes to the right of the avatar. Somehow Joe realized this must be the login selection process for entering the game. Shrugging his shoulders, Joe began to speed through the menus, the knowledge of how to play the game and what attributes to choose were solidly in his mind, which convinced him even more that this must be a dream. Within minutes, Joe had almost completed the avatar creation process. On the giant screen now stood a perfect replica of Joe, minus the extra belly weight and with larger muscles. Joe paused as he entered the information regarding personal life for his game avatar. Everything in his head screamed that he should recreate his marital status and number of children, but instead he entered 'single and no kids'. He figured it was just a game, so a few variables could be changed for the few hours he was inside the simulation, right?

Joe watched the cursor flash above the 'Enter Tygon' button. He took a deep breath and pressed the mouse.

The screen became a bright white light which leapt off the screen and enveloped him, knocking him backwards forcefully onto the ground and causing him to lose consciousness.

===

"Joe, can you hear me? Hey, come on, buddy, wake up."

Joe opened his eyes and tried to sit up.

"Whoah there, man." A firm hand on his chest kept him from rising. "Take a second and lay there. You had a nasty fall."

Joe looked around. He was lying on the floor surrounded by kitchen equipment. It took him only a moment to remember where he was. "I had the craziest dream, just now," he said.

"Really?" a blonde man with an unshaven face and crooked teeth smiled down at him. "I thought you never dream?" he said.

"Yeah," Joe nodded. "I don't, normally, but this one was so real."

"What was it?"

"I was playing a game," Joe said. "I was standing in front of a big screen selecting my character."

"Sounds cool," the man said.

"Not really," Joe admitted. "I ended up making a character that looked identical to the way I do now, and I was going to play a game where I lived a regular life."

"Yeah," his co-worker said, "that doesn't sound very cool at all. What was the game called, do you remember?"

Joe frowned, "I think it was called Tygon 3.0," he said.

"Cool name, at least."

"Yeah, I guess," Joe shrugged. "I kinda like the name of our world better, though."

"True," the blonde guy helped Joe stand. "Earth is a better sounding name, for sure."

80

"**Hello? Is anybody here?**"

The young girl looked first in the kitchen, then in the dining and living rooms. Next she walked to each bedroom and called out, searching for signs of the rest of her family.

She heard sounds coming from the basement, so she walked to the doorway and stopped at the top of the stairs.

"Hello?" she called down, but no one answered. She hesitated a moment. Her brother had played this game before, hiding in the basement to scare her when Mommy and Daddy weren't home. She shook her head and walked bravely down the stairs. It was better to be scared by her brother downstairs than it was to be alone up here, she decided.

There was no one in the main room, but the door to the storage section was open. She walked over to shut it. Mommy always said to keep it closed so the cold air didn't get in.

She grabbed the handle and quickly tried to shut it, but it wouldn't close. Looking down at the ground she saw a shoe... no, it was a foot, sticking out from the storage room.

The little girl pushed the door open and her mind froze in horror. Mommy and Daddy and her brother were all lying in the storage room in a pile, wearing their new VR helmets and not moving. She wondered why their legs and arms were laying in weird directions, and she knew something was wrong.

Before she could move, a hand grabbed her from behind and clamped hard over her mouth. She tried to scream and get away, but the hand was just too strong. The little girl started to cry.

"What have you got there, Hank?" a woman's voice said from across the room. The little girl was spun around and found herself looking at a woman with black hair and a pale face. She looked like a mean lady, especially her eyes.

"Guess they weren't all playing," a rough voice said from behind the girl. The little girl stopped crying; she was now too scared to make a sound.

"What should we do with her?" the man asked. "I don't much feel like killing anyone, specially a little girl."

The woman tapped her finger against the side of her head and narrowed her eyes. "Let's take her with us. Maybe we can sell her before we get sucked into the game." She walked closer and leaned down in front of the little girl. "Don't worry, little one, we will take you with us." Her smile didn't make the girl feel safe.

"I think you'll just leave her be," said a voice from the top of the stairs.

All three heads turned towards the steps. An old man was slowly walking down them. He was dirty, with long stringy hair and black beady eyes. He was smiling, but his teeth were crooked and yellow. For clothes, the man wore black garbage bags; the tattered and frayed bottoms of the bags ended just above his knees and he wore heavy black boots with thick soles and no laces. His hands were covered with strange looking gloves; the little girl thought they looked like a bunch of red bottle caps all held together somehow. They clanked and made a singsong sound as he swung his hands from side to side.

"Get lost, old man," the woman said. "This is none of your business. If you come to the bottom of those stairs, you're gonna get hurt real bad."

The old man chuckled and shook his head from side to side, his long hair swishing back and forth in a ridiculous wave. "I don't think so, kids." He said. "When my foot hits the bottom step, you two are gonna put your hands down by your sides and walk quietly up the stairs and out of this house. If the people in that other room are dead and you killed them, then I'm gonna come looking for you. When I find you... well, now, I'm likely gonna make you hurt real bad. Remember that as you walk out of here in a second."

"Doddering old fart," the woman sneered. "You're really starting to pi..."

Suddenly the woman stopped talking and put her hands to her sides. The little girl felt lighter as the man behind her let her go and walked towards the woman. Both of them quietly walked past the old man, who was now standing on the bottom step, and climbed the stairs as they'd been commanded.

The little girl watched them go. Once they were gone, she turned to look at the old man.

He smiled and winked at her. His teeth were ugly and his face was wrinkled, but the little girl could tell he was a very nice man who wouldn't hurt her. She smiled and walked towards him, taking his outstretched hand and walking with him up the stairs.

He led her to the kitchen and she sat down at the table.

"You look hungry, Emily," he said kindly. "Let's see if we can't find you some food before we get out of here."

"Where are we going?" Emily asked. "Are Mommy and Daddy and Cort coming with us?"

The old man shook his head as he reached up into a cupboard and grabbed a loaf of bread and a jar of spread. "I'm afraid not, sweetie," he said. "They had to go live in the game for a while."

Emily said nothing more as the old man made four sandwiches and plopped one down in front of her. He started to eat a sandwich himself, and smiled when she picked hers up and began to eat.

When he was done, he picked up a knife and held it in his palm. Emily continued to eat her sandwich, but she watched him curiously. Slowly the knife rose up into the air a few inches above his hand.

"Wow," she said. "Can you show me how to do that?"

"Maybe I can, Emily. We'll have to see."

"Am I dreaming?" she asked. "Are you somehow inside my dream?"

The old man grinned at her and the knife started to slowly rotate in the air. "Maybe you're inside my dream, little one," he said.

Epilogue

One hundred floors above the ground, Brandon looked out into the darkness, gazing at the bright lights of the cityscape as they twinkled far below him. It was 3 AM, but like most nights, Brandon couldn't sleep.

Always alone, He thought to himself. He used to preface that thought with, after all these years, but he wasn't always certain how many years it had been. He'd lived thirteen years in the dream, thirty in another simulation, and seven here. It was confusing to think about who he was or how old he should act.

He knew his real body, the fit, gangly, frame of a teenage orphan, lay comatose in the real world on a table deep underground. From what he'd been able to piece together from his Father and Cooper, the odds of returning to that body were very slim.

"Billions of people rely on me to save them from death, but they have no idea that they're even in danger." He said aloud to relieve the pressure that seemed to be building with increasing intensity, threatening to overwhelm him.

His teammates were counting on him to lead them to success; it was something he'd always done so well. After years of leading, they followed him with unshakeable belief and faith in his abilities, just as he relied on them for theirs.

Brandon thought of the other Elite leaders and he knew they could never accomplish what was being asked, what was being demanded. Brandon knew it was up to him; this game was his to win or lose, and no one else's.

"This requires decades of precise moves," he said. "Each delicate step leads to the next. If enough steps fall out of sync, the entire game crumbles and we all die."

Everywhere he turned, people saw Brandon Strayne as the leader. The great businessman and inventor, the brilliant strategist who could pull miracles out of the air at will. Thorn believed in him, and his team believed in him.

Tygon believed in him.

Brandon believed in himself... most of the time.

He sat down on the floor and crossed his legs. It was 3 AM, and he was alone. He buried his head in his hands, taking deep breaths in an attempt to allow the stress and pressure to flow out. Hot tears formed in his eyes and began to drip onto his lap. Softly he hummed a tune; a song he could remember someone singing to him when he was very little. Maybe it was his mother who sang it to him; he liked to imagine that it was.

Soon he would stand, and when he did, Brandon knew that he would be strong enough for two worlds to lean on him once again.

For the next couple of minutes, however, he was just a thirteen-year-old boy who was very alone, and very frightened.

Time passed, and Brandon rubbed his eyes to clear the tears away. He stood purposefully, straightened his shoulders, and walked to his desk to get back to work.

===

The screen went blank.

The man didn't move. He sat staring silently at the monitor, watching the cursor flash purposefully.

Thorn sat behind him, respectfully quiet to let the information sink in.

The man began to lightly chew the inside of his top lip, blinking slowly every few moments as he stared.

Thorn remained motionless. This was an important moment, and he knew that the best thing to do… was nothing.

After a long time had passed, the man slowly raised his hands and removed the headphones and placed them softly on the desk.

Thorn was nervous; he wanted to speak, but he didn't dare.

Finally, the man looked at Thorn. His eyes were dull; sad, almost.

"Is there more?" he asked, his voice barely more than a whisper.

"Not that I can show you at this time," Thorn said. "The rest you know. Brandon spent the next twenty-eight years building the Game into what it became. He rose to full power, becoming the most powerful man in the entire world."

"Yes," the man nodded. "I guess you're right. It's not the real world, though; it's a simulation. Just like the Game he created."

"It's real for those who live in it," Thorn said. "It's real for Brandon."

"Those who live in it are NPCs," the man shook his head. "They aren't real at all. Empty shells programmed by the mainframe that runs the simulation."

Thorn shook his head. "How can you say that? You've just sat through hours of video watching Brandon's entire life story until he reached twenty. You saw numerous NPCs throughout; did they look empty to you? They're as real as anyone could ever be."

The man laughed. "Why did you show this to me? How can any of this help?"

"That's how it was set up," Thorn said. "When Brandon died, someone was going to have to be brought up to speed to move the plan along."

"He's not dead."

"He should be."

The man swiveled his head to look again at the blank screen.

"Who's the shadow?" he asked. "The one near Brandon all the time inside there?"

Thorn shook his head. "I don't know."

"What do you know?" the man snapped. "I thought you were the genius who created all of this? It seems you made a terrible mess."

"Yes," Thorn said. "That's usually what happens. We create and implement things before we understand what can go wrong. Then we try to fix the messes we've made. That's what I'm trying to do."

The man nodded. "So what's next?"

"That's up to you."

"Why?"

"Because that's what Brandon told me he wanted. He wanted me to search you out when he was finished his part of this simulation. He wanted you to take over from where he left off and continue on."

The man stood up and walked towards the door with an angry scowl on his face. "That's ridiculous. You should never have shown me this; now I'll be of no use to you."

"You're our only hope now."

The man stalked over to Thorn and moved in close. At the top of his lungs he roared, "HOW CAN I DO ANYTHING? I'M JUST A STUPID NPC!"

Thorn said nothing. The man shook his head and strode angrily towards the door and opened it. Before he could exit the room, a soothing woman's voice stopped him.

"It doesn't matter what you are, Trew," Sylvia said gently. "You have to help us save the world."

Trew turned around and smiled tiredly. "Save which world?" he asked.

Sylvia chuckled softly, the sound of her voice echoing off the walls. "As many as you can, dear boy. As many as you can."

To be concluded in Virtual Prophet...

Printed in Poland
by Amazon Fulfillment
Poland Sp. z o.o., Wrocław